Antoine A Raphael

I0562112

Harmony and Contrast
The female impact
(A story)
Book I

Part One

1

Everything looked so wonderful in our classroom: the tenderness of its light blue walls, my fellow students' cheerfulness and optimism, even Dr. Shaw's "dry course". Oh, yes, everything looked wonderful! At least to me, Peter Young, it did. The only way I could explain my compelling optimism was that in my shirt pocket was an unopened letter I had picked up before from the dean's office, on my way to Dr. Shaw's class. From that letter, I anticipated heavenly inner thoughts and more heart to keep on living. Of course, my wishful happiness pervaded everything around me.

"Well, Peter!" Dr. Shaw said, "You started saying something about prejudice during our last meeting, but since it was terribly late, we had to stop our class discussion. Your premise—as far as I can remember—was worth considering. We wouldn't mind your expatiating on it."

I was very surprised, and my mind was straying miles away, in New York: I was thinking about Fay and wondering what she was doing. Furthermore, I had completely forgotten what I was about to say during our last class meeting, except that it was about intolerance. Anyway, I had to take a stand (above all against prejudice). For, if there was any hatred in my heart it would be of bigotry in general. In other words, I was contemplating not only prejudice about difference in complexion (the most prevalent and the silliest of all), but also a wide range of others. People of the same ethnic group misjudge each other every day. Difference in education, fortune, power, size, appearance, ethics, doctrine, gives rise to prejudgment and, eventually, to injurious negativism.

"It's beyond me," I started, "that intelligent persons spend all their lives seeing others through the distorted prism of prejudice. What's so discouraging is to find out that supposedly well-educated persons, several of whom are policy makers and leaders, walk right into the trap."

I pause for a while. There was a dead silence in the classroom. I knew Dr. Shaw and my fellow students were eagerly waiting for the logical inference to be drawn from my premise.

"It's discouraging," I went on, "because we happen to realize that, in spite of all the objective thoughts we've been exposed to through schooling, we can't prevent ourselves from being opinionated."

I had another pause before adding, "It's paradoxical too: prejudice comes from the Latin compound 'prae' and 'judicare', which means to judge beforehand, without the knowledge of fact. In other words, it's an expression of ignorance in the fullest sense of the word. Then a supposedly educated person, who practices prejudice, wants deliberately to put aside his exposure to positive knowledge and to rather use ignorance as a way of approaching reality. Hence—as would argue an existentialist à la Sartre—a prejudiced person acts in bad faith, because, from time to time, he must have some doubt about his unfounded beliefs, but still, being addicted to his crooked manner of seeing reality, he wouldn't do anything to try a more objective system of thoughts. By so doing, he closes himself completely to a broader human dimension his formal education has entitled him to."

I didn't know whether my argument made sense or not. I was almost certain there was a much more academic approach to the problem. However, I had just expressed my feeling about the whole subject.

"Who would like to comment on Peter's argument?" Dr. Shaw asked encouragingly.

I sensed a certain inner excitement from my fellow students. In fact, there was a legitimate reason for their being a little disturbed: I was the only black student in Dr. Shaw's class, and my fellow students might feel more or less personally concerned about the stand I had taken. To make matters worse, they had to be cautious of what they had to say (from an intellectual viewpoint); for, either they acquiesced to my line of arguments or they kept a low profile. Of course, they were free to hold any wild opinion—as any lay person would do—and to bluntly sustain that prejudice isn't synonymous with ignorance and does constitute an acceptable way of evaluating human beings. If they advanced such opinion, there would be nothing anyone could do. It's a class of free speech.

All in all, no one wanted to make the first move.

Suddenly, Michael Day held up his hand. Believe it or not, I had intuited he would be the one to make that first move.

He happened to be a talkative fellow. He enjoyed elaborating on everything and above all on subjects nobody understood. Now and then, one thought he had reached the peak of his chattering power and decided to put his mouth at rest for a while (to everybody's relief), but soon after, he would say, "Well..." and go on and on.

Likewise, he usually saw reality through rose-colored glasses, except that he didn't care for *Negroes*. He enjoyed repeating, whenever *Negroes* couldn't hear him railing against them, "They are nothing but pains in the neck". Rumor had it that he was advocating a strange doctrine which put forward that, before creating mankind, God decreed the fall of *Negroes* and the salvation of *Whites*. Did he really hold such a view? Nobody knew. However, if he did, he would have been joking; for, how can such transcendent Being sink into spitefulness and discrimination?

Now he argued, "I don't understand Peter's position. He lays stress on the fact that we shouldn't be prejudiced, while it's a fact that we are. It appears as if Peter would deny the world existence or, like Descartes, he would sustain that maybe reality is a dream. This is an attempt to avoid facing reality and to reject the compelling weight of facts. Listening to Peter, I should have asked myself whether or not we are sitting here in this classroom and are having a live discussion on prejudice. Frankly, I don't understand this line of reasoning at all. It doesn't make any sense. But it's a land of freedom. Everybody has the right to have an opinion."

Dr. Shaw looked at me furtively, through his thick glasses.

The good old Dr. Shaw!

He had the reputation of being a great debater and always wishing for a *profitable* discussion. He usually expressed his amazement at an educated person's bias judgment. How many times hadn't he been engaged in academic discussions with his colleagues and his students, on the college premises, in the streets, everywhere? I imagined that his house, once in a while, was changed to a literary salon. He had never missed an opportunity to remind us, "You must find out an idea *good* and *bad* sides. There is no absolute truth."

Of course, with such objective-mindedness, he would be disappointed if I didn't try to refute Michael's "strong" objection or, at least, to decipher its bad sides. There had to be so many too choose from! Although my intention of leaving the classroom as soon as possible to read Fay's letter was hardly resistible, I couldn't afford to disappoint Dr. Shaw who thought highly of me.

"Michael, your objection can't hold water," I argued. "You have set forth what you call facts or the compelling power of facts, and believed that we should be pleased. But, in a human context, facts by themselves are meaningless. They become meaningful only when they generate meaningful actions. In the same line of reasoning, facts are meaningful when we try to channel them towards significant patterns of actions, higher types of behaviors, which tally the kinds of beings we believe to be."

Finally, I concluded, "If my argument is acceptable and that prejudice happens to be an expression of sheer ignorance, it will be up to intelligent beings to try wiping it out from their patterns of actions and thoughts. They won't succeed if they adopt your approach, Michael. You sound as if prejudice is what we call a necessary evil we will have to accept peacefully. 'Necessary evils' have been known to be rejected by reasonable people throughout history. No, we don't have to accept them at all! Indeed our rejection of them is an expression of human dynamism."

Dr. Shaw smiled. Then he looked around and was pleased with the expression of satisfaction radiated from my fellow students' face, but Michael's.

Since there weren't any more "speakers", Dr. Shaw made his final observation, "Peter's argument is a justification of my belief that an idea must have *good* and *bad* sides, depending on the angle it has been appraised from. All you have to do is to think hard, and the truth will emerge from your mind."

We all laughed heartily.

He went on, "Please, my friends, don't ever accept anything for granted. When you write your papers, always have the following thought in mind: *the most appealing argument can be challenged*. The way you deal with such a thought will please me a lot. Remember that. My course is the open door leading to objectivity and good judgment."

He paused for a while to allow us the time to *digest* his observation and his expectations of our literary compositions. Then he went on, "Next time we will touch on the *immoral aspect* of prostitution. We will try to find out whether two persons who agree to exchange 'sexual service and remuneration' can be said to be immorally inclined. Think about it over the weekend. We are talking about two adults, two consenting adults. They are 'free' to do whatever they want to. They meet somewhere and decide to have sex, provided one pays for it. How could these two consenting adults be said to lack moral orientation? Would we be justified to have doubt about their freedom of choice? Now, it's time to go."

Our young minds already started to bubble over this topic and we were exchanging conspiratorial glances. We looked forward to another exciting class discussion the week after. Since the session was closed, I was as anxious as my fellow students to leave the classroom and I was about to dash away when Dr. Shaw called my name. I thought, "Damn!" before stopping short. I then turned around to face the professor. At the sight of his smiling face, my discontent vanished.

"I read over your midterm paper and found it very interesting," He stated. "There will be a small reward (too small, as far as I am concerned) for the best paper in the entire college system and I am willing to submit yours for consideration. I am sure it can hardly be defeated. Yet I need your consent to my suggestion. What do you think?"

I didn't answer right away, because I was speechless. I was redis-covering my creative power, which took me by surprise. It was a long way from evil days I had fallen on the year before, in New York.

"Do you think I stand a chance, Dr. Shaw?" I asked.

"Absolutely yes," he answered. "You know I wouldn't bother if I wasn't certain."

"Then, Doctor, let's try it. We have nothing to lose."

He reached for my hand, shook it and promised, "Very well, Peter, I am going to notify the contest committee. I will let you know what happens."

I rushed headlong towards the porch, which was unusual: I was a *much cooler* young fellow. I couldn't resist to the moment of joy that greeted me! The world wasn't so bad after all! I had received two great pieces of news in one day: Fay's letter and the submission of my paper for a literary contest.

Once again, I felt being a dynamic subject, which was crucial to me.

A few days before meeting the "objective-minded" Dr. Shaw and my "lovely Fay", I had undergone the pangs of loneliness and despair. I was often plunged in nightmarish thoughts. I used to imagine I was lying at the mercy of blind forces and to indulge in silly ideas such as: "What would happen if the world turned upside down? If the sky got near our planet and pushed down and flattened people, animals and things? Would I feel everlasting pain after death? How about the Supreme Being? Is It good, benevolent, wicked?"

I had sincerely believed that I was unlucky to live too long. I was disappointed to find out precociously that I was wrongly led to think that the world was evolving according to a harmonious curve, that the new generations stemmed from the old ones, and that the former surpassed the latter in intellectual, moral and political stature. But, instead, I was the powerless witness to the debasement of morals and the immersion of the world in a breathtaking descent into a new era of barbarism. The well-celebrated human evolution gave all the signs of retrogression, so much so that the exclamation of victory emitted by science, the homely of religion, the conceit of economics, politics, sociology and other branches of knowledge, were nothing but hidden and subtle weapons used to decimate and push mankind headlong in the depths of despair. The proof being that the elements of the new generation displayed more inhuman sadism, cruelty and lack of fineness and urbanity.

However, since my encounter with the "objective-minded" Dr. Shaw and my "lovely" Fay, I felt that I belonged to the company of wonderful human beings. The most compelling proof was that I was slowly rejecting my pessimism and becoming an *actor*, an *irruptive consciousness* capable of altering courses of action, of *yearning for novelty*.

While I was running down the street to *Martin Luther King* Pavilion, someone shouted my name. I stopped short, turned around and saw Michael Day. "What does he want?" I wondered. He was surrounded by a number of my fellow students who meant to *comfort* him and pursue the discussion we had started in class. But I was in no mood for such "foolishness". I had to read Fay's letter. The desire to do so was too burning, too overpowering to be postponed any longer.

"Sorry!" I yelled back. "I must attend a very important business. I will be at your disposal tomorrow. Today, I will be a lousy debater. Believe me. It has to be tomorrow! But under one condition: Dr. Shaw must be there to serve as moderator. His presence will certainly prevent things from going out of hand."

I started running again.

I finally reached the pavilion, stepped into it, walked hurriedly across the hall and stopped at my room doorstep. I opened the door; I was happy to notice my roommate's absence. "All by myself with Fay," I whispered, "That's perfect."

I took the letter out of my pocket and, with a knife, sliced the enveloped open. The sight of the knife brought me a quick feeling of panic. After having calmed down, I pulled the folded soft paper out of the envelope and opened it. I recognized Fay's handwriting immediately.

The letter started with the word "Honey", which brought me a flood of sweet memories. I pictured the lips whispering it and wished I could be there, in New York, by Fay, to take delight in receiving all the *honey* of her love.

Then, the letter continued in a motherly tone. Fay couldn't stop *reminding* me of taking care of myself. I was, so to speak, her *creation*. She didn't want me to suffer a setback to my hopes of becoming a professional. She knew that I would *live up* to her expectations, but she refused to leave everything to chance. So, like an *alien* from outer space, she kept on *checking*.

Of course, her *motherly interference* was a little inconspicuous. She wrote:

Honey, you are a human being and you can make mistakes. However, I am certain you won't do anything wrong deliberately to jeopardize a broad future opened up to you. I want you to feel that any words of encouragement from me do nothing but strengthen in you what you have wished to do in the first place. I didn't mean to embarrass you or express some kind of mistrust of you. But I love you so much that I can't even imagine you might get hurt again.

The letter then swung to a much more affectionate mood (which I liked better).

I dreamed of you the other night. It seemed to me that you were an ancient sage with a long silver beard. You were sitting on a big rock and haranguing. You didn't pay me any attention. I was a perfect stranger to you. Nevertheless, I wished you could look at me, speak to me, touch me, be closer to me...Your indifference to me hurt me so bad. Suddenly, I saw a huge scorpion going up to you. I jumped and tried to grab that deadly insect; but it stung me. I was glad to save you, although I knew I could die of the venom secreted into my blood stream. And then you looked around, saw what had happened to me and became interested in me. You got excited, cried loudly and cradled me. I woke up.

I don't know the meaning of my dream, but I don't really need it to tell you that I love you so much that I will be happy to die for you. Of course, I would rather live to listen to the sweet words you had said to me the day before your starting for school, in the West Coast. Don't you remember? We were standing by the bedroom window, my head resting on your shoulder. A nice breeze was caressing our faces. We were mad with joy and love. You said then: "Darling, do you see the sun shining? This is for our love, just for our love. However, if for any reason, the sun isn't rising for a while, our love will be enough to warm us up. Maybe all the loves on earth will act the same and will warm up the whole planet". Such imaginary event wasn't likely to happen, but the words were so sweet in my ears, so divinely innocent, that I cried.

No one before you had ever had enough time to tell me sweet little things; things I haven't been acquainted with; poetic, intangible things. You have struck the light of love in my heart, which has never stopped burning, filling me with a fresh stream of life, a new

17

perspective from which I see reality and entertain the belief that goodness can still be reached and practiced.

We will always be together, won't we? You can imagine what it will be when we are "really together". If I am in love with you, while duty keeps us apart, then, what will happen when the time comes to live with you, to be kissed by you, fondled by you, to listen to your sweet words, day in, day out, forever?

Finally, Fay's letter was getting more and more intimate: it swung from the abstract tenderness to the *very nature* of our relationships:

What have you been doing? Do you miss me? What's the part of me you are missing? Is it my cooking? No, I don't think so. You are a cordon bleu yourself! I think my kisses get you confused. You like being confused by my kisses, don't you? But my teasing you doesn't leave you indifferent either. Even though you have called me so many times a "little pretty devil without the horns", I get the impression that you've enjoyed every minute we've spent together, haven't you?

Oh, how many wonderful moments are we missing? It could be so much better to have you beside me, in bed, doing all kinds of crazy things, instead of writing to you and filling your mind with exciting

memories. But what can we do? Our temporary separation is for a
good cause, for a brighter future for both of us.
Receive, with my billet doux, one billion kisses and my entire soul.

Your Fay forever and ever.

I was out of breath. I knew that Fay was in love with me, but I just
came to realize to what extent she was. And I had to admit that, having allowed me to spend some time with her, in her New York apartment, she had already appeared to me like someone out of this world,
a superhuman being that wouldn't pay any attention to human social
conditions and backgrounds.

If she had to go by the circumstances surrounding our first acquaintance to have an opinion about me, she would see in me nothing
but the very picture of human trash. While I am writing my story today, I still refuse to believe that I was (although against my will) such
a despicable character. I am still ashamed of what I seemed to be.
Perhaps I will be for the remaining of my life. In fact, I wonder if Fay
and the others, familiar with the predicaments I was in, will ever forget what I was. But what I am afraid of the most is that Fay, out of the
goodness of her heart, would only feel sorry for me. Her compassion
would hurt me so much.

However, by the same token, I have kept asking myself how she
manages to love me, despite appearances to the contrary. Indeed how
can someone love someone else, single him out and have complete

trust in him? Very often that someone is a perfect stranger, a black hole, who often acts against his better judgment.

I remember that young woman who depended completely on her aunt for support. She fell in love with a merciless cab driver. She became pregnant. Her aunt was furious and wanted to put her out. Neighbors and relatives talked that brave aunt out of it, provided that the niece *got her act together* and *behaved herself in the future.* Three months after delivery of that child, she met again *her cab driver* and was pregnant again. The aunt was exasperated, but was once more talked out of her decision to put her out. And this pattern of action continued until everybody agreed with the aunt to throw her *passionate stubborn niece* out.

This blind commitment of somebody to somebody else has always puzzled me. And although, to some extent, I am a little that *somebody else* now, I am still puzzled. For example, Fay, taking chance on loving me, puts her career and her life in possible danger.

As we go along, I will tell you the reason for my thinking this way.

2

I wasn't indeed such *abominable person* I've just alluded to. Oh, no! I was rather bright and disciplined. I used to believe that if everybody thought and behaved like me, the world would be a lot better. From primary school to college, I was a straight "A" student. I was capable of understanding easily whatever subject matter I was exposed to. I was also polite, respected acceptable values of the community and rejected a generation gap notion. As far as I was concerned, society was a continuum, a harmonious amalgamation of intelligent beings, helping one another, communicating their endless experiences to one another.

My prodigious intelligence amazed everybody; but since I was modest, I didn't arouse my school fellows' jealousy. This reminds me of the prizes and medals I used to receive. They were certainly teachers' obvious ways to reward the clever students, and, by the same token, to discourage (maybe unwillingly) the slower ones. I couldn't rate such practices when I was a kid, but, now, being a little remote from that moment in my life, I strongly believe in their dehumanizing values.

Of course, the teaching profession didn't know anything about hypothyroidism, hearing and vision impairments, malnutrition, autism and many other detrimental factors which could lead to cretinism or mental retardation. The slower students had to be exposed, punished, accused of being inferior in intelligence and, finally, dropped like bags of potatoes.

Once a month, the whole school gathered in the huge auditorium to witness the giving of prizes and medals to the "greatest".

Certainly, it was fun to go to school at that time, above all for us, the "gifted ones", unaware of the slow ones' plight, who could make the most of learning and adapt to the multiplicity of experiences we were being exposed to, we believed it was such a *big deal* to carry so many large books. Most of us didn't have bags and we had to arrange our books in a way that we could carry them all. As the time went by, it became quite a challenge to even go to school in such a way; for, at each grade, new books were added to previous ones. But we were proud to show ourselves with our *book loads*.

On our way to school and back home, it was as if we were marching down the street, by the Christian Sisters' School, to be admired by the uniformed girls. Their waists were girded with belts of different colors, depending on the grade those "angels" belonged to. They were whispering secrets in each other's ears. Even if we didn't know what they were talking about, we strongly believed it had to be about us (in flattering terms).

At the City College, I was still maintaining my "A" average as a freshman and during my second year. My papers were among the best. They were often read in class by my professors and won me eulogistic remarks from college officials. I was considered one of the "students with clear thinking".

Things were going smoothly until I reached the third year.

At first, it didn't appear from Dr. Miles' behavior toward me that he was an evil character. As had all my professors reacted, he noticed my "clear thinking" and seized every opportunity to ask me questions. But little by little, I found out there would be a hard time for me in his class.

My trouble indeed started on a warm Friday. I was tired out when I entered the classroom. The wind was blowing hard on my way over: it raised the dust, whipped my face and left me practically blind and out of breath. I was about ten minutes late, and the classroom was packed with students.

Dr. Miles, as soon as I had sat down, began to read the "best papers" of a previous class assignment. I was surprised but not mad at the fact that my paper wasn't among the "best".

I could have been so far a straight *A student*, but I didn't expect to always submit the best papers to all my professors. Additionally, I remembered an old saying repeated over and over by my late father, "Other times other ways". He meant to tell me that I had to stop taking things for granted. But, still, I was very uneasy, so were my fellow students who had known me for nearly three years. We had just learned that I could write something *not too good*. Nevertheless, we were ready to forget about the "incident", but Dr. Miles wasn't. For some unexplained reason, he wanted to *humble* me still further, which was against all recommendations from modern psychology. He gave each student his paper back, except that he held up mine and, while smiling with a shade of resentment and disgust on the corners of his mouth, he declared, "I have Peter's paper. I don't know what I can make of it."

I was dazed, not so much because of a bad mark I obtained for the first time in school, but above all because of my first exposure to spitefulness and sadism embodied by a supposedly well-educated person. A mixed feeling of anger and disappointment slowly took over my entire personality.

My dear Dr. Miles, however, hadn't finished yet. He went on, "All I can say is that Peter has tried to be cute. He has made in vain an attempt to emulate William James, using a flowing style to deal with a scientific matter. But William James was a genius! You will never be equal to him. No, no way!"

I couldn't stand Dr. Miles' sneer any longer; I raised my hand.

He shouted, "What?"

"I understand that you can disagree with me on my way of seeing things," my voice started to express anger and frustration. "I don't have the monopoly of absolute knowledge. However, Dr. Miles, so far, you haven't said anything objective about my paper. As far as I can remember, I've tried to state clearly my feeling and my understanding of the topic. If I am wrong, I am sure you, as a critic, must know why I am. You wouldn't allow yourself to make a free statement, would you? I will be very glad if you make us all aware of what I have done wrong in my paper, so we can learn all from my mistakes. Surely, you must have strong reasons for disliking my paper. What are they?"

I drew a long breath to keep calm and I went on, "Furthermore, I don't try to emulate William James. Although I have heard of that famous psychologist and philosopher, and that I have been eager to read his works, I have never had, however, an opportunity to fall on one of his books. Therefore, my alleged emulation of that author's style happens to be my own. If it reminds you of his, that isn't my fault."

"Listen, Peter!" shouted the professor. "I will not tolerate your impertinent behavior. You said yourself that you don't possess the monopoly of absolute knowledge. You are here to learn."

I was too excited to stop. There was no way I could respect a professor who didn't respect himself. "Correction, Dr. Miles," I maintained firmly, "even when I was attending primary school, I wasn't told that learning was a unilateral mind stuffing process. At college level, learning presupposes to be commensurate with students' abilities to grasp reality objectively, critically, and to participate in class discussions and in the way teaching should be handled. It can't mean that a professor must discourage his students by submitting them to his satirical and abusive remarks. Your attitude is counterproductive, as far as teaching purpose is concerned..."

"That's enough nonsense in one day," insinuated Dr. Miles while looking at his watch. "You've just spoilt my day, Peter!"

"I thought you were about to say that I've just spoilt your fun at my expense," I yelled out.

I was pervaded by a feeling of unexplainable guilt. I thought that perhaps I had done something wrong; perhaps I had touched unknowingly in my paper on a sensitive subject; perhaps I overreacted to Dr. Miles' attitude toward me. It was possible that he treated all his students in the same manner; which was a strange way (I would say), but that was his way, his *idiosyncrasy*. Although it would be more idealistic that an instructor shouldn't be allowed to use his idiosyncrasy in a classroom, I didn't think, however, that teacher's unbecoming action was the end of the world. I had just overreacted (I thought). Shouldn't I go back and apologize to Dr. Miles? But why should I? I did nothing but write a paper according to my feeling and my understanding of the subject. What's the value of any composition if it doesn't reflect—at least in part—the feeling of its author? I also resented the confusion of my style with William James', as if I had committed a plagiarism.

At that time, I was living at Aunt Emma's. When I arrived at the front door, I was too nervous to take my keys out of my pocket. I rang the doorbell repeatedly.

After she had let me in, she inquired, "What's wrong with my Peter?"

I was about to relate the classroom incident, but I changed my mind: I didn't want that sweet woman to be concerned about my trouble. I replied instead, "Nothing, Aunt Emma. Maybe this is one of my gloomy days."

"I know you Peter," her voice betrayed a sense of warning and urgency. "Usually you are cheerful and less explosive. This is the first time I've seen you in such a bad mood."

Indeed she was right.

I calmed down a little and even smiled. I didn't think it was fair to make my *sweet Aunt Emma* miserable because someone else had abused me. To *restore harmony* in the house, I asserted, "You know, Aunt Emma, with age, new aspects of my personality are revealing themselves. I am getting more pensive, more concerned about the state of affairs and my future."

She hugged me tight, sensing that something wasn't too right. "Let's hope you are not hiding something from me," she implied. "Usually, we confide in each other.

"By the way, I've been waiting for you to have supper. It's time now; I am starving. Let's go to the dining room. I made some rice and beans, just the way you like them."

I did my best to eat, but I wasn't really hungry. I had a lump on my chest. But how could I handle Aunt Emma's displeasure to my refusal of eating? I would sound like telling her that she was no longer a *cor-*

don bleu; which would be a lie. She cooked well and a lot of food (too much food!). Additionally, I would do all in my power not to hurt her. She was so good to me. After my parents had died in a car accident, she spontaneously invited me to live with her. Then she did her best to soothe my sorrow and make me regain my cheerfulness, which I had preserved until that evening Dr. Miles hurt my feelings so bad.

As soon as I had finished eating, I excused myself and went back to my room, which was in the attic. I undressed, took a shower and went to bed, hoping that I could fall asleep.

In fact, I did believe in sleeping and had never stopped welcoming it. For some indefinable reason, a good night sleep always made me see the real from a brighter angle (on waking up). My feelings, as well as my perceptions, judgments, memories, seemed to become clearer and sharper, and were ready to start anew.

When I woke up, the sun was already up. I smiled: it was Saturday. I didn't have to go anywhere. I anticipated new pleasures on opening the window, on going back to bed and on letting in the cool morning breeze for an hour or two, on reading few chapters of a novel I had borrowed from the college library. I was high-spirited again and was glad to follow my instinct about the goodness of a night sleep.

I also hoped that Dr. Miles' idiosyncrasy would give me a break the following week.

I was hoping in vain. Dr. Miles' animosity against me would worsen.

On that Monday evening—I remember—, I left home earlier than I was accustomed to. I tried to put all the odds on my side to avoid being late and in a state of nervous tension. As a matter of fact, I had legitimate reason to act that way: the sky was suddenly covered with black clouds. The meteorologist, on the radio, had announced a passing shower and probably a lasting rain if the southern wind reached our horizon. It was an atmospheric situation to follow closely from moment to moment. There wasn't any clear weather pattern.

I was lucky indeed. As soon as I sat down in the classroom, it started pouring. Dr. Miles came anyway. "It seems I have to be content with the few of you who have come," he stated.

I presumed that everything was going well: the rain, the small number of students and the gentle smell of the soil which had not been wet for months until that day, brought in the classroom an ambiance of intimacy like the one making people feel closer to one another.

Dr. Miles asked us to open our books and to read a kind of father's lament over his son's death. The professor, to speed up the process, read it himself slowly. When he finished, he set the open book on his desk and asked, "What can you make out of that imbroglio?"

I said to myself there had to be something wrong with that man's personality. He had picked up the text himself as one which was worth considering, but still he asked us what to make out of "that imbroglio". He sounded as if the text was meaningless. If that was the case why had he selected it?

No one answered. It seemed we were afraid to jump into the pool in order to avoid sorting out an *inextricable imbroglio* and making ourselves look ridiculous in the process.

"Well, Peter," Dr. Miles picked me out from all the students, "do you give your tongue to a cat?"

We all burst out laughing.

I thought hard, trying to remember the point raised by the author. I then commented in a very cautious manner, "I only want to go by the poem you have just read; and I notice a great deal of fatalism in it. It seems the author advocates that fate controls everything that happens, and that one should admit that everything that happens is inevitable."

"Is there anyone who wants to comment on Peter's remark?" Dr. Miles asked.

He looked round and said, "Yes, John."

The so-called John raising his hand to participate in a class discussion was surprising. Usually, he was a taciturn fellow who spent the entire semester without saying one single word. We always wondered about the possibility for him to even have a passing grade, since he couldn't be judged from his eternal silence. But he had always made it. How? That's a mystery.

"I disagree with Peter," he said. "The author isn't a fatalist."

Everybody frowned upon John's utterance. I couldn't help saying to myself, "Just like that! That man must be crazy. How can someone, who respects himself, make a fool of himself by opening his mouth for the sake of it?"

Then I spoke up, "I understand John that you disagree with me, but whit's your reason for disagreeing with me?"

John looked at me as if I were a strange bird. It seemed he was unable to understand my reason for not accepting his mere statement as a sufficient argument. He reminded me of that brat on TV, who answered a question by just saying: "Because" and walked away smilingly.

"No, John!" I thought. "This is not admissible in an academic setting. We, college students, are expected to bubble over with excited ideas."

There was a dead silence in the classroom. We could hear a fly passing by if there was one. Indeed the situation was apparently so embarrassing, so gross, so *non-collegiate*! Something had to be wrong with John. I felt sorry for him. Yet, Dr. Miles sided with him! That was even more astonishing. What could be getting into that professor's mind, which changed him to an unrefined person? How could he decide to throw away all the wonderful ideas to which he was certainly exposed into the garbage can, just to give me a hard time? What did I do wrong to deserve his anger? Shouldn't he behave with more dignity, more decorum and self-restraint, which would be worthy of his education and his professorial status.

"I am afraid, Peter, but I must agree with John," he argued in a falsely and irritating drawling accent. "What he wants to say is that the author of the lament couldn't conceive of a fatalistic character for the simple reason he was a Christian."

"Good Lord!" I exclaimed, in spite of myself.

"That's right, Peter," he argued mockingly. "Remember, you don't have the monopoly of absolute knowledge."

"But, Dr. Miles I am not the only one who recognizes that Christianity contains a great deal of fatalism in itself," I pointed out. "Karl Marx said that religion is the opium of the people. He was aiming above all at the Judeo-Christian faith he was acquainted with. He also meant that the religiously oriented person takes the world as giving and there is nothing else he can do about it. Holdback, Büchner, Feuerbach, Schopenhauer, Nietzsche, Sartre wouldn't disagree with Marx. As a matter of fact, when the Christian himself says that he has to submit to God's will, he is not too far from taking a fatalistic attitude."

Dr. Miles stood up, pulled out from his suitcase our papers for the previous week's assignment and started returning them to us as if I wasn't talking. When he reached me, he said, "Peter, you believe you are smarter than anyone else and that you can't be wrong! That's bull. Your presumption doesn't play with me. Here is your paper, and you have an 'F'."

"Oh!" My fellow students shouted out in unison.

I was completely baffled. However, I did have the courage to look at Dr. Miles' marginal notes. I couldn't believe my eyes. Those notes were nothing but considerations which didn't have anything to do with the value or the merit of my paper. An annotation recommended, "You should have left a larger margin for comments". Another one advised, "I would rather write maybe than perhaps". A comment surprised me when he stated, "If I agree to you...," I repeated in my mind, "...Agree to you! What's that?"

As for the essence of the paper, Dr. Miles flatly rejected my recognizing that a human being possesses three aspects: a social one, a biological one and a psychological one. The marginal comment went on, "As far as I am concerned, a human being has only two basic aspects: a social one and a biological one. The third one you come up with is just gibberish. In this matter, I sympathize with the materialists."

Henceforth, this pattern of Dr. Miles' negativism toward me continued. My subsequent papers were irrevocably underrated by him. My failing his course was then ineluctable; for, my final score had to be the average grade of my short papers. I was caught up in a stream of total hopelessness. I felt totally disoriented and that I was like hanging in the space.

My fellow students, though they sympathized with me, were afraid to speak up to avoid that mad professor's reprisal, which made me think about the unsteady and slow walk of democracy. Only John—to my surprise—came to me and gave me a positive piece of advice. That day, he stated clearly, "Peter, I have nothing against you. You know, you are by far more intelligent than most of the students I've met. We come from a long way, and I know what I am talking about. I can't figure out why Dr. Miles is giving you a hard time. You don't deserve this kind of treatment. You are serious-minded, interested in learning, respectful. I didn't even understand Dr. Miles' siding with me the other day. For, I didn't make any sense; I was frozen with fear. I didn't even complete my thought. That was crazy...I have been thinking about this senseless situation the whole week. Peter, you should go and explain your problems to the dean."

It was thoughtful of John to understand my predicament, overcome his shyness and choose to advise me on that matter. Human nature is so unpredictable! We thought we knew John and pictured him as an idiot, but he rather possessed unrevealed qualities. In fact, without his advice, I wouldn't remember the dean's office. How could I have been interested in the raison d'être of such office before? I had never experienced failure and professors' harassments in my life.

I went to the dean's office the day following my conversation with John.

A slender pretty woman asked me to have a seat in the waiting room. Then she opened a door and disappeared. Five minutes later, she came back. "The dean is waiting for you," she informed.

I pushed the door slowly. It creaked a little bit; but, being determined to go all the way, I pushed it wide open. There was the dean! He could be forty-five years of age. His personality reminded me of a sated bear. He was sitting comfortably on a high-back rocker handsomely covered with gray velvet. He kept on reading a book open on his crossed legs, so he didn't pay me any attention or he pretended not to see me. Finally, he closed the book, put it down on the desk top and rocked himself back and forth, holding his neck with his hands.

All of a sudden, he asked, "What can I do for you, Peter?"

He had just noticed that I was still standing and said, "Oh, I am sorry! Have a seat."

I sat down on a chair set in front of the desk and faced him. He glanced sidelong at me.

"Well, I don't even know where to start," I spoke up. "If you look into my records from the time I was a freshman up to now, and if you pull my file on my previous schooling, you will see that I've been a straight "*A*" student. However, it seems that pattern has drastically changed, ever since I've taken Dr. Miles' course."

I breathed in deeply before going on, "I would imagine that, at least, once, I haven't been able to cope with a subject matter. If that was the case, I would do my best to overcome such hurdle. But all indicates that Dr. Miles doesn't even give me the impression that I should hope for improving my understanding of his course..."

The dean raised his hand to stop me and asked, "Can you be more specific?"

I told him about Dr. Miles' ironical and personal comments on my papers, about his deliberate siding with other students during our class discussions, about his derogatory remarks...

The dean stood up. I did the same; for, it was clearly an invitation to walk off.

"I am sorry that you have been singled out by Dr. Miles," he declared. "Usually, he is a very sensible and concerned person. I will investigate the matter, and the problem will be corrected—if need be."

I left with a funny impression that the school authority would do absolutely nothing. Later on, some of my fellow students would confirm my apprehension, telling me that the dean was known for being the "chicken" on the campus. So, there was no way out. Meanwhile, Dr. Miles' mistreating me kept worsening to the point that attending his class was nothing for me but a torture chamber.

My persistent sense of unexplainable guilt had also made matters worst. I wondered about what I might have done wrong unknowingly. But I couldn't find any acceptable answer. Maybe I was dreaming; I didn't believe what was happening to me. How could I deserve someone's animosity? I was just interested in going to school, being an excellent student, keeping my *A* average. How could that be the wrong thing to do?

Like a windmill, I was spinning hopelessly, aimlessly.

3

I had just found out that I was *vulnerable* and couldn't bear pressure. I failed one course and thought it was all up with me. I was like a perfect machinery they silenced by pulling the plug or like an off-centered universe drifting away toward a gruesome destiny. I began to have doubts about my intelligence which had allowed me, for nearly eighteen years, to deal with the problems of life. I no longer thought I was a subject; instead I was experiencing a feeling of being fragile, lifeless, static, lonely, abandoned in this immeasurable galaxy.

Of course, at that time, I had often heard people quoting Plautus' truism again and again: "Homo hominis lupus. [Brother turns on brother, man is a wolf to man]." But I was totally taken by surprise by the wolf and quite unprepared, because of my ingenuousness, to react like another fierce and savage wolf. I couldn't believe that, as a man, I had to end up acting as if I was in a jungle. Yet I couldn't both resign myself to behaving like a lamb and let them eat me up. So my only reaction was to try to escape from the corner Dr. Miles and people of his kind pushed me in, and to walk away as far as I could to avoid sinking into madness.

Yet my option didn't please me at all; I didn't experience any sense of victory and, instead, I was fully conscious of my agony of defeat, of my being a lamb in a kind of way. I had to walk away from my ideal, my plan for the future, my only hope for a better life. I wouldn't belong to that select group of professionals, the leaders of mankind.

What should I do? This question kept spinning in my head like a senseless top. I could go to Aunt Emma and try to ease my mind of my worries. But what would this step lead me to? I would only find a palliative to postpone the advent of my failure and humiliation. Of course, Aunt Emma would do her best to appease me. First, she would serve me a big piece of chocolate cake on a golden wide-rimmed saucer. I would eat the dessert with relish. Then, the delicious taste would fade from my palate, and I would sink again into my gloomy thoughts and despair. I imagined that Aunt Emma wouldn't admit *defeat*. She would then remind me of my departed parents who had expected so much from me. Though they passed away, their dream of having a son they would be proud of had never vanished with that well-meaning woman being around to go over it again and again. "We, the Young's," she often repeated, "believe in ideals and take things seriously."

By the way, I had never questioned her about my foreign back-ground. What part of West Indies did we come from? It was a mys-tery. All I was allowed to know was that my mother was nine months

pregnant with me when she immigrated with my father to this country. My birth certificate, to make matters worst, omitted my parents'
birthplace. My *dubious accent*, however, told me something about my
foreign root. Yet, I wasn't the kind of person who would go and look
for roots and backgrounds. I was content with being there, being conscious of reality, going to school, living at my sweet aunt's house,
letting myself immerse in the matrix of existence. I often repeated that
I was a citizen of the world; my brothers and sisters lived throughout
the planet. Anyway, at that time, as a lover of ideals, Aunt Emma (my
late father's sister) would be flabbergasted by learning that I had
dropped out of school.

It was exactly what I did. I had been staying away from school for
a month. I received letters after letters from professors and college
officials, but I didn't take trouble to open them. "What do they want
now?" I once whispered. "Nobody cared before. And I don't want to
be a punching-bag for their amusement?" All I needed was to have
my peace of mind.

Some peace of mind! It was rather a total surrender. I had never
been so anxious before. For the first time in my life, I went from one
crisis of anxiety to another and dreaded suicide and madness. I was
constantly lost in nightmarish thoughts.

What should I do? Again, I had no answer, except that I was in
bed, alone, facing myself. All around me, I saw nothing but insur-
mountable hurdles, impossible schemes, childish solutions. Suddenly,
an image came to my mind! It was the image of something or some-

one which overshadowed all the other images because of its positiveness, its aiming at a tangible being: it was the image of *Yolanda's world*. I did my best to get rid of it, but it kept coming back to me with a compelling, forceful appeal. Finally, it occupied every inch of my consciousness, to such a par that avoiding it or denying it would be a vain undertaking.

I met Yolanda when I was a freshman at the City College. Instinctively, we stroke a friendship with each other, which we kept alive, even after that *Amazon* had dropped out before the end of the second semester. The last time I had seen her, she looked like a beautiful blossomed flower. Indeed, all in her appearance had indicated that she was well-off or was about to be, which wouldn't be surprising, considering her parents' wealth (at least, according to what she had told me). That day, she beckoned to her girlfriends to wait for her. Then, she welcomed me with her usual overpowering warmth. She kissed me, hugged me, squeezed my hair and whispered sweet words to my ear (to her friends and passers-by's big surprise).

Everybody believed we were more than good friends. However having been interested in nothing but studying and activities about school, I had strongly disapproved of her decision to drop out. We had heated arguments about that. To avoid my "fussiness", she chose to stay away from me. It could be the reason why—I thought—we hadn't fallen in love long time before. But since I followed in her footsteps by leaving school, I didn't see anything that was opposed to our being closer to each other.

Her image was definitely neat in my mind.

She was a potpourri of races: blue eyes, straight hair, fat lips, light skin, robust Hottentots' hips sustaining a delicate waist. She could be confused with a Mulatto, a White, an Arab, a Hispanic, a Black, an Asiatic—what else? One day, she tried to let me into the secret of her *dubious nature*. She explained mechanically, "My mother is Black; my father half-Hispanic, half-Black; my grandmother, on my mother's side, is Indian; my grandmother, on my father's side is Italian; my grand-father on..." I remembered begging her to stop, because I couldn't keep up with such a labyrinth of races.

I dialed her telephone number. She picked up the receiver after two rings and answered in a sluggish tone, which formed a contrast with her buoyant personality, "Who's it?"

I didn't answer right away; I knew that my first word would lead me one step towards trouble. I intuited it, but I was destitute of will-power and couldn't restrain myself from uttering the following words, "This is Peter."

"Oh! Peter, Peter, darling," she said mellifluously, "where have you been? How could you stay away from me for so long? You are no good! You should be ashamed of yourself!"

She took a pause and then went on, "I am expecting you with all my heart, my soul, my body. Oh! Peter, all that time! You don't even know what you are missing!"

"What am I missing?"

"Me, baby, a woman who's bubbling over with energy and crazy with love for you and…"

"Yolanda, please, I am coming."

I hung up.

While I was getting dressed, I thought of my shyness about dealing with women. I read a lot about sex and the various implications involving in it, but, at that time, I was practically "untouched", a *novice*. Of course, my theoretical knowledge of the matter enabled me to put my fellow students at a false scent: I had to save my face since they were involved in *romance* to such a par that they were blasé.

I took a taxi and gave the driver Yolanda's address.

She lived in a two-bedroom apartment medium size building located in Richmond Hill section, in Queens. I had never visited her there, but, from my knowledge of the area, I thought it was a delightful neighborhood with clean streets, green trees on each side and serenity following the peak hours.

The taxi stopped. I was day-dreaming and didn't realize that I had reached my destination. I paid the driver, got off the car and walked to a marvelous two-story building. I scanned the area and spotted Yolanda's apartment. I rang the bell. The door was wide open, and I was welcomed by a young and extremely beautiful woman. She squeezed me, kissed me, nibbled my ears, my cheeks, and, finally, pushed me on a settee nearby.

"Yolanda, please, calm down!" I uttered imploringly. "I am all yours; there is no need to molest me. Listen to me, if you don't want me to call the police and file an 'assault and rape complaint'. Please."

She calmed down. However, while I had *the floor,* so to speak, I didn't know where to begin. Meanwhile, she lay down on the settee and gently put her head on my lap. I felt her hair, and she closed her eyes.

"Yolanda...," I uttered.

"Yes, Master," she replied jokingly.

"I have dropped out."

"So!"

"Do you understand the meaning of my decision?"

"Yes, baby, I understand your problem perfectly, because I experienced it two years ago. School..."

"No, Yolanda, you don't understand my problem. My leaving school means that I give up the dream I've cherished since my childhood to become a respectable professional. Do you understand me?"

She shrugged her shoulders.

"It hurts me," I went on to say. "I am still obsessed with that dream."

"Then go back to school," she suggested in a slightly irritating tone.

"I can't"

"Why can't you?"

"Something had happened to me over there, and I can't go back there without losing my face."

"In that case, come to the woman who adores your face."

"Yolanda, you don't understand my dilemma? If you love me, you should feel sorry for me."

Her face wreathed in smiles. Apparently, I had rubbed her the right way. She pulled me and kissed me on the lips.

"Why?" I asked.

"I am so glad that we are having this conversation," she admitted.

"I don't understand."

"You've just given me the answer to what I've suspected long since."

"What is it?"

"You care about me."

"But, Yol, you know that I do."

"I have the certainty now."

"You do?"

"When I dropped out of school, you took pity on me. You were even mad at me. At that time, I couldn't understand the meaning of your anger. Now, I know that you did care about me and wanted the best for me."

"That's true, Yol."

We kept silent for a while. We listened to a soft tune on the radio, which seemed to soothe our unexpressed frustrations. Then, she felt my face just to sense something tangible.

"Yes, darling, I understand your problem," she mentioned. "But (between us) school is so boring. There, they teach values they don't even want to carry out. So, that's a waste of time."

She turned over, on her side, and buried her head in my shirt, which she had unbuttoned partly. Her voice turned sepulchral and bluntly confessed, "I can't keep up, anyway, with all those theories; above all, I find out that I can make it with the little education I have. To tell you the truth, I have no time to lose. I happen to be a woman of action. Do you understand me?"

"But what am I going to do, Yol?" I asked desperately. "What could I tell Aunt Emma?"

Yolanda sat down and cast an amorous glance at me, which made me shudder. "You will do what I am doing," her voice was very confident. "From now on, I am your new Aunt Emma."

"I don't know, Yol, you make it sound so simple."

It seemed indeed so promising to be free like a bird, owing no explanation to anyone, leaving behind homework and Dr. Miles' sneer and spitefulness. Oh, yes! I couldn't stand that *baboon!* Just thinking about him turned me irascible. I believed I would have killed him, if I had been going to school. Then, my abandon of studies appeared to me as the lesser of the two evils.

I went back to Aunt Emma and took leave of her. It wasn't an easy task. She wanted to know what I intended to do. "I've found a part-time job," I explained. "It's closer to my school."

That was a lie, and I felt so ashamed. I realized then I was getting on the wrong side of the road.

My aunt asked, "Peter, are you going to leave me by myself? What's going wrong with you? What do you need a part-time job for? I am able to support you until you finish school. I am drawing social security and pension benefits. That's enough for both of us. I don't understand youngsters in these days."

Her complaint made my heart bleed. I was torn between two desires. On the one hand, I wanted to feel free, and Yolanda seemed to give me a helping hand towards that (though the outcome wasn't certain at all). On the contrary, I sensed some clouded future waiting for me. On the other hand, I wished to remain a dutiful nephew, especially as Aunt Emma tried to bring me to reason. But I couldn't listen to reason, since I didn't want to hurt her more than I had already done by informing her of taking leave of her. So, to stay would mean to inform her of my quitting school. No way! I had much rather she remained with the wonderful image of me as a young bright man.

"Aunt Emma, I appreciate your willingness to help me," I stated. "In fact, I'll never be able to repay you for what you've done for me. However, I've to start doing things on my own.

"Besides, I am not going to leave you completely by yourself. I'll visit you almost daily. If things work out in the end, I'll buy a car, will be able to travel faster and will attend different businesses, including visiting you and going errands for you."

She came up to me and kissed me on the forehead. Maybe she realized that I had grown up, and that she had to let me go. "God bless you, my son!" She said in a sad tone. Then she walked away to her bedroom. I thought she was crying.

I packed a huge traveling bag (a gift from her) with clothes and books, and hurried away. I didn't want to change my mind and confess my problems to that sweet old lady. I just couldn't do it! I was ashamed but full of the "Young's pride"

I went and joined Yolanda in her apartment. She was waiting for me. She relieved me of my bag and pointed at the dining room. As she was proceeding towards the guestroom to put away my bag, I noticed her powerful hips, her promising legs and her feline motion. "Oh, she is more beautiful than I thought!" I whispered. "She is a goddess of charm. Peter, my friend, are you sure you are not dreaming?"

My heart beat fast. I understood that I was entering the world of manhood. Things were *looking good* by the minute, and I thought it was silly of me to unduly exaggerate my dropping out of school. That *young woman* was certainly right to believe that one should experience all the gamut of pleasures and above all when one was in the springtime of one's life. Anyway, I hoped strongly that she would be right.

I pulled a chair and invited her to sit down. I kissed her on her neck. She shivered. I went around the table and also sat down on the opposite chair, so that we faced each other.

47

She said abruptly, "What are we waiting for? Let's eat."

I was terribly hungry and reacted at once to her invitation to have dinner. I ate like a wolf. When I finished I raised my head and caught my hostess looking at me intensely.

I was so embarrassed! I had violated all the rules of basic propriety.

She seemed not to notice my *boorishness*. She asked instead, "Why do I have to love you so much, Peter?"

I didn't answer. These types of questions require no answers.

She added, "It may seem weird, but I have never stopped believing that, one day, you will be close to me, as if you were the only man in the universe. Why have I entertained this belief? I can't tell."

She paused for breath and then continued, "Peter, as you can see, I am doing fine. But, because of you, I don't want to go beyond what is necessary in my line of activity. To go all the way will jeopardize my chance to have you with me. You know what I mean, don't you?

"To tell you the truth, what I am doing is not the kind of activity I think you will approve of one hundred percent; although I don't see anything wrong with my line of work. A job is a job, as long as I haven't sold my body and soul. But, knowing your straightforwardness..."

"But what would your parents say about your line of work?"

"I don't care about them. They should go to hell!"

She stood up, came to me, on the other side of the table, and sat on my lap. "I am sorry Peter," she whispered. "I am truly sorry. I

shouldn't speak to you like that; except your presence makes nervous."

Shortly after, she explained, "My parents are filthy rich. But that's
their business and their money. I must show them I can also manage
without them and do well in the process."

I looked askance at her. Her eyes flickered, and like a spark, I had
the whole picture: her reality appeared to me in its disturbing bare-
ness. She had been dealing in illegal activities and probably had drug
experiences (either as a user or a dealer). I felt like guilty of something. How could have I let that happen to her? I should have paid her
more attention; I should have been with her before she had taken the
wrong turn. I believed I was too selfish, too interested in school,
while, all around me, there was a wave of sufferings and human tragedies. Poor Yolanda!

That day, I promised to do whatever in my power to help her.

"Pete, this is what I don't like with you," she asserted abruptly.

I was surprised at her ability to guess what I was thinking about.
"What?" I inquired for conscience's sake.

"You are always lucid, always understanding things right away.
Your intelligence doesn't leave anything out, which can make someone uncomfortable, nervous to be with you."

"Yol, I am not implying anything."

"No, you are not implying anything, but your constant awareness
of reality makes an active woman like me a little vulnerable—if you
get my meaning."

"Hum!"

"There's nothing wrong with dropping out once in while to reach euphoria."

"What!" I shouted. "Break it to me in plain English."

"Well, baby, from time to time, one should withdraw from the real world to experience a feeling of well-being."

I didn't know what to think. Here I was far away from Aunt Emma, deluding myself that I was doing something meaningful; but, instead, I believed I was caught in the middle of a huge illegal enterprise. "Poor Yolanda," I kept saying to myself, while I should havd said, "Poor Peter."

"Pete, don't worry," she carried on. "I can afford it. I receive my fatty and double-trouble free of charge. I am a storekeeper and a good one, believe me! But I want you to know I don't quite live in *Narcoland*. I just need a little push daily, as you need a cup of coffee. No more, no less. At least..."

I was speechless and stared into the distance. The more she was using the drug jargon to confuse me, the more I was afraid of my new environment and lifestyle.

She proceeded shamelessly, "Now, you know me better than anyone else. You have to make up your mind. I don't expect you to do anything I am doing. You can be with me, and that will be so much satisfying. I need you Peter. You are the only decent man I am willing to be with forever. I love you very much, otherwise I wouldn't wait for you patiently, religiously."

It wasn't too cold, considering we were in the middle of February. The window panes were covered with vapor. Yolanda stood up and took a piece of rag to wipe them up. Then she called me, "Look, Peter, it's been snowing, and we haven't noticed it."

I knew she tried to divert my attention from worries caused by what she had avowed. But she didn't have to do that. I joined her in her apartment, didn't I? I had broken with school and Aunt Emma. I had already committed myself to that *voluptuous young lady*. It was my mistake. Hence I was laying at her mercy.

I joined her by the window, looked through the panes and saw big white snow flakes falling thick and fast. It was lovely. The city looked like a huge crystal bowl full of people, vehicles and houses which seemed to emerge from a dream. Without noticing it, I was in a romantic mood. I touched Yolanda on the shoulder. As if she was waiting for my touching as a signal, she grabbed my hand and pulled me against her. Gently, but firmly, she made me walk backwards, feet against feet, and parted lips joined. The last thing I knew I was flat on my back, in bed, and she was on the top of me. For the first time, I noticed how astonishingly strong she was. She held my arms open and fondled me until she was fully conscious of my willingness to follow her on the road to love.

Those moments of sexual acquaintance introduced us to a world of intense emotions and pleasures; above all, we didn't have to go out for anything at all. Once a week, Yolanda called a supermarket, ordered what we needed, and, one hour after, a messenger delivered the bags of food. Whenever I had the opportunity, I gave a ring to Aunt Emma or I visited her and brought her cakes, ice cream and boxes of crackers. I never stayed too long with her, because I tried to avoid giving her any explanation of my conduct. In fact, there was nothing to explain, since I didn't have any control over what I was doing at Yolanda's, neither over what I could expect from it. Moreover, I was always eager to join my hostess. She was a center of sexual delight, and I was eighteen years of age, at the peak of my sexuality kept too long muzzled and unperturbed.

4

t first, I was dreaming of a dragon thundering and gar-
gling. It was standing between me and a window opened
on to a meadow and a river over yonder. As it twirled its
tail and posed a threat to anyone in its way, I trembled from fear and
woke up with a start. Then I perceived a gurgling. I turned over on my
side; there was no sign of Yolanda! "Good Lord!" I exclaimed.
"Where can she be?"

I jumped out of bed and rushed to the bathroom. There she was
leaning over the toilet and vomiting!

"Yol, you should have called me," I suggested. "I didn't know that
you were sick. Let me help you."

I seized her round the waist, from behind, so my hands could
squeeze her stomach, exactly like Aunt Emma used to do when I was
sick and vomiting. I was thinking about the know-how we have
learned from our family surroundings.

I jokingly inquired, "Do you think your *fatty* and *double-troubles are* making you sick? Yol, you must take care of yourself. The primary keeper of your body as a temple is you."

She had one more spasm; then she rinsed her mouth, turned around and faced me. She was still a little winded. "Pete, don't be stupid!" she shouted. "What are you talking about? I know my body is my temple and I revere it. I've been taking good care of it. But I am not made of steel. Once in while, I may feel uncomfortable."

She rested her head on my shoulder like a child who has just made an ultimate effort not to sleep. Then, having caught her breath, she pushed me gently against the closing bathroom door and went on, "Pete, do you really think I would put such deadly stuff into my body, my beautiful body which I revere like a temple? I thought you knew me better than that. I only drink water and, occasionally, a glass of fruit juice. I don't smoke and I am not certainly on the booze. I was just joking the other day when I let you think I was under the influence of drugs. To tell you the truth, I was introducing you to the street jargon (for your own good). You never can tell, one of these days, you might find it very handy. The way to big money now leads to narcotics."

She blindfolded me with her palms and kissed me quickly on the lips. "Pete, don't look at me like that!" she screamed. "I am not crazy. I am simply realistic. I find myself in a world which is going on in a certain direction. To go against it would be foolish of me."

We remained voluptuously embraced for a while, and she kissed me tenderly on the neck and rubbed the back of my head. Then she suggested, "Pete, what I am going to tell you is not an expression of madness. I've never been more lucid in my life. So, hear me out.

"I have a more scientific way to explain the whole drug business spectrum."

"Is that so!" I cut in.

She proceeded didactically, "I read a lot, since I have plenty of time to do so. And I do believe the Darwinian natural selection is still going on, although we don't pay it too much attention. In the hierarchy of beings, only the most suitable for the imperatives of reality have made it. It could be that those hooked on drugs fall into the category of the unsuitable, the unfit for the requirements of reality. Then, from the very beginning, they weren't born to be strong and enjoy longevity. If they didn't reach the *Narcoland*, they would have buried themselves anyway in something no less destructive and deleterious: alcoholism, gang war, guerrilla warfare, bloody ethnic cleansing, mercenary activity, prostitution—and so on. They seem to be always walking on the wrong side of the road. They are not intelligent and must wallow in vices, then in the realm of nothingness, where they belong. The drug pushers, acting as simple agents for the evolution process by natural selection, do nothing but comply to the sickening and deadly wishes of the hooked.

"If this picture wasn't accurate, then it wouldn't happen at all. That natural selection has to be carried out all the time. Indeed it's going on naturally, despite the belief that we are reasonable beings and we should know how to behave wisely.

"I am telling you, Pete, the world is a jungle, in which only the most intelligent of us will survive. I am not talking nonsense; I've been around and I know a thing or two.

"Still lots of pushers are no better. They can only afford to *shoot* themselves with no out-of-pocket money. But, in the long run, their dooms are sealed.

"I am intelligent enough to be aware of all this. I would be naïve not to take advantage of such profitable business. However, I let everybody believe that I freak out from time to time. I even pretend to breathe uneasily because of my sniffing "dangerous substances". This is a strategy of survival."

I didn't know what I could make of her *scientific explanation* and her *strategy of survival*. My idea of Darwinism was certainly much *less realistic*. I thought that evolutionary fitness wasn't as fast and perceptible as she put it. I knew about the extinction of species from books, reports, televised documentaries, museum fossils and videos. However, Yolanda, who had never received any scientific training, had just "informed" me that evolution was more rampant than ever and was going on alive right under my very nose, and I had been an unconscious witness of it. I promised myself, from that point on, to keep a closer watch on reality.

My only doubt about her expertise came from the fact that she was too beautiful, voluptuous and suspiciously indolent, and she smelled

too good early that morning to be an *authority* in any branch of knowledge. But I could be wrong, considering the new breed of scientists
several of whom could be beautiful, dazzling, voluptuous young
woman with Einsteinian brain.

"Let's suppose I buy your explanation, Yol," I conceded, "what
could make you throw up?"

She looked at me with her falsely languid eyes. I shivered. No
scientist can look like that. She answered in a suspiciously provoca-
tive way, "You've made me sick!"

"I have! How could it be possible?" I protested in a bland but genuine manner. "I was sleeping when you felt sick. When you got up
and went to the bathroom, I was dreaming of a dragon giving me such
a scare. Remember, I joined you in the bathroom and found you sick."

"No, no, no! You were awoken when you made me sick! Believe
me!"

"No, I don't buy that. You are joking, are you? I wasn't conscious
of doing any harm to you. I wouldn't deliberately hurt you, Yol."

"Maybe you weren't conscious of what you did to me, but you
were awoken. I make no mistake about it."

"Yol, darling, what are you talking about?"

"Pete, you are responsible for my discomfort. I am pregnant."

"Good Lord!"

"Is that all you can say? Aren't you going to kiss the mother of
your child?"

I was so disturbed that I did whatever she asked me to do, like a zombie. For a novice, I was already doing too much! I had never had sex before, but as soon as she had shown me the way, I turned into an insatiable stallion. However, I didn't think for one minute that a new being would come out of the fury of our passion. How could I forget this imperative of nature?

I was confused.

Of course, it was a nice feeling to know that a *little angel* was developing in a woman I cared about, and who gave herself entirely to me. Indeed that woman, being young and beautiful, possessing the gift of seduction and the talent for making money, could have turned on the richest and the most powerful man in the world. Don't they say that a woman may conquer the planet with a smile only? But that young and charming woman had been waiting for me patiently to carry my baby. Such devotion touched me deeply. Notwithstanding, I didn't welcome the idea of having a child at that moment. I wasn't ready, neither was she (I thought).

I opened the bathroom door and went into the living room, trying to make some sense out of all this. She followed me there. I was deep in thought. She was kind of disappointed to my apparently halfhearted reaction. And she had the right to be discontented with me—to say the least. I thought I owed her an explanation, to appease her and make her aware of the fact that she wasn't at fault, and I wasn't unhappy. Her pregnancy was simply the result of our passion and the dictum of nature. My behavior, indeed, bordered on ungratefulness and insensitivity.

"Yol," I uttered.

"What is it, Peter?" her voice turned irascible. "What's wrong? I want to know! I thought I was bringing you the good news. What is it, Peter?"

"Yol, take it easy. We are not having a dispute. I…"

"Don't tell me to take it easy. I want to know what's wrong. You have reacted as if you have just received a death sentence. I don't understand you at all."

"Well, I sense some anger in your voice and I prefer not to say a word. We will talk when the time is right."

"When will the time be right? What should we talk about? I am listening. You haven't said anything meaningful to me. I know that you are smart, lucid. I am listening. You've started it, you've to finish it. I am not going to calm down until I know what's in your mind."

I was puzzled: I didn't expect her to flare up. She had to be under some kind of pressure. However, it seemed I had to say something, which would make matters better or worst. The status quo wasn't recommended at that moment.

"Do you think, Yol, that we are ready for a child now?" I finally asked.

She grabbed me by the shoulders, pushed me hard on the sofa and held me down.

"Yol, what do you think you are doing?" I complained. "You are hurting me. We are not having a fight, but a dialogue to make sense out of our situation. You must stop! What's wrong with you? Please."

I couldn't afford to be angry. I had to keep calm, to compel myself to keep calm, to avoid an ungracious reaction I would regret all my life. I kept saying to myself, "You should be calm. You have to be calm. Don't forget that you need two angry persons to cause the irreparable. She has the right to be angry. She's just found out she is pregnant and she is in a state of confusion. And your lukewarmness doesn't help the situation. Be calm."

"I am tired of your sermonizing me," she shouted. "Really, I am. Who do you think you are? You are no better than I! Do you hear me? Whatever I am doing is the result of my choice. Can't I make up my mind on what I want to do? Do I need your permission to act in any way I want to? Who gives you the right to sit in judgment on me? Tell me, for Christ's sake!"

She loosened her grip, but her face was still expressing anger. Then she referred to the matter *at issue*, "Peter, what do you mean? You'd better explain yourself. I am not going to take this crap from you. Are you trying to play God now? Is it in your power to decide when I should have a baby or not? Tell me!

"In fact, you act like a Super God. The True God creates us to have children. You, on the contrary, don't expect any as a result of our relationship. If you didn't want any children, you shouldn't come to my home and make love to me."

I had to cool off. The last thing I needed was a quarrel with her. In fact, I felt ashamed and sorry to make her upset. She tried to be helpful. Besides, I was a guest in a way; I had no right to impose my ethical values on her. And speaking of ethical values, did I have any? If I did, what could they be?

"Sorry! I am confused, Yol," my voice turned pleasant, assuaging. "I don't know what I am saying. Do you forgive me?"

"How can I forgive you if I don't know what you have in mind?"

"I have nothing in mind. Forget that I even raised a question."

"If you mean that I should have an abortion, forget it."

"I don't mean that. I..."

She brightened up.

Her changeableness made me think about her childlike resiliency.

She stood up, then sat down on the sofa and, with motion of the hands, invited me to do the same. "Peter, let me tell you something," her voice was didactic, "you shouldn't take me for granted. I am a grown-up woman with a mind of my own. If I didn't love you, I wouldn't let you come and live with me; I wouldn't wait for you, patiently. What else could have made me behave this way?

"Powerful and wealthy men are after me. They have offered me castles in Spain, all the gold in Peru, pies in the sky. But I don't trust them. I feel they are simply after my body and my youthfulness. I figure out that, following them will lead me to a tunnel of despair. And what makes me resist to the falsely exciting life they have tried to lure me to? Your image. It has outshone them all. Why? I haven't got the faintest idea. It happens to be one of the mysteries of existence. But I do love you and more than you can imagine. Then how could you expect me to get rid of a being as valuable as a baby coming from you? Would you still have respect for me if you learned that I aborted your child I was pregnant with? Listen, this is the biggest gift I have ever received in my life. I am certain I'll give birth to a boy who'll be your very picture in all respects. You deserve to be duplicated, don't you ever forget it. You may not believe me, I am not depraved. You are the first man I've allowed to share my bed. I do have a sense of value, which you keep reinforcing in me."

After a short pause, she added regretfully, "I was the one who lost my temper and did the cursing. You were the embodiment of wisdom. However, put yourself in my place and you'll understand my reaction to your apparent lukewarmness."

We kissed and made up. Everything seemed to be in order except that I couldn't get out of my mind the idea of our unfitness for having a baby at that moment. In my case, I felt that I wasn't praiseworthy: I was a college dropout living on my girl friend's illicit activity.

Time was flying. I had been living at Yolanda's for about a year. Meanwhile, she was getting heavier and clumsier, and could give birth to the baby soon. Her maternal instinct already appeared and started to spread out on the entire apartment. She wouldn't let me help her to do anything at all. She cooked, did the washing and all the cleaning, and, above all, she personally attended her *storekeeper func-*

tions. It was her *livelihood,* and she seemed to be uncompromising about it. Nonetheless, I sensed that she was actuated by nobler feelings: she wanted to protect me from something evil, to make me keep my "purity" and my positive *image* untouched, so she could—so to speak— come back to it with a sense of re-immersing herself in an *atmosphere* of *greatness.* I was grateful to her for holding me in such high esteem and I will be for the remaining of my life.

One day, the *messenger* came to pick up *things* from her. He was the same one that I had seen coming daily, since I had been living in her home. She opened her unusually large refrigerator and pulled a parcel form the vegetable compartment. She could hardly bend forward. When she drew herself up, she made a painful face.

"That's it, Yolanda!" I declared firmly. "I can't stay here and let you hurt yourself. I am a man, not a puppet. I'll attend your business (at least until you get back on your feet)."

She looked at me with her falsely innocent eyes. "You are not going to like it," she warned me. "But it seems that I have no choice. The simplest task seems to make me out of breath. Since you make me sick, you must take care of me for a while. Isn't it right, little daddy?"

She kissed me tenderly on the lips. I kissed her back. We felt so close to each other! Then we became aware of the *messenger's* presence. We turned around and looked askance at him.

He smiled and left. We couldn't tell whether he approved of our closeness or not.

I sat down on the sofa and asked Yolanda to join me. She lay down at full length on the seat, her head resting on my lap. I touched her enlarged abdomen and felt, for the first time, the fetal movements.

"Now, you notice," she observed.

"Yes, I do," I replied

"Pete, I am so happy to carry your child. I thank God for the day you came and shared my life.

"Hum!" I only uttered.

She took my hand and squeezed it. I sensed a pleasant flush of warmth emanating from her.

"Pete, listen to me," she stated suddenly. "What I am going to tell you is extremely important.

"Don't ask questions. I don't ask questions myself; I am just a *storekeeper*. I don't even know what they are doing or selling. I am honest. I imagine their transactions must be illegal. One doesn't have to be a genius to figure it out. But everybody is dealing in illegal activity. For some unexplained reason, crime pays lavishly, as evidenced by many crooked people's wealthiness. This is the only way one can make a living. It's like a disgrace to go to work for a company or the government and to receive a fixed small income. I repeat: in these days, one can never live comfortably by being a fixed wage-earner. Somehow the policy makers give us enough money to barely survive. So, they have started the generalized demoralization and despair spread all over the world. Indeed Rent and other bills are due before you know it, every month, like a deadly curse. Interest rates are outrageous. The prices of commodities and services are skyrocketing. One has to make a lot of money to keep up with this kind of galloping inflation."

I was listening to her like a little boy who knows better than his mother, but keeps silent in deference to her.

"But, Yol, at least, out of curiosity, you should try to find out what you are involved in," I cut in quickly. "Don't tell me that you are totally unconcerned? I won't believe that."

"Listen, Pete, I am too young to be interested in what people are doing with their lives," she argued in such a natural fashion that I shuddered with apprehension. "That's no concern of mine. And I am sincere. I don't want to lie to you. Really, we are too close to have secrets between us. I am not a politician who may tell you a nice story to have your vote. One wants to commit suicide, that's his prerogative. He wants to live, that's his prerogative too. If I intervene in one's decision about his life, he will have the right to ask me for assistance, which I am unable to give him. Maybe I'll change when I turn older. All I'm interested in now is to survive for my baby and you."

She kept silent for a while before going on, "Anyway, to come back to what I was saying, I don't ask questions. I don't even question my role in the whole business. Why should I be concerned about something like that? I am just a blind soldier carrying out senseless orders. I don't get paid to think; for, I am not in a business that requires cerebration. And I have been often reminded of that in a clever and understood fashion. Furthermore, I wouldn't spend my time thinking about something as stupid as what I am doing. Once a month, I drive to a warehouse to pick up light boxes. I am supposed to keep them unopened in transit in my refrigerator (a huge one, isn't?) or anywhere else they are safe from *prying eyes*. In return, I occupy this "suite" and receive enough money to live like a princess. I don't kill anyone with my bare hands; this, I will never do, except in self-defense. What I don't see I don't know. I don't have any guilty conscience. Do you understand me?"

She paused for breath and then proceeded, "If you want to help me, all you have to do is to take one light box out of the refrigerator and hand it over to that stupid *messenger* (whenever he shows up). No more, no less. I was expressly told not to give him more than one box a day. Why? I can't tell. I believe that box contains *raw material* that could be processed to respond to the clients' daily needs. By the way, I was hired because of my ignorance of what's going on. A *female employee,* a friend of mine recommended me for the position. I didn't sell my body or my dignity. Is it clear, Pete? Believe me, I've given you a safe and sound body, an ingenuous soul and untapped passion."

I kept silent. There was nothing to say. She had covered all the grounds. I had accepted her presents I could no longer refuse: a *safe and sound body*, an *ingenuous soul* and *untapped passion*. Whatever the course of action, it was too late for me to go forward or backwards. Almost a year earlier, I had solicited and obtained her friendship and *savoir-faire*. In return, she needed me, I couldn't abandon her. That would sound too ungrateful and contrary to my belief in the give and take relationships among normal people.

Moreover, she was carrying our baby. I had a strong sense of responsibility, like this of a *paterfamilias*. My "duty" was to do whatever in my power to support the mother and our baby.

That day, we stayed for hours on the sofa. She stopped her *monologue*. Words were no longer necessary: we understood each other and had the intuition of what was going on.

Someone rang at the door. I stood up and went to see who it was.

A couple of guys (one White, one Black) stepped in and made themselves at home. There were tall and slender. Both wore all tailored three-piece suits, matching shoes, ties, and large hats a la musketeer. In fact, they removed their hats and bowed to Yolanda showily, as if they were two royal escorts in person.

I made a quick look through the window and saw a fancy car parking alongside the sidewalk, which attracted a crowd of admirers among the passers-by. There was no doubt about whom it belonged to. Those guys were too extravagant to drive an average vehicle.

"Yolanda, so many things have happened to you since our last meeting," the black visitor insinuated in a very falsely sweet tone. "We thought that you were keeping a low profile. That's our mistake. You've been instead very busy."

While he was talking, he pointed Yolanda's stomach out with his chin.

"Paul, just leave me alone!" she said.

"Oh, don't be shy!" he insisted. "I meant to compliment you. You are fulfilling your womanly functions."

The visitors invited themselves to the armchairs in the living-room and sat, with the legs wide-open and stretched out, as if they were masters of the universe.

"Yolanda, I am proud of you," remarked the white visitor. "You know we all love you. You are a valuable asset to our association. We trust you and never have any reason to complain. Despite your pregnancy, you keep carrying out your duty to perfection. That's truly commendable."

"Well, Tony, I couldn't do it without Peter," she acknowledged. "By the way, he'll keep things going while I am pregnant."

"Who's he?" Tony asked.

I was astounded that the man was referring to me as if I were a piece of furniture.

"Tony, you must know that I wouldn't entrust the first comer with my *delicate function*," she replied jokingly. "Peter is the father..."

Suddenly, Paul and Tony stood up, came up to me and shook hands with me. "Welcome, brother!" Paul said.

"Yolanda is a loving, beautiful, sensitive woman," asserted Tony. "She needs a considerate man—you know what I mean—to love her, protect her and make her feel good. You must be the man she's been waiting for (there was a suggestion of bitterness in his voice). Welcome, Peter! And, I tell you! You do a good job; you don't have to worry about problems in life!"

Suiting the action to the words, he removed a long wallet from his jacket inside pocket, took a wad of large bills out of it, and gave them to me. "Accept this as a token of my friendship and appreciation," he added.

Shortly after, he and Paul were on their way out. Just as they were closing the door behind them, the former stopped short and, with a pointed finger towards Yolanda's stomach, asked, "By the way, when is the bambino due to be with us?"

"The doctor said in about one month," replied Yolanda.

"Good. Please, notify me of that, and I'll send him my welcome present."

"How do you know it'll be *he*?" asked an all smiling Yolanda.

"Mum, you wouldn't dare give us a sister now!"

Both visitors burst out laughing.

Yolanda and I heard them laughing all the way down the street.

5

I carried out Yolanda's *duty* to perfection, which consisted of opening the refrigerator, pulling a light box from the vegetable compartment and giving it to our *messenger*. That man, with a clockwork precision, showed up daily. Did they cut his tongue for security reason? Sometimes I was thinking of speaking to him to prove his muteness or not, but the vow of silence I was put under by Yolanda would curb my curiosity. One day, after he had received the parcel, he delivered a letter to me and left. "Should I add shyness to his muteness?" I thought.

Yolanda took that letter from me, sliced the envelope open with her finger nail and read the address where "delivery of the goods" would be taken place.

"There won't be any problem to find the place," she assured. "I did go there once."

"What do you mean?" I inquired in a puzzling tone.

I could never get accustomed to our "line of work".

"Oh! I've forgotten to tell you that the place of delivery isn't the same at all time," her voice expressed apprehension and regret at the same time. "It changes, once in while, to different areas (maybe for security reason or something like that)."

"I see."

My voice betrayed a certain asperity. Her attempt to clear up the situation had saddened me instead. I was wondering about the type of relationship we were going to have. She was so involved in schemes totally alien to me, which I would never condone willingly! Would I ever get rid of the nagging feeling that she had so many deadly secrets hidden from me that, in the long run, I would develop a distrust of her and I would always believe that she would be a perfect stranger to me? Such thought hurt me, above all when I knew she trusted me herself despite her secretiveness.

Maybe she sensed my dilemma; for, she said in an apologetic and sad voice, "Peter, there's nothing to worry about. I know all the places of delivery. I'll accompany you."

I walked away into the kitchen to fix us some breakfast.

The following day, we left early in the morning to the *delivery place*. I drove carefully: her due day was drawing near. She could barely walk and often was out of breath. Her stomach had enormously distended, and it was quite a challenge for her to go on a trip to some distant warehouse.

After driving for two hours or so, we reached the warehouse located in an area unknown to me, which wasn't surprising, considering, before my involvement with her business, I had almost lived like a *certified hermit*: I had spent my entire existence between school and Aunt Emma's home, to such a par, one might think I wasn't a native of New York. Because of my seclusive life, I wasn't good (I am not still) at finding my way around the State.

A bearded tall white man recognized Yolanda and welcomed her. "Uh-huh...Yol!" he shouted. "You must be ready to deliver of that angel you are carrying! That's a boy!"

She smiled against her will.

The bearded man went into a recess under a staircase and returned shortly after with a large box. I imagined it was light since he was carrying it easily with one hand. When he reached us, he eyed me suspiciously before turning the box over to me (with an obvious reluctance).

"One can never be too careful," he couldn't help insinuating. "You have to, above all when your life is at stake."

Again I remembered the muteness attitude recommended by Yolanda and received the *precious parcel* with no comment whatsoever. Then we drove back home.

No sooner had we entered the apartment, she screamed. I ran to her help and held her by the shoulders. She looked so frail! I was so scared!

"Yol, what's wrong?" I inquired.

She drew a long breath and answered, "I think it's almost here."

"You think so?"

"But sure. I am the one who's carrying it. If I said it's not far from...uh, uh, uh!"

"I am going to take you to the health center, now!"

"I think you should. The pains are becoming regular...uh, uh, uh! I won't go without my bag...uh, uh, uh!"

I thought that women's minds worked differently from men's. Yolanda was having excruciating pains and could barely stand up; and yet, she had enough strength and lucidity to remember her bag.

I wondered how many men, in such a stressful situation, would think about a bag.

"Don't worry, Yol, I will take care of everything," I assured. "I'll take the bag. I know where you keep it handy. I'll drive you to the health center. I am going also to call Dr. Joel...Let's go."

She took one look at me, shook her head and smiled.

I giggled: I suggested to her that we should leave, while I didn't fulfill any of my urgent promises.

"Yol, you must understand my emotive state of mind," I uttered apologetically. "Just be a little patient and I'll do my best to take care of everything. Remember, it's going to be my first child too!"

She kissed me and touched my face. "Go ahead! I'll be patient, little daddy," she said. "I understand."

It was a nice gesture on her part, managing to transcend her pains in order to be sweet to me. She infused new heart into me. As a matter of fact, few minutes after, we were on our way to the health center she had been attending since the beginning of her pregnancy (with her bag full with female toiletries).

When we reached the emergency room, we were pleased to see that Dr. Joel had been waiting for us. He looked weird and tired in his aseptic green uniform. He didn't waste any time and helped her to the maternity quarters located on the fourth floor.

I was sitting in the waiting room, hoping for the best. One hour later, Dr. Joel joined me. He sat down and stretched his legs. "I am exhausted," he whispered. "We've been having a busy day."

I made no comment. My mind was empty and couldn't put words together to form meaningful sentences. I decided to keep my mouth shut to avoid making a fool of myself.

The obstetrician asked, "It's going to be your first child, isn't it?"

"Yes, it is," I answered.

"Oh, don't worry! Yolanda is in good hands. She's put to bed and is being prepared by the nurses for an aseptic delivery. I've just examined her personally and believed that very soon she'll have a healthy baby. It's better not to hasten her delivery, so no instruments will be required. We believe it's better for women to have—what they call—normal, natural delivery.

"Your wife is still in the first stage labor. Some pain killer was given to her. The head nurse will call me as soon as her cervix is fully dilated. So, at this point, it's going to be a coordinate action of the medical staff and Yolanda's willpower.

"She can use her abdominal muscles to help along the contractions..."

I was listening vaguely to Dr. Joel's obstetric explanation. Indeed I was in a daze. I felt as if I was dropped in the middle of the ocean of life, lying at the mercy of a blind destiny. So was Yolanda. Poor Yolanda! It was my fault if her life was imperiled. I should have let her alone. I should have resisted calling her after I had dropped out of school. I should have faced my problems alone, like a man. My reaching out to her was maybe responsible for her predicament. If I panicked and abandoned her! Would I behave in such manner? No. I didn't think so. I was a man of my word. I would stand by her for better or for worse. Those doctors and nurses, did they know what they were doing? I wished I could be with her to help her breathing, to encourage her and make her feel that she wasn't by herself. But I was too scared; I would faint and embarrass her unnecessarily. She would be well. She had to be. She didn't deserve to be harmed in any respect. All things being considered, she was a good person. As the time went by, I understood her better and discovered the positive aspects of her nature: generosity and love (although she was afraid of acknowledging them). She was good to me, wasn't she? Of course, she made the wrong move by getting involved in something illegal, but I was sure that she would get out of that mess. I guaranteed she would. I would take care of this matter personally.

I whispered, "My God! Why hasn't she delivered yet? No, she won't die!"

I had to murmur the last sentences as a prayer to cast out the pitiful representation of a *Yolanda* lying down dead, like a piece of wood. I recognized at once that my vision had to be wrong: it pictured a life-less image which had nothing to do with the *voluptuous young woman* I knew. She was bubbling over with energy instead, with a compelling desire to live, with *untapped passion*. She wouldn't die. No. She had to live for her baby, our baby (if not for me). If she lived, I would do whatever in my power to free her from her dangerous environment, from Paul, Tony and their friends. I knew those people. They were nothing but human trash, despite their deceitful appearance of supe-riority and stylishness. They were dispensers of death and hopeless-ness. I would be so glad if the proclamation of God's existence cor-responded to reality and that such a Great Being was alive and well. I would be so glad, the more so as He would stand up as a Universal Soldier delivering a swift and just punishment to that deadly gang, or even as a rectifying Cosmic Judge saying in a powerful and clear voice: "No" to all the criminals who plagued the world and brought violence and death to innocent people. How could Yolanda get in-volved with these hoodlums' insane schemes? Poor Yolanda! She was on the wrong track for sure.

She claimed to live comfortably! Poor Yolanda! She was instead like resting everyday in her coffin, waiting to be wasted one of these days.

"Mr. Young, Mr. Young, Mr. Young!" Someone, not far from me, shouted.

I turned round and saw a nurse. Maybe I showed an idiotic smile on my face, for she looked at me with pity.

"I've been calling you for the longest," her voice betrayed annoyance. "What's wrong with you?"

"Oh, I'm fine." I replied.

Then her facial expression changed and seemed to forecast good news.

"Congratulations! You have a son," she announced.

"I have a son! A son! A son!" my voice sounded like a broken record.

"Yes, you have a son. Mother and baby are well. Let's go."

The nurse went on ahead and led me to Yolanda and the baby.

I bet Yolanda had known her baby gender, long before his birth, but she had been content with only giving me some vague hints about it.

When I entered the room, I saw the mother. She was glowing with happiness, charm and beauty. However, I didn't perceive the *new being* immediately. And, puff! Like a revelation, it was there! It looked like a rabbit. "Was I like that once?" I wondered. "Of course you were; so was everybody. What's going to happen to this *little man*? Is he already a person? He won't be a bum, will he? No, he will be fine. Twenty years from now, he will be a handsome young man ready to conquer the world."

At that time, I used to wonder about the *bag persons*, the alcoholics, the drug addicts, the homeless I used to see on the train, at night, or in dirty streets. They smelt like horses. They had no place to go, no food to eat, no claim on reality, no bright future to yearn for. It's one of the worst human tragedies. Their bodies were infected and covered with deep wounds and ugly ulcers. They were not the pictures of the ideal humanity, to such a par that *normal people* tried to avoid their company, to express feeling of revulsion in their presence and to often hide them from tourists' views. Had those homeless ever been babies, little angels? Had they ever been washed, powdered and pampered? What went wrong with them?

Those sad thoughts crossed my mind when I was face to face with the *little man* begotten by me. I didn't think he would be a bum. His angelic face seemed to destine him for a better lot. Yet, I was conscious of the fact that his cherubic look wasn't a guarantee of success in life. But what could I do to ward off an eventuality of failure for him? I had no power to prevent the worst from happening to the *little man. Poor little man*! He didn't ask to be born. I thought that he should remain in the realm of nothingness, so he wouldn't be exposed to Paul, Tony and their likes' misdeeds.

Tony! That man's name resounded in my mind like a knell, a grinding machine or a brewery delivering bitterness, disgust and despair. Certainly, my son wouldn't be called Tony. He wouldn't be called Paul either. The latter's name would always remind me of the former's. I was used too much to associating them with each other, to think of them as two complementary pieces of a deadly mechanism. No, I wouldn't call my son either Tony or Paul. I was absolute sure of that. I believed Yolanda would let me pick out my son's name. It was the least I could ask her for.

I was almost happy to decide something meaningful to me about my progeny.

"Pete," she said.

I became again conscious of her presence and answered apologetically, "Yol, the little man had held my attention. You did such a good job! They said you were courageous. I am glad that you could manage without me. I was so scared! I didn't want to embarrass you. Do you forgive me?"

I kissed her. She hugged me. "I won't let you go, monster," she said joyfully.

We remained embraced for a while.

"Pete, I gave you a hard time," she whispered: "I cursed you, I yelled at you and I even did violence against you. You must understand that I didn't mean any of these things. I was nervous, that's all."

"I knew, Yol," I conceded.

"I am glad you did. That makes my heart less heavy."

We remained silent for a while. She squeezed my neck and kissed me repeatedly on the face. Suddenly, she asked me, "By the way, how are things going on over there, at home?"

"Yol, your guess is as good as mine," my voice betrayed a certain disconcertment. "Remember, we've been together since this morning."

"That's true. Well, Paul and Tony might fly into a rage if they call and don't have any answer," she insisted; "above all on a day we have picked up goods which belong to them. They are not among the nicest people in the world."

I was on the verge of losing my temper. I couldn't understand the reason why she had to spoil our closeness.

"They'll keep calling until they reach me while I am home," I vented my frustration. "Is there anything simpler than that?"

Paul and Tony, those men would drive me crazy if I did nothing about them.

"What's wrong?" Yolanda asked.

"Nothing," I replied.

"You turn bitter. I don't recognize my sweet little Peter."

I kept silent for a while. Then I suggested abruptly, "Yol, if I have nothing more I can do for the baby and you, I believe that I should go back home."

"I think so," she conceded sadly. "But I am sorry that the world can't be upright, the way you would like it to be. I know, Pete, I know. You are a sensitive and bright man. But, be patient with me. One of these days I'll live up to your expectations. I have to if I want to be close to you all the time."

I kissed her good bye and walked towards the exit.

Her car was parked not far from the health center. I took the wheel and drove away. I lowered the glass door by me. A fresh breeze welcomed me. I felt better already. It was the beginning of March, and the weather was full of surprises. In the morning—I remembered—, It was *nasty*. There was a blizzard. Visibility, while driving, was reduced due to fog hailstorm and snow. I had to guess my way through a maze of cars and people. Gradually, the snow had changed to cold rain. Some streets were flooded. However, on my way back home, I noticed that the rain had stopped for the longest and that the sun was radiating everywhere. The trees displayed their stripped branches like fleshless human arms.

By midday, the whole city offered a summery appearance. Children were running like hares on the school playground. They screamed like a bunch of birds. As to the adults, they were having a walk, breathing in the fresh air, talking about this and that. Some wore too warm clothes; some, too light ones. Young women took advantage of the sudden warming up of the weather to carry short pants and skirts, as well as low-cut blouses, to the enjoyment of young men's eyes (and old ones too, but in a more discreet manner). I understood those pretty women's feeling, since, for three months or so, the harshness of winter had prevented *any body exposure*. It was for them some kind of revenge on Mother Nature. They didn't care, so long as they could be out strolling around, when the weather allowed it.

By the time I reached Yolanda's apartment, it was so warm that I had to open the windows.

I was all by myself. I welcomed such opportunity to reexamine the priorities which *my old lady* and I might have to work out for our child's sake. Besides, I was beginning to enjoy solitude, not so much because I was unsociable, but because I found out that solitude was often less hollow, less discontinued than companionship. In social gatherings, speakers often bump their thoughts against each other, with no hope of reaching a compromise. In solitude, on the contrary, the mind wanders freely, in the context of harmonization of thoughts with one another.

The phone rang. I jumped: I was on the moon, in the land of fancy where my mind was venturing, dreaming about an ideal world, a possible one, if mankind made an effort to work at it.

I picked up the receiver.

A male voice, with a shade of anxiety, uttered, "Hello, Peter. Are you Peter?"

"Yes," I answered.

"This is Tony."

"Oh, dear, Tony again," I thought. "What should I do? That man is getting on my nerves. Wherever I turn, his presence was there like spreading gangrene. Why Yolanda had to get me involved in such a mess? What could have prevented her from making a better choice of friends and work environment? She couldn't have been in such a desperate financial situation! Oh! I remember! She had her *pride*; she didn't want to go to her parents for anything at all."

"What can I do for you?" I finally asked aloud,

"I like that, Peter," that man said. "You are a business-minded person. No time to waste."

He kept silent for a short time before adding, "I called several times and didn't have any answer. Did you pick up the goods?"

"Yes, since this morning," I replied almost harshly. "There was nobody at home. We were busy at the health center."

"What's for?"

"How can you ask me that?"

"Oh! I've forgotten. Yolanda has the baby, hasn't she?"

"Yes, she had a boy this morning."

"Good."

He hung up.

Definitely, that man was weird. He might even be out of this world. For one thing, he didn't show good judgment to ask me why I had to go to the health center; unless Yolanda's pregnancy meant so little to him that he had forgotten it completely. As a matter of fact, people, usually, don't go to hospitals for the fun of it. "I must do something about the whole matter," I whispered. "I am not going to let Yolanda and our son lie at that man's mercy. They have to be kept away from such a nightmarish environment. I'll have to do it the hard way, though I'll suffer myself."

I went to the bedroom and started to look for Yolanda parents' address.

It was the first time I invaded her privacy. I was also hoping it would be the last time.

6

I thought I would have a nervous breakdown if things continued at the same rate. A month had elapsed since I had mailed an anonymous letter to Yolanda's parents. I was hopeful that letter was disquieting enough to alarm them and decide them to take some appropriate action.

I wrote:

Mr. and Mrs. Clinton,

It's painful to me but I have to send you this letter. You don't know me and had never met me. I happen to be Yolanda's schoolmate. Recently, we have been very close to each other. No matter what happens to me, I can't stay there and watch her destroying herself and, in the process, someone else she loves very much.

They are in great danger. I am incapable of guessing the magnitude of such danger. Words can't describe it.

I know that you cherish your unique child. Now if you want to save her from an awful destiny, I will advise you to come and get her in any way you can.

Don't tell her that I am the author of this plea. She will kill me.

A concerned friend.

If Yolanda's parents took my letter lightly, their carelessness would lead to many unpleasant eventualities.

First, they could confide in some corrupt authorities who would then warn Paul and Tony. I imagined these had built up connections in high places. The outcome would be disastrous.

Second, Yolanda could be contacted in writing by her parents who might believe that a scolding letter would do. She and the criminal association could arrive at the conclusion that I was the person who had written anonymously to Mr. and Mrs. Clinton. I was a new comer, wasn't I? The association had never experienced this kind of problem before.

Third, Yolanda, our son and I would remain forever at Paul and Tony's mercy.

The mere thought of being at the mercy of those scoundrels drove a breath of warm air throughout my body. For, in such eventualities, all my vision of the future would vanish forever. "No, no," I whispered, "I must hasten my freedom from these dogs, one way or another".

So, until then, the parents' silence to my anonymous letter seemed to prove the inanity of my worries. In the meantime, I was remembering the content of that letter and was ashamed of myself. I couldn't prevent myself from feeling that I was a spy, a double-crosser. I was laughing to Yolanda, playing with her and our baby, being nice to them, and still I betrayed them.

I felt even guiltier, on recalling my first meeting with that woman. I'd been so desperate and unable to conceive of any escape from my predicament at the school, and I had even thought of committing suicide. Then she welcomed me in her house, initiated me into her secret business and carried my baby. Yet I betrayed her.

She held me in high esteem and told me that my personality outshone people of wealth and power she had met, and yet I betrayed her.

However, I had to find a way to prevent her from being headed for greater disaster. Undoubtedly, she imagined that she was having a nice time, a life of pleasure. Yet, as far as I was concerned, she was rather engaged in a deadly game which could shorten our lives any moment, in case Tony and Paul had their suspicions about our intentions.

I didn't think she was as intelligent as she believed, at least with respect to morality which, being a conformity to the rules of right conduct, requires a high level of intelligence. Perhaps she had enough intelligence to join a criminal association and make the best out of it: a *castle*, costly furniture and a life of *princess*. She was smart enough to give others the false impression of being addicted to deadly drugs.

But did she really make an intelligent move? A lot of narrow-minded street youngsters have got it into their heads that they are smart to be deceitful; a lot of statesmen also claim to be intelligent because they outwit their opponents and drive their subjects to despair. None of them are intelligent in the human sense of the word. What they are doing barely goes beyond lower animals' activities. Don't animals outsmart their preys? Don't we expect more from human intelligence, the power of sublimation? Of course we do, under normal circumstances. Indeed we expect it to be more constructive than destructive, to serve as an instrument of genuine progress, and a stepping stone to promoting communication and understanding.

I am not saying that it's easy to try being lucid all the time. I know that sometimes it hurts to be lucid, to keep being considerate and to restrain oneself from pleasurable experiences which one knows might turn sour in the long run. In fact, at the time of this story, the worst part of my nightmarish situation stemmed from my constant heedfulness of reality. I never stopped being conscious of my flirting with my doom. Consequently, in spite of my concern about others, I had to strive to remain consistent with myself, to do violence against my feelings, to repress the bestial part of my nature, which kept suggesting to me that society should be taken as a jungle, where only individual survival made sense, only the primary needs had to be satisfied, only the biological values should be taken into consideration, regardless of the cost of action. In a context of primal nature, all these postures could have been adopted without any remorse.

However, as far as I was concerned, it was too late for me to be subdued by uncontrollable drives. I had been exposed too long to values practiced by genuine human beings through the ages: uniqueness of a person, human dignity, the tendency of the mind to transcend immediate reality, man as a bridge between ignorance and knowledge, between mediocrity and greatness, between being and becoming.

Thus I was involved indirectly in criminal activities, and yet I abominated malfeasance in any respect. I didn't stand a chance to survive, with such an awkward attitude, unless I endeavored to escape from my criminal environment. It was as if I wanted to get involved in misdeeds without willing to get involved in them. The *absurdity* of my position was blatant and couldn't continue without engendering trouble I wouldn't be able to handle.

But I wouldn't leave Yolanda and our son behind. They had to be included in the escape plan. Yolanda was nice to me and reminded me that life is full with alternatives. My son, well, he was another I, a projection of me in space and time. Leaving him behind would be turning my back on myself.

I had then legitimate reasons for writing anonymously to Yolanda's parents. Not that I didn't look for another way of life and alternative; but that young lady was adamant in her refusal to even think over my exhortation to change her field of activity to some more lawful one.

In fact, one day, I had a dispute with her on her involvement with Paul and Tony. We were sitting on the sofa, in the living room. Peter junior was in my arms. She was so angry at me that she grabbed the baby from me and went to sit down on a chair, far away, in the dining room.

I remembered having only said, "Yol, now that we have a child, we can't allow ourselves to behave inconsiderately. We have to think about his safety, his future and, above all, about our duty as parents to act in a way that will make him proud of us. We can't allow ourselves to teach him badness. Remember, parents are the first role models that can shape the children's minds while they are malleable, adaptable and waxy."

She yelled out, "What are you talking about? This is what I hate with you: you've been talking all kind of nonsense. I don't see anything wrong with what we are doing."

"How do we know that?"

"How can our ignorance of reality make a difference? We grab what we can. Isn't it a law of survival? We are not creators of this world and certainly not responsible for the turn it takes. We have no choice but to follow the trend."

"You just don't want to understand," I pointed out. "You close your eyes and your ears to deliberately avoid facing reality. I must tell you that ignorance is not a permanent state of mind. The refusal to know is something else."

"Peter, you know, you are a pain in the neck! Nobody can have you as a useful associate. You are capable of ruining any plan for the future. Don't tell me that I've made the biggest mistake in my life by loving you!"

"Thanks!"

"Really, I don't understand you at all. You think you've got the absolute and final answer to everything. Reality is this or that, according to your omniscient mind. You have complete mastery of the alpha and the omega of what needs to be known. But I have a question for you: where else can you make as much money as you are making now?"

"That's not the point."

"What's the point? Damn it!"

"The point is that we don't know the source of our money."

"So! Who cares?"

"I do."

"That's your damned business."

"If it's my business, I am entitled to know."

She stood up. She had a mean expression on her face. I was really concerned about the safety of Peter Junior. She could, in a fit of rage, throw the baby at me. I thought then I should try to placate her before she resorted to something so awful.

"Listen to me, Peter," she screamed, "is it the way you intend to pay me back for letting you come to my house, where you live like a prince? Not only you want to cut off my livelihood and my child's, but also you want us to be killed. What kind of ethical philosophy are you professing? For its sake, you want to cause harm to people you said you care about. I can't figure you out."

She had a good point. My insisting on knowing all about our line of activity might endanger our lives, which would be downright stupid.

"I do care about you," I argued for conscience's sake. "If I didn't, I wouldn't question our behavior and our future. I would either go along with you or walk away. But don't you think that we should know what we are embarked on? For, if, by any chance, we are instruments of death, we will be as morally ugly as the killers themselves."

"Come on, Peter! You are living in a dream world. People don't put obstacles in their own ways as you do. You are impossible, self-defeating. But you can't have it both ways. You can't enjoy the benefits of our *kinds of activities,* which you find fault at, and think that you can still come out smelling roses."

"No, I am not self-defeating," I protested. "If I was, I wouldn't think about the dangers we are putting others and ourselves in. I think you are totally wrong about me. Our relationship means a lot to me. We don't need to live in abundance to have a wonderful time together. I am concerned about our dignity, our sense of value, our status as members of an intelligent community. We have each other, don't we? I can find myself a regular decent position somewhere and bring home money coming from the sweat of my brow and not from innocent people's blood. It may not be as profitable as what we are engaged in now, but we won't have either to keep watching our back, living in constant fear, day in day out. All I ask you is not to destroy our chance to happiness by insisting on living carelessly. Don't you care about the future of our relationships?"

"Of course, I do," she answered.

Peter Junior was soundly sleeping. I relieved her of him and took him to his cradle, in the bedroom. About five minutes later, she joined me. She kissed me. I kissed her back. The fire of our passion rekindled. When we came back to our senses, she asserted as if she hadn't stopped talking for quite a while, "...However, until you can find a very good job to take care of us, I won't make the mistake to cut off our livelihood. This is the only way, Pete, my darling, the only way. Only then you'll find out what a loving and passionate woman you have in your hands. I'll make life sweet for you. I'll do things for you, which both you and I couldn't have dreamed of. I'll be entirely yours."

I had the intuition that the course of events was about to speed up. The apartment looked so strange, as if I didn't belong to its setting and that I was viewing it through a mirror or in a dream. Why was I feeling this kind of distortion of reality? I couldn't tell. Yet I firmly believed that a painful experience remained to be undergone. What would be the magnitude of it? Who would be hurt? Was I experiencing an illusion or the power of foresight? I couldn't answer those questions either. Yet, although such premonitory feeling was compelling in me, I held it to be devoid of any bearing on the coming state of affairs. For, since I was nervous, after I had written anonymously to Yolanda's parents, I ascribed my concern about the future to my confused mind full with guilt and apprehension. Anyway, to get rid of my vexation, I joined Yolanda in the bedroom and started to tease her. We then played, laughed, kissed each other. At times, I took our son in my arms and kissed him all over his stomach and his neck. He laughed heartily. Once in a while, his mother fell on my neck and kissed us both. It was a happy and sad occasion at the same time. We looked apparently like an ideal family finding happiness in its small universe confined in the apartment; however, such happiness was bound to be short-lived. We should rather be crying than laughing.

My guilty conscience was haunting me in the middle of that short moment of cheerfulness. I said to myself, "I am a monster; I am a Judas in person. I am no good. I am playing with Yolanda and my son, laughing with them, while I am on the verge of parting from them. This can happen any minute. Perhaps her parents may have been in town. Did I do the right thing by sending the anonymous letter? Why didn't I wait longer and see what would come out of the situation? It could be that I didn't take all the facts into consideration."

The door bell rang over and over. I felt a pinch in my heart. That painful experience was about to happen! My intuition about it was so vivid, so lucid, that it took the complexion of certainty, as if I was a witness to a scenario. "Goodbye joy of living in this apartment with Yol and Peter junior," I thought, "but also goodbye Paul and Tony and the other vermin! Yol and our son are going to be safe. They are going to be fine."

"Yol, are you expecting a visitor?" I asked

"No, I am not," she replied. "That stupid messenger has been here. I don't know. It may be a salesman or a kid trying to sell something."

The door bell kept ringing.

Finally, I stood up and suggested, "Yol, let me see who's in such a hurry."

With the baby in her arms, she cautiously followed me at a certain distance. I turned round and looked at them. I tried to smile; I made a painful face instead. "Don't worry, you are going to be all right," I uttered unconvincingly. "I'll see to that."

I opened the door slowly. A policeman showed up. Then two other ones came in. They spoke all at once and sounded cacophonous. Finally, the one I had seen arriving first asked, "Is it Yolanda Clinton's residence?"

At first, I didn't answer, because I didn't know the purpose of their visit. If they had traced Tony's gang to that woman's activity, I would have to do my best to conceal her identity and give her time to run away.

The policemen looked at each other and were puzzled over my silence. One of them came up to me and stated, "Sir, we don't want any trouble from you, Do you understand me?"

"I don't intend to give you any, Officer," I stated. "Why should I?"

"...Therefore, you should cooperate with us..."

"I think I should. In fact, I've always cooperated with the police, since I am a law-abiding citizen. However, I am curious to know why you are inquiring about a certain Yolanda Clinton. I believe I am entitled to know."

Again the policemen looked at each other. Then they nodded assent to each other. The one who had spoken to me continued, "Sir, we have reason to believe that Yolanda Clinton lives here. We want to see that she speaks to her parents without any disturbance whatsoever."

"Since you've stated your business more clearly, Officer, there is no problem whatsoever," I replied cheerfully. "By the way, where are Mr. and Mrs. Clinton?"

The policeman, seemingly in charge, ordered the youngest one to go and pick up the parents. "There are in the lobby," he indicated, "by the manager's office."

Ten minutes later, the officer came back with the visitors.

Mr. Clinton entered first. He was tall and muscular. He was wearing a gray suit which fit him like a glove. I noticed his *tangled* and *dubious* ethnic origin Yolanda had tried to *decipher* to me before. He contemptuously looked about the living room.

Then Mrs. Clinton came in. She looked so young that, juxtaposing her and Yolanda, they would certainly be confused with two siblings.

The daughter shouted, "Mother, father, what are you doing here? Who gives you my address? I don't need your help! Go away!"

The father grabbed her and shook her violently. The mother ran to ease her of the baby. "Please George, don't make a big scene," she suggested. "Let me go and talk with Yolanda in the bedroom. I am sure something meaningful will derive from our conversation."

The father let go her daughter's arm. "I give you half an hour, Bonnie," he bawled. "Remember, I have a court order. I don't want any more nonsense from that young lady. I am warning you."

He pulled a folded paper out of his jacket inside pocket and held it up, as a reminder.

I went and sat down on the sofa. I turned into a living target: apart from the presumed superior officer, the policemen and Mr. Clinton were staring at me with obvious animosity. I felt naked in spite of the clothes I was wearing. But what could I do? I couldn't start talking like a fool in an attempt to clarify the situation. To clear myself from any wrongdoing, I had to reveal my real identity, to claim to be the person who had sent the anonymous letter. By so doing, I would heap on myself their anger and Yolanda's. I didn't want the latter to remember me as a double-crosser. In fact, I didn't believe I was a double-crosser at all, considering that my action could turn out to be a blessing in disguise. But Yolanda wouldn't take it like that. Usually, people on the wrong side of road want to keep on going deeper into trouble. They don't appreciate any attempt to make them change, until it's too late. So, I kept my mouth shut.

Likewise, my confession would incriminate the woman I cared so much about. I didn't believe I should go that far.

About half an hour later, Yolanda and her mother came out of the bedroom. The latter was still carrying the baby. She gave me the impression to be a very sweet and considerate person. Her moderate attitude had certainly come handy. I felt that, without her, the whole situation could have ended in tragedy.

Yolanda was dressed to go out. She held a trunk in her hand. I imagined that she was ready to leave with her parents. She said abruptly, while drawing near to me, "Mother, I would like to speak with Peter in private."

Mr. Clinton stepped in the middle of the living room, pointed a finger at me and shouted, "Who's that man?"

Yolanda didn't answer.

For some unexplained reason, people had confused me with a piece of furniture or a dog. First, it was Tony, now Yolanda's father, who didn't think they could ask me to identify myself.

"I am talking to you, Young Lady!" Mr. Clinton shouted.

Then turning around, he asked some kind of general question anyone could answer, provided that he knew what was really going on, "Can someone fill me in. I am in the dark here. What's going on in this apartment?"

His wife walked up to him and looked him in the eyes. She seemed to have the power to mollify him under any circumstances. And, apparently, she knew part of the answer. "Please, George! Control yourself!" her voice had never lost its softness. "Your quick temper won't make the situation any better. What you are about to hear won't please you. Yolanda obviously has a child, our grandchild. Isn't he cute? His name is Peter Junior. His father is this young man."

"That's great! Just great! That's just great!" the husband yelled out. "What did I do to deserve this kind of treatment? God, I am not questioning your wisdom, but try to enlighten me. I am in complete darkness."

Then he walked up to Yolanda and stopped few inches away from her. I was in state of tension, not being able to anticipate his next move. He gave me the impression of being unreasonable. He was capable of assaulting his daughter. If he did, would I stay there doing nothing? Would the policemen intervene and remind that hot-tempered father the fact that we were in America, where corporal punishment were supposed to be banned for quite a while? Would we end up in a tragedy or an outcome that would go out of control?

Fortunately, that man didn't give full vents to his anger. Instead he went on, in a falsely calm voice, "Young Lady, is that the way you pay us for all the trouble we have gone through to raise you? You know what you've done! You've forsworn your catholic faith, the family religion for generations! You've sex before marriage! You've given birth to a natural child! His father is a bum! He is going to be one himself. You've become a fallen angel, a jade! You are a disgrace. I wish you had never been born."

"George, why do you have to fuss so much?" Mrs. Clinton interjected. "What's done is done. Now we have to do our best to correct the situation. We still have time and the means to do so. That young man..."

"Oh, no," the father's voice reverberated through the apartment. "I don't want this bum, this dog, this vermin, in my family. He has done so much harm to our only daughter. He has managed to make her follow him on the road to crimes. Yolanda is leaving him exactly where she gets him. I'll make sure that she and the baby stay away from depraved human beings like him."

Yolanda had never stopped looking at me with an imploring expression on her face. I put myself in her shoes and I understood her.

"Father, I am not a fallen angel and a jade," she argued firmly. "All these negative images are figments of your bloody imagination. You've confused me with someone else. I've given myself up to the only man I've ever loved. So, I don't consider myself a woman with no morals."

She breathed deeply before adding, "I am willing to follow you. It seems I have no choice. But I must have a word with Peter alone in my bedroom. This happens to be the only condition I raise for now."

She held my hand and said, "Come on, Pete. We must have a long talk."

We went into the bedroom.

7

"Pete, thanks!" she whispered, while she pushed me gently against the wall. Then she hugged me, kissed me and nibbled at my ear lobe. "Your usual common sense and sound judgment have come handy."

"They have, haven't they?" I asked with a shade of surprise in my voice; because I remembered being changed to a mute statue, at the mercy of events my anonymous letter had put into motion.

"Yes, they have. I silently entreated you to remain calm during the 'ordeal', and you behaved accordingly," she explained. "You never can tell, you may have prevented a tragedy. Thanks!

"Let's hope the situation will keep being unfolded without any aggravation. That irascible man is capable of turning any situation into a disaster."

Then she turned into a talking machine I couldn't stop, I didn't want to stop. Later on, I would welcome it, because her voice would fill the impression of inner emptiness following my feeling of betrayal I was experiencing.

"That's true. My father has always been a quick-tempered man," she went on. "There's only one person who has the power to calm him down: my mother. You can imagine how hard it was for me, as a child, to tolerate his crabbed personality.

"The point I am trying to make is that he doesn't single you out to heap abuses on you. Oh, no! That's the way he treats everybody; the more so as he can afford to bully people and get away with it: he has plenty of money.

"Money, you know, allows everything, even arrogance. Now, you understand why I want to be free like a bird. I don't intend to be bossed around any more by this martinet that's my father. I don't have patience anymore for his abuses.

"Yet I don't even have the faintest idea of the course of action I am going to take now. My parents, coming into the picture, have messed up all my plans. I hate to think that I am going to live again under my parents' guardianship. Pete, I hate it, I hate it, I hate... I am a quick-tempered person too. When I can't have my wish, I see red and I am capable of doing something awful, regrettable. Can two sour personalities live under the same roof?

"However, Pete, to avoid a tragedy, I must follow them to Mississippi.

"What I mean is that my father is not as sweet as you. Your sweetness is a sign of generosity, compassion and love. You can love any person, any woman, because you are fond of anything which reminds you of mankind. But I'll kill you if I ever find out that you love another woman. Do you hear me?

"Pete, darling, I see in you the ideal image of what I have always expected from a man: sweet firmness, intelligence, consideration. You are my 'ideal father', the one I dreamed of having, day in day out, when I was a child, whom I could go to and entrust with my problems, my fear, my joy, my vision. I am exactly the opposite of you. I like that so much. We complete each other; we form a wonderful couple, a real couple. You have the brain and the foresight; I have the boldness and the inventiveness. Isn't that great? We can, banded together, have the whole world in the palm of our hands."

She kissed me on the neck. I put my arms around her waist. I wished we could stop the time and remain in that posture forever. But I was aware of the fact that the bitter side of reality would soon catch up with us.

She started to talk again, while rubbing her nose on my neck, "Oh, Pete, I am sorry, I can't do anything to counter my parents' decision. They have a court order. God knows what my father told the judge to get him on his side. So, I am going to leave you (at least for a while). It's a painful decision. It seems someone has betrayed me by sending an anonymous letter to my parents, which has informed them of my involvement in illicit activities. If I challenge them, I will endanger your future. You may even go to jail. My father is a rich and powerful man. Do you understand me? Do you see the irony of life? You know how people think. They may believe that you are the one who gets me into that mess or whatever that is, while this is the other way around. You've been adamantly against my line of activity; you've done your best to talk me out of it. But no one will believe this kind of equation. Everybody is willing to admit instead that men are always the catalysts for action, the corrupters, having loose morals. And I love you so much, Pete, that I would remain miserable for the rest of my life, if I became indirectly responsible for your being harmed.

"I am going to follow my parents to Mississippi. From that point on, I'll persuade them of my ability to take care of myself. Finally, they will understand me since I am almost eighteen. At least, I'll leave Peter junior with them for a while. However, I won't stay away from you too long."

She paused for a short time. She breathed deeply, sighed and continued, "Pete, there is plenty of money in the bottom drawer of that dresser. Where I am going, I have no need for it. So, take it and get out of here. And—I am warning you, I am begging you—don't look back. I repeat: don't look back! If you stay, Paul and Tony will become suspicious of your intentions. They might think that you and the guy who has betrayed me are the same person. From such a premise, they will infer that you are a government agent. They are paranoid and see plots everywhere. You know how it goes with people who have skeletons hanging in their closets. Indeed Paul and Tony have a lot of skeletons all over their houses. They will kill anyone standing in their way. The reason is simple: they don't intend to give up their opulent lifestyle.

"Here is my parents' address. You'll write to me, using your initials. You'll tell me where you stay and I'll join you there as soon as possible. Then we'll go into business for ourselves. It doesn't have to be something contrary to your sense of morality and decency."

I didn't say a word, I couldn't say a word: her gift of the gab had reached an overpowering stage. I had just discovered that she was the type of person whose intellectual faculties increased tenfold under pressure.

She went on, "Pete, the time we have spent together in this apartment is the best I have ever known in my whole life. I am sure it can keep on going if you want to. As for me, I love it and am willing to follow you to hell if this is the price I have to pay to be with you forever. I'll never be tired of you. Isn't it a sign of true love? You are intelligent and kind. I wouldn't be surprised at learning that you had sent the letter to my parents, just to keep me away from trouble. You are capable of this act of abnegation, aren't you?

"No, I don't think so. Your betrayal would sound as if you didn't enjoy being with me. That would be a lie. I know you care about me, enjoy being with me. I am the first woman you have ever known. I have introduced you to the tunnel of love, and you turn out to be a fervent student, a wonderful lover, a man who drives me crazy (she giggled). The remembrance of our frenzied passion is fresh in my mind! You want to be with me, don't you, Pete? You wouldn't send me away, would you?"

I felt like an icy knife slicing my back. Was I wrong about her? Wasn't she more intelligent than she looked? Could it be, by any chance that, like quite a few people, she pretended not to care about others' problems because she believed it was hopeless to do so; that she couldn't make a dent to this valley of tears; that her apparent selfishness was tailored on the ragged fabric of life? Indeed, since time immemorial, human beings have been wolves to each other. Bloody wars have cut short so many lives. Leaders have reduced their subjects to poverty and despair. The rich have remained rich and powerful. Revolutions have just misplaced or rearranged the power and fortune in favor of small groups of lucky or unscrupulous people. The newly wealthy have started doing the same thing: the spreading of animal selfishness, the perpetuating hopelessness on earth and the parallelism of social and economic conditions. Then why should we care about others if the course of events has been engaged in a vicious circle? Maybe Yolanda belonged to that category of persons who appeared to be indifferent to the future, since there was nothing they could do about it.

However, I couldn't trust her, I couldn't submit to trust her, though it could be a sweet, appealing decision for me to make, considering her beauty, her body, a source of exhilarating pleasure, her buoyant personality, her way to set me in *trouble*. Yet, her indifference to others, feigned or not, was, to me, unacceptable. I believe that, being alive, we should care about the future because this is our own. How could I be deliberately indifferent to it? Now my future looks so unsure and shaky without others' futures. In fact, this lack of common purpose happens to be the downfall of this world: there are too many plans, too many individual or clannish plans to the exclusion of the others, so, their disharmony, their mutual destruction, their inefficiency become inevitable and put the planet in danger of annihilation.

As a matter of fact, to be morally inclined, we must act in a certain manner which makes us deserve the status of a person, a status contingent upon the faculty of reasoning, choosing, transcending the past and present levels of conduct. Such moralistic attitude must be constant. And this constancy, this continuity derives from the habit of trying to live up to sets of values. Morally speaking, we can't behave in a certain manner today and in a different one tomorrow. We can't say that premeditated murder is awful today and welcoming tomorrow, depending on our moods, our caprices, our personal interests. Is it possible for someone to spread death and miseries around him today, and generate welfare and happiness tomorrow?

"Pete, what are you going to do in the meantime?" Yolanda inquired abruptly,

I shrugged my shoulders.

She started to talk again, "Pete, you are so naive and so wrong about human beings. They don't deserve your self-sacrifice. So many great leaders have died for nothing. Either the masses are too sluggish or too blockish to recognize and protect their true friends, or the latter are neutralized or mesmerized by opportunists and cold-hearted men and women of action. As a matter of fact, the masses don't want to be saved. They have been brainwashed with a philosophy of resignation, of complete submission. They look happy, content with their situation. Not only they don't care to lead a miserable way of life, but also they have the assurance of living eternally happy after death. As an author explains, they are making the biggest investment one can think of. They will laugh all the way to heaven and will get the last laugh. Only great minds, pragmatic minds want the fruits of progress and technology, now, on the planet and not in some kind of wonderland which may have never existed, in the first place. Please, Pete, be pragmatic and be among the winners who can appreciate the full meaning of existence. Don't waste your time. Don't behave as if all the cares of the world are on your shoulders. Humanity is bad, apathetic. How can they force you, a bright student, to give up school, your ideals and your vision? Can you believe that? That's your business, Pete, if you choose to remain a naive person.

"In other words, you must be a fighter in the kingdom of men and women. Indeed a real fighter shouldn't be having scruples. Imagine a boxer who wouldn't swing and jab; who wouldn't even kill in order to prevent himself from being killed! A manufacturer who wouldn't be engaged in fierce competition! With your intelligence you can outsmart those presumptuous rascals who think they are better than anyone else. You can be on the top of the world. Pete, think about my suggestions to go into business for ourselves, get married and have the future opened up to us."

Mr. Clinton's voice resounded in the living room, "Yolanda! It's time to leave!"

She pushed me towards the bed. I fell flat on my back. She lay down on me and started to cry bitterly. Tears were falling on my face and into my eyes. At that moment, I felt something close to love for her. But I didn't want to love her for her own sake, for our son's and mine. I had, anyway, one good and legitimate reason for restraining my love for her: we were too far apart in terms of our respective outlooks on reality.

But I would miss her. In fact, I started missing her by anticipation. She was the loveliest, the warmest and the sexiest woman I had ever met. She was the first woman I had ever been close to. She could have been an excellent mother, a wonderful lover, a perfect wife, in the proper environment.

I also started to weep. I cried because I knew perfectly that I was missing the opportunity to have that exciting woman. For reasons beyond my power, I couldn't turn such an opportunity to account. Then it was so frustrating in entertaining the belief that a better solution to our awkward predicament was certainly within my reach, but I couldn't conceive of it.

"You are a man, Pete, you shouldn't cry," she said mellifluously. "I want you to be strong, to love me and protect me, one of these days."

She dried my tears with her lovely palms, while she was still sobbing.

Suddenly, she stood up and gave herself up to her parents.

I didn't know what was getting into my head, but I wished she could stay with me. I made few steps forward and reached for her hand. However, before I could say something to her, Mr. Clinton pulled her, then pushed her towards his wife, grasped hold of my shirt collar and smacked my face repeatedly.

The Policemen intervened, so did Yolanda and her mother.

Yolanda held my bloody face in her palms and asked alarmingly. "Pete, are you all right?"

Then she turned round to face her father and stated, "How could you hurt an innocent man? He is an innocent and decent man, and doesn't deserve this kind of humiliation and treatment. Do you know him? You don't know him! How can you allow yourself to look down on him? I don't understand you at all."

Mr. Clinton brushed her aside. Instead, he eyed me offensively. He then shouted, "Haven't you done enough harm? Just leave my daughter alone! Go and get your head blown up by tugs of your kind. Now listen to me, I can be very tough and make life miserable for you. You should be happy that I want to leave things the way they are. I know what you intended to get my daughter involved in. You have introduced her to your world of crime and deception. You could be willing to turn her to a prostitute. Believe me, man, stay cool if you don't want to spend the remaining of your rotten life in jail where you belong. Remember, I have friends in high places; I am capable of giving you a very hard time. Stay away from my only child or I swear I'll kill you."

The Policemen pulled him towards the exit.

Yolanda, Peter Junior and Mrs. Clinton had disappeared, waiting somewhere in the street.

I was about to sit down on the sofa with a view to feeling easy in my mind, when the door which wasn't locked, reopened slowly. The assumed superior officer reentered and came up to me. He put his hands on my shoulders and paternally said, "Son, we know exactly what's been going on. But Yolanda's parents don't. You have been wise to remain cool. Try to understand Mr. Clinton's anger. Yolanda is his only child. He would like to see her becoming a decent person. Let the fury of anger die down. Go away."

I nodded to him. He started out again.

The apartment became noiseless and, consequently, devoid of its human significance. I lay down on the sofa and looked vaguely at the ceiling. Then I realized the poignant fact that I was already missing Yolanda, above all when her perfume was still pervading the air, a scent which used to put me in a romantic mood. Thus, our *little universe*, the apartment, turned into a cold tomb without her.

Come to think of it, that apartment had been our only *universe*, the place where we gave free rein to our passion. I don't remember any time we went out to have some fun. No, that isn't quite true. We did go out once to *enjoy ourselves*.

Few days after our son's birth, we were really tired of sitting in the house. The *messenger* had received *his parcel*, and we hadn't expected any visitors. We took the baby and drove at random. We went far beyond George Washington Bridge and another one erected across the longest waterway we had ever seen.

We stopped in a region devoid of dwelling. It was just the countryside: trees, grass, hillocks, the blue horizon and valleys. It was a lovely scenery we contemplated as far as our eyes could reach.

We sat on the grass. She was carrying the baby in her arms. For the first time, I fully noticed her instability, indeed, her changeableness. Sometimes she showed a stolid expression on her face, sometimes, a joyful one; sometimes, she appeared like a submissive, lascivious woman; sometimes, she reminded me of a martinet, ready to jump at my throat. I wished I could read her mind to elucidate the nature of the conscious or unconscious forces which were pulling her apart. I wish she could be transparent, so all the changes occurring in her could be easily seen through in vivid colors.

In one bound, she stood up. I did the same, being unaware of her following move. I took the baby from her. She came closer to me and held me tight as a castaway would grab the only life-saver bough in sight.

Few minutes after, we sat down again on the grass. We looked at each other with amorous eyes. Then she lay down. She seemed to be happy. She surrendered herself to somnolence. The sight of her beautiful body bathed in the twilight greeted my eyes. All in her revealed her undeniable femininity: her insignificant gesture of lassitude, the gentle scratching of her eyelids with her polished finger nails, her capricious smile, her regular breathing, her touching my arm just to acknowledge my presence. Why couldn't I accept her the way she was, with her weakness, as well as with whatever positive she could offer because of her inventiveness, her boldness, her spirit of adventure? Why did I jeopardize her *action plan*, her way of life, her heedlessness? I said to myself that day, "Oh, my beautiful lady, it's not my fault if I make you suffer. It's not my fault if I am a joy killer, a spoiler. I don't know how to make you happy. It seems that all of you longs for happiness. I also yearn for the joy of living, except that we disagree on the means to achieve it. I don't believe in the sacrosanct value of money. You do. You want to live in the present with all its excitements. I want to live fully in the past with its lessons of wisdom, in the present and in the future, with their hopes, their expectations. I purpose to give you what my person can keep creating anew: my inner warmth made of transcendence, spontaneity, optimism. It's inexhaustible. It can always rekindle my love for you. This is what I would like to give you. But I wonder if you want to accept it."

That day, she jumped up and asked me to drive her back to Queens. Her sudden decision took me by surprise; I was temporarily at a loss for words. I wondered if she wasn't more mentally unbalanced than what I had believed until then. For conscience's sake, I whispered, "But Yol, I thought you were enjoying yourself. What could make you change your mind so quickly?"

"Please, Pete, let's go," she insisted urgently. "Don't ask questions. I have no positive and intelligent answer to give you. But I don't want to be here another second. Let's go."

On our way back to the city, I could see, from the corner of my eyes, the tense expression of her face. At times, she shivered.

"What could be responsible for such a big change in her mood?" I wondered again. "Was she once victim of a traumatic experience which she suddenly remembered?"

As we were approaching Queens, she became less tense. On our reaching her apartment, she brightened up. "Pete, I am so hungry," she said. "Aren't you?"

"Yes, I am," I replied.

She cooked steaks, strained beans and mashed potatoes.

After we had finished eating, we went to the living room, sat down side by side on the sofa and watched television. The baby was fast asleep.

"Pete," she acknowledged, while putting her arm around my neck, "I've been a pain in the neck. Say it!"

"Yol, you are a wonderful and charming young lady," I replied.

"Oh! I am, am I not?"

"Yes, you are. Don't you ever forget it."

"I am so glad to hear it."

Shortly after, she added, "I was silly wasn't I? I spoilt our fun this afternoon. I am so sorry about that."

I touched her leg. She quivered. "That's quite all right," I said to make her at ease.

"No, that's not all right," she insisted.

"Oh, what is it?"

She smiled and then giggled. "Pete, you are not going to believe it:" she went on.

"Why shouldn't I?"

"I am so afraid of snakes!"

"You are, aren't you?"

"Yes, I am. I am so afraid of these 'creatures' that I don't look up words in illustrated dictionaries to avoid stumbling on pictures of these disgusting animals, which will give me great mental discomfort for a long time.

"Likewise, I don't go too the zoo, so I don't have to see reptilians and snakes. Their sight disturb me a lot.'

"But, as far as I can remember, we didn't see any," I pointed out for conscience's sake. "The setting was so charming and peaceful that I wouldn't mind spending the rest of my life there."

"I know. But, while I was lying down on the grass, my imagination played tricks on me. I pictured to myself a snake creeping towards me. I can't explain the origin of such silly idea in me, but it's the scaring vision I had. I believe that the expression 'snakes in the grass' and my imagination threw me into a panic. Isn't it silly?"

We laughed heartily at her "vivid imagination". That was really funny. She reacted like a baby, "my baby".

I felt it was my duty to protect her against snakes, reptiles and rascals of all kinds, above all the ones walking on two feet, like Paul, Tony and their kinds.

Well, I should have consented to her "plan" and made the best of it. That could be so much enjoyable in the long run. But it was too late. She had to be in Mississippi by then.

8

I finished packing up bag and baggage. Then I went and fetched the money mentioned by Yolanda before she had left. When I found it, I couldn't believe my eyes: there were more than six thousand dollars in large bills, not counting smaller ones.

First, I hesitated for a moment. I remembered the old saying: "Nothing is free. What's the catch?" Then the lure of profit dulled my usual prudence, and I took all the bank notes as well as the small changes.

"Not only I can survive while I am looking for a decent job," I whispered, "but also I will be able to find an acceptable place to live. Who knows? Wisdom tells me not to rush things. Of course, I don't want to go back to Aunt Emma's house. I have to let her live quietly, without the aggravation my new lifestyle might cause her. I will probably give a second thought to Yolanda's suggestion of going into business for ourselves and getting married. But, it has to be a legitimate business permissible by law. However, being aware of the difference between our general outlooks on reality, I believed that my answer to her suggestion would be a negative one. She would never agree to give up the kind of activity which was handsomely profitable to her. She would never depart from her belief that being a wage earner was a disgrace and a straitjacket. She would always be leery of my invitation to a life of morality and wisdom, a life of moderation, in harmony with social norms. In fact, I wondered if I would see her and the baby very soon. Despite everything, alone in *my apartment*, their images were the only points I could focus on at that moment.

I stayed in bed for hours. My mind was filled to the cracking point with compelling thoughts interweaving, repulsing and attracting each other, reinforcing my sense of hopelessness and stillness: no sooner premises on sweetness of life, human perfectibility, the ultimate triumph of good over evil, had reached my mind, the opposite of them arose from remembrance of bitter experiences, human pervasive weakness, a rotten state of affairs.

Finally, I stood up, grabbed my traveling bag and made my way towards the front door. Before I opened it, I stopped, turned round for a final look at the apartment with *Moses' eyes facing the promise land*. Indeed, that place was full of potential happiness and positiveness. It was waiting for decent people with vision and fellowship. It was unconscious for being a medium through which criminals were spreading strong ingredients of death. I knew that if it depended on me and my striving for moral conduct, I could have enjoyed moments of joy in such *lovely residence*, where our children could have grown up soundly, where..."Heck!" I exclaimed. Then, I opened the door.

I cried out with pain when a giant black man struck me with an uppercut: his closed fists were each almost as big as my head. Another swinging blow delivered on my sternum made me roll over the carpet, in the living room. I had difficulty breathing. I knew I was on the verge of death if that brutal treatment went on with the same violence.

The aggressor grabbed me and carried me to the sofa as if I were a straw. Then came in Paul, Tony, the *messenger* and other members of the death team. I saw them approaching like grotesque beings: their heads seemed unusually big to me.

"So, Peter," stated Tony in a falsely whining voice, "you get rid of Yolanda and plan to carry the *loot* away. I know your type. I didn't trust you at all. The minute I saw you, I knew you were trouble. But you are messing up with the wrong people."

I was out of breath, and it took me quite a while before I could utter something unintelligible.

"Listen, Peter, start all over again," suggested Tony this time in a deceitfully conciliatory tone. "We can't understand you, and without a good excuse, you can say bye-bye to life. So, tell us something believable. We have all the time in the world. You should know that we are the nicest fellows in the world. We don't kill our friends, but we crush our enemies."

I had enough time to pull myself together, the proof being that I tried hard to answer *satisfactorily* to Tony's indirect question. "I can do it, I can do it," I kept saying to myself. "My life depends on my answers. They are not the smartest people in the world. According to Yol, I can hoodwink them. I hope she's right."

I hemmed and hawed for a while. Then I cleared my throat. My voice became audible enough, and I risked, "I don't know what you are talking about."

It was just a meaningless statement anyone could have uttered. But considering my *audience,* it was enough.

Paul stepped forward and shook his fist at me. "Don't play games!" he shouted. "We mean business. Don't play with us. We are in no mood for that now. We saw Yolanda and her kid leaving with people and cops. The only person who knew where she lived and what she was doing was you. Now, why didn't they also put you under arrest? Well, I don't have to be a genius to find the answer: you've sold out your old lady. Therefore..."

He drew a long breath and went on, "And why would you do that for? Again the answer is obvious: you want to double-cross Yolanda and us, and put us out of business. You know that you are crazy to even think of something like that. You are a dead duck."

With a motion of the head, he beckoned to the *giant to* get into action. "Eddy, do your work," he added. "Make sure he is unrecognizable."

The giant raised his arm to strike again. With a wave of the hand, I made them know my *willingness* to *cooperate.*

"Go ahead!" urged Tony. "You may try to buy time, but your dooms are sealed. We will never trust you again."

"You get me all wrong," I said firmly. "Why would I double-cross you?"

I was perfectly aware that, so far, I hadn't expressed myself in a convincing manner. However, I thought if I kept repeating exactly what they said, I would be able to enter the track of their minds made of vapid clichés. By so doing, I might save my bacon.

"You know very well that I am not a fool," I pointed out. "I won't be deliberately in your way. Why should I do that for, while we can go hand in hand? Tell me, why should I try to double-cross you?"

"You are just trying to gain time," said Paul. "It won't work, man. It's clear that you've sold out your old lady, and that's wrong, man; that's bad. Yolanda is a sweet and innocent girl. She is a *good store-keeper*. What kind of man are you to betray one of the sweetest and most beautiful women in the world? Just for that, you deserve to die. Besides, you've hurt us, man. We have to start all over again looking for a place to store our stuffs. Do you know how hard it is to keep things safe? Man, you have no chance to survive after pulling a stunt like this; you have really hurt the whole family."

"But who told you that I sold Yolanda out?" I inquired. "In fact, nobody betrayed her at all."

"Then, tell us what happened."

"Her mom and dad were looking for her all over New York, man. They have the prerogative, as parents, to act this way. They haven't heard from her for months. Finally, with the help of some cops who happened to be Mr. Clinton's old partners and friends, they found Yolanda's address. By the way, Mr. Clinton used to work for the Police, you know. They came over and coaxed their daughter into going away with them for a week or so. Believe me, she thought that was an excellent idea, taking some vacations she richly deserved. She thought that I was capable of filling in for her. Her mom will help her with the baby. Did you see her living the premises handcuffed?

"Of course, she would have told you all this herself if she had the time, but her parents insisted that they should leave at once. They had to catch a plane. Therefore, my friends, you get it all wrong. It wasn't necessary to get me almost smashed by your gorilla. All you should have done was to ask me questions."

Everybody seemed to mellow, except the giant who maintained a dour expression on his face. He looked like a bizarre evil being escaped from some distant uncivilized planet. His head was oddly big and round, maybe full with anything but brainy stuff. His lack of intelligence was written all over his face. Additionally, tremendous spasms spread over his body. All his muscles contracted; his legs hammered heavily on the floor; his face twisted; his nostrils dilated. He was the very picture of a rhino on the verge of charging.

"Just be patient, Eddy!" Tony recommended, who had also sensed the giant's nervousness. "I know you are eager to let him have the excess of your anger. Be patient."

Then, Paul took Tony aside, in a corner, to "talk things over". They could be discussing how they were going to kill me.

While they were gesticulating, I praised myself for not only keeping my composure, considering that my probable death was near, but also for being still able to notice the harmony in which those partners in crime were living and the mutual respect in which they held each other. Common interests seemed to blunt the asperity of *racism* in them. I wished their unity could have been motivated by more transcendent reasons. Then I would be the first one to welcome its symbolic value. Unfortunately, the growing impression I had of Paul and Tony's association coincided with something evil. Indeed, the inhuman way in which they were dealing with me did nothing but reinforce my first impression.

They came back and sat down, each, on the armchairs facing the sofa. The other members of the gang remained standing (maybe out of respect).

"I can buy your story," said Tony abruptly. "Yolanda's parents may want her to spend a week vacation or so with them. Come to think of it, we have never given her any time off. You know, Paul (he turned towards the latter), that's an excellent idea. From now on, we are going to come up with vacation schedules for our staff. So far so good (he was facing me again). I am willing to buy your story. However, how can you explain that you were leaving with the 'loot' in your traveling bag?"

"What are you talking about?" I yelled out. "What loot? You will find in my bag some clothes, books and money belonging to Yolanda, which I didn't want to leave in the cabinet drawer. I was about to spend the night at my cousin's."

I was temporarily relieved of anxiety. If my ethical philosophy didn't consist in refusing to hurt others deliberately, I would have taken the "loot" and would be in a deadlier situation. Of course, I suspected Yolanda of keeping something lethal and highly profitable to Paul and Tony, but I wouldn't touch it with a ten-foot pole. What for?

It was a big plus for morality. It could save my life.

"Open the bag," said Tony to the *messenger*.

The latter unzipped the bag. Then, with great care, he removed each cloth, unfolded it and shook it.

The books were also submitted to the same scrutiny.

In those people's business, one could never be too much *careful*. Little bags could have been starched by me in the clothes and books. These, above all, couldn't be judged by their covers. They could be boxes disguised as hardcore's.

Finally, the bottom of the bag was thoroughly explored, and its protective plastic was sliced open.

When the *messenger* concluded his search, he drew himself up and, *proudly*, pronounced the redeeming word, "Nothing."

He looked at me with an absence of animosity. He could have developed some kind of sympathy for me, since I had never given him the impression that he was subhuman.

Tony stood up and came up to me slowly. At that moment, I realized how fragile and precious life was. The coming course of action was absolutely unpredictable to me. My life could be ended any minute. I would soon receive the final blow and would become absolutely unconscious and I would turn into a dead piece of meat. The neighbors would smell something foul and would call the police. They would get rid of my carcass. I thought, "Would I be absolutely unconscious? How about what they call the *soul*? Would it be a witness to my body decomposition, a cool, unconcerned witness, devoid of power on the materiality of things?"

Maybe I was delirious, but in the silence my conscience, I caught myself praying to my *soul* for some miracle: "My Soul, are you going to leave me at this crucial moment? Are you going to let these monsters destroy a temple from which you have been contemplating transcendent values? Are you a coward? It was you who have shown me the road to greatness, love, serenity. Are you going to let me die with the feeling that you've been wrong? My Soul..."

Tony stopped few inches away from me. He stretched out his arm, rubbed my hair repeatedly and, finally, said, "Peter, I am very sorry! You are on the level. Your bag is clean, and the loot is still in the refrigerator. That means you've been telling the truth."

I didn't know when the order was given, however, the *giant,* the *messenger* and the others left suddenly.

"Listen, Peter," uttered Paul, "no hard feelings."

"No hard feelings," I echoed him.

After a moment of dead silence, Paul and Tony seemed to be ready to take their leave of me. The latter recommended, "Peter, you can't leave the apartment unattended. That's the way it has been with your old lady, that's the way it will remain until she is back to duty. So far, this is the best storehouse we've been able to find. It's unsuspected. Business is good this way; we don't want to change the setting."

He plucked my sleeve with one hand and passed his card to me with the other one. "Here is the location of the place of operation," he explained, while his finger pointed at the written address. "Come over this Friday to visit us and you'll see for yourself. Meanwhile, be a *good warehouseman.*"

I was back to square one. My curse, started with Doctor Miles, kept me in its clutches. "It could be that superstition starts this way," I thought. "A sequence of events occurs at the same time in someone's life. The next thing you learn is that a supernatural explanation of these random events is given. Indeed, it's so strange that it hasn't been quite clearly explained why a trail of fortunes or misfortunes can strike someone over and over. This is one of the mysteries of life, like these of life itself, of death, of destiny. Nobody can elucidate their rationale, their unfolding in the stream of history."

Destiny, for no apparent reason, kept imposing on me the company of Paul, Tony, the *giant,* the *messenger* and other members of that deadly association. Did I have a mission to fulfill unknowingly? Did the force of goodness choose me to act as a foil to that organization evil influence?

The *messenger*, in particular (despite his unsuspected sympathy for me), put on my nerves with his reptilian eyes, his idiotic face and his impenetrable silence. He responded to my questions by mechanical gestures. "Do you want to have a seat?" He looked at me straight in the eyes and walked backwards, towards the wall and stayed quiet until I handed the "package" over to him. "Do you want to make sure everything is ok?" He turned around and walked away.

Paul, Tony, the giant, the messenger and people of their kinds, made me think that we should see humanity in terms of degrees. I argued loud enough to hear myself thinking, "One would deserve more or less to be called a human being according to his ability to think. I mean that one should be more or less capable of pertinent and original thoughts. One should also be a moral being, realizing a compromise between his actions and others' interests. All this presupposes that one should transcend his drives and instincts. At the most, one would deserve more or less to be called a human being when one strives to draw near, by his actions, to the above-mentioned ideals."

Certainly, Paul, Tony, the *giant*, the *messenger* and their kinds would be at the bottom of a human diagonal scale if it could be impartially established. I wondered if an act of injustice was possible against them since they were rotten to the core, they were in the business of hurting others and they hadn't shown any remorse. They had to be guilty by anticipation and by nature. Their presence would never be a plus to the ontological process. But (the irony of reality) I had to bear their company, let things die down, allow Yolanda and our child enough time to be far away from those deadly mammalians. Then I would manage to sneak off to some distant State.

I smiled: I represented to myself what would happen when, on the day of my departure, the *messenger* would knock at the door and have no answer. He would be excited for the first time in his life. His heart would start beating fast, at the prospect of going back to his bosses without *his parcel*. He would step back to see if he had mistaken somebody else's address for mine. He would look about the street and would convince himself that he was in front of the apartment he had been having his parcel from, daily, for over a year then. He would go back to the doorstep. He would keep knocking at it, over and over, while jumping up and down, like a poisoned rat or a neurotic one caught in an experimenting device. Then a click would set his mind conceiving a new type of action, and he would temporarily escape from the vicious circle consisting of knocking at the door, jumping up and down, looking about: he would call Paul and Tony.

Escorted by the giant, they would join him and start all over again the *knocking sarabande*. They would turn furious, would be talking nonsense and drooling like Pavlov's dogs. However, the stimulus, for a change, would not be meaty powder, but rather some crazy stuff kept in Yolanda's refrigerator.

I imagined that a neighbor would become suspicious of this kind of rite made of knocking at the door, uttering nonsense and drooling, and would call the police. That would be the end of an association of dreadful monsters.

I was hoping strongly that my imaginary course of action would turn true.

I was beset by a new wave of sad thoughts. I wondered about my involvement in criminal activities. It didn't make any sense to me. I wasn't a criminal type. I disdained crimes of any nature.

Likewise, I was born in a decent family. My parents used to raise me in an atmosphere of love, understanding and compassion. I was growing up bright. What did happen to me? Oh, I remember: Doctor Miles' prejudice! But was his animosity enough to put me on the wrong side of the road? I should have changed school. I should have at least joined the army. Though I would hate taking orders and would certainly hate shouting senselessly: "Yes, Sir! No, Sir!" it would be better for me to join the army. Would it be better, really? I don't think so. I didn't think so, at the time of this story. I believed that, joining the army, I would have missed many sleeping hours. I wouldn't enjoy being awakened in the middle of the night by a trumpet, a bugle or something like that. This type of behavior would look purposeless and unnatural to me. A good night sleep belongs to Nature's *master plan*. Above all I feared I could be sent abroad to fight, kill and be killed. That was so much against my philosophy of life. In fact, why should I go abroad to fight, kill and be killed for reasons unknown to me? Why should I kill perfect strangers? We couldn't communicate well, since we didn't speak the same language. We didn't know each other's names. We didn't wear the same outfits and didn't love the same way. We didn't share the same experiences and patrimony. We didn't have any personal dispute. We ignored everything about each other. What could make me start wishing these perfect strangers evil? Ah! The order to wish them evil, to maim them, to destroy them, would come from my superior officer who would have received it from his commander who would have received it from someone else. By the time it reached me, it would become so impersonal, so cold and unemotional, that carrying it out would be senseless or would say a lot about my own sadism and lack of humanity.

No joining the army wouldn't be the best solution, because I would be provided with sophisticated means to do even greater harm to mankind. I could be destroying cities, human beings, hopes for a better life.

However, rubbing shoulders with Paul, Tony, the *giant*, the *messenger* made me sick to my stomach.

At least, in the army, I would, once in a while, enjoy the intelligent conversation of some of my peers. In fact, the confrontation of armies often starts with summit meetings. Only, later on, the staccato of words is changed for the staccato of machine guns.

With the criminal associations, it goes the other way around. Their members submit you to a battery of blows, first, and then they bore you stiff with their stupid clichés.

While the army might have some constructive items in its agenda, only to knock them off at the end; a criminal association, on the contrary, starts with destruction and carries it all through around.

Anyway, at the time of the story, I wouldn't like to join either one of them (willingly, joyfully).

For one thing, I got stuck with my unwilling job, a job which brought me a disgust of myself. Sometimes, I smelt myself as if I were rotten; but all I was inhaling was my deodorant. The rotten smell had to be emanating from my mind, my sick mind, my rebellious mind.

9

The meteorologist was right once in his forecast: as he had announced, the rain started a little after midnight. There was a gusty wind carrying along all kind of rubbish. Forked lightning streaked the night. I wouldn't like to be in the shoes of people who were caught in such a dreadful setting. I believed that Apocalypse wouldn't be less disheartening.

Though I was sleepy, I got up to close the windows. When I woke up again the sun was shining outside. I jumped up, went to the bathroom and had a shower. I made myself some breakfast and was on the point of eating when the doorbell rang.

I went and let the *messenger* in.

I noticed something unusual about him: his face showed some brightness, indeed, some intelligence. His motion turned casual. It seemed that man was suddenly touched by the grace, free from worries. I bet that he would try to communicate with me that day.

Hardly had I said that to myself when he mentioned in one go, "Tony asked me to remind you that today is Friday, and that you have to be at the place of operation. This is where you are going to be paid. Dig it, my man?"

I was astonished. That man could speak after all.

"Be there on time," he added.

He smiled and was evidently content with the fact that he was able to convey a verbal message in such a clear manner. If my presence could operate this *miracle*, then my life, after all, had some *meaning* and *purpose*.

"That's nice, Mr. Messenger," I observed jokingly. "Keep up like that and you are going to be all right."

He pulled a face, walked sideways towards the front door, opened it and disappeared.

Shortly after, I sank into solitude again and faced myself and the predicament I was in.

I became aware of the fact that human consciousness is restless. It's always engaging in and considering the surroundings with their multifarious elements. But these mean so little to it if they are deprived of their human significance. This lack of human significance explained the reason why the apartment no longer *concerned* me. Indeed, Yolanda and my son, Tony, Paul, the giant and the *messenger*, weren't there to impose their buoyant and dynamic presences (in their respective ways). Thus, as soon as I was alone, my consciousness was robbed of its human interest. It couldn't keep focusing on pieces of furniture, paintings on the walls, motion pictures showing on the TV set. Instead, it turned towards me as a unique center of human trouble and palpitation. It was then in the dumps.

I no longer liked being lost in thoughts. It was a mental rumination, going back and forth to the self-consciousness. I needed to go away, where I would no longer be the only food for my thoughts, where I would meet decent people with whom I would communicate, share permissible experiences.

As soon as I had made that wish, I became pervaded by a feeling of well-being, indeed, an exultant sensation, so much so that I felt that my escape from the apartment, set as a devil's island, had to be realized without delay. "I must leave this place before it is too late," I asserted loud to convince myself of my decision. "I will not wake up in this house next week."

I turned more relaxed and fell asleep.

Hours later, I woke up with a funny feeling that I was living in a strange world. The furniture, all around me, seemed to be just put there by some whimsical beings. My effort of recollection brought me a sense of déjà vu. What was going on with me?

Since the world looked so strange to me, I didn't feel I belonged to it. I was one too many in it, and my time of breath, my last one, would come soon in order to settle the balance of population.

I was thinking about my heart which could stop any minute, any second. There was no guarantee in this respect. Yet, I didn't anticipate any harm to come from it, to such a par that I thought apologetically, "My heart, I can't blame you. You've been serving me as a motor for eighteen years, without an overhaul, without any complaint. You have always made me strong. You are the best partner I have ever had. You've never abandoned me, and, today, I have the impression that you will do your best to prolong our partnership. If they don't disturb you, you will go on and on."

Then where did I have this doubt about my "immortality", that I was about to experience my last breath, while I still had the impression of having been *built like a rock*? But, because of this deadly impression, I started to take interest in the surroundings as if I would see them for the last time. I went to the window and started to contemplate the sky covered with a shade of blue and gradually changed to a hesitant gray in the horizon. I was elated to see a flying airplane. The weather was so beautiful and sunny that I was able to distinguish the colors of the craft fuselage, its profile and its propellers.

I took a walk (maybe my last one). Under the bridge flew cloudy water, in which were gamboling ducks and other smaller web-footed birds.

An endless stream of people came and went in all directions. Buses zoomed from stop to stop.

I opened my eyes on the tiniest creatures; I listened to the slightest audible sounds; I interpreted the least significant gestures; everything, that day, appeared charming to me, worthy of interest. The fear of seeing, experiencing, touching, smelling this profusion of beings in reality for the last time, had intensified my perception; for, I couldn't think of any other means of being conscious of reality, apart from what we called being alive. Life after death concept had never been appealing to me.

Then, some point in time, while I was walking, my interest in reality died down. I went back home, sat down on the sofa and concluded that I wasn't growing up in the matrix of time and space. I was still, alien to duration, left there like a rock.

Either I was a rock or pure thought, but I wasn't living (at least in the very sense of the word).

Living means engaging in action to fulfill the goal of being: to persevere in life. In fact, an exiting being is senseless if it possesses no craving for perseverance in living. The perseverance in living presupposes that the existing being must go on with any means available to it. If the means are made of weapons, ambition, hatred, selfishness, mystification, one should be willing to use them all naturally, profusely, remorselessly. They could be true pictures of reality, because not too many people seem to find anything wrong with them, to balk at them, to be disposed to reward those who find faults at them. Then if they revealed true pictures of reality, I wasn't living, since I was rejecting too many means placed at my disposal throughout my existence.

Along with all this, did I care about living? No, I didn't. What for? I didn't have any fixed plan in life to carry out. I didn't think I had any purpose. I didn't feel connected to anything positive on this planet. I wouldn't certainly take my unwanted *warehouseman's position* for a worthwhile catalyst for living dynamically. It was quite the contrary. It was the main cause of my despair. Again I was there, like a rock. Once, I did have a vision to be a professional, to give a positive contribution to mankind struggle for life, to share decent experiences with others. But I couldn't live the way I wanted to. I was denied such a right at school. I was denied it by a woman who, I thought, could have seen reality my way. I was denied it on the street. Instead, others imposed their rotten and disgusting ready-made patterns of living on me. I was in a jam because I refused such patterns. They weren't too challenging for me, an *animal-man,* holder of a sophisticated brain with millions of cells and impression possibilities, with an imagination aiming at the infinity, at the sky and the lights; an inheritor of the universe, which had the privilege of being conscious of its origin and its Promethean role. These patterns imposed on me didn't go beyond the activities of all living beings, great or small ones, which kill, maim, betray, associate, dissociate for food (their fortune) and for an exclusive spot (their power). All that living beings need, to function this way, is to be more or less powerful, more or less daredevil like a cheetah, vicious and sneaky like a snake, heavy and strong like a rhino. Indeed, we do have similar needs to satisfy. Henceforth, very often, like the lower animals, we don't want to go beyond the mere satisfaction of these needs. We unleash on each other their destructive effects, with no remorse. Yet, the sophisticated nature of our brainy system makes us brag about our transcendent origin, about the fact that we are all subjects, not objects, the only privileged creatures of God. We claim to make an effort to deliberate over our decisions before acting, but the results of our deeds let to be desired and keep re-minding us of our bestial origins. Wars, spreading all over the world, are certainly a triumph of matter over mind, a total absence of delibe-rations, a systematic effort to return to the wild.

It was strange and revealing the way I was comparing men to low-er animals. "How silly I am to think it could be otherwise," I whis-pered. "Aren't we animals? Aren't we the products of evolution? How naive I am to think that we wouldn't have some strong characteristics inherited from our not too distant relatives!"

I went to the bathroom and took a shower. I put on my clothes and drove to the "place of operation". I had some difficulty locating it; for, twice, I passed by the *CANDY AND ICE CREAM STORE* which was situated exactly at the address written down on Tony's personal card, but I didn't see any sign of a business which needed to retrieve a bag of stuff, daily, from Yolanda's refrigerator. I thought I had mista-ken the street for another one, which was possible since I was in a state of mind capable of confusing my perception of reality. For one thing, I couldn't believe that Tony, Paul and company would have made such a big deal about a candy and ice cream store. Furthermore, such modest activity couldn't be lucrative enough to allow Paul and Tony to live an opulent life, to wear three-piece suits, with large hats à la musketeer, to drive the fanciest car I had ever seen. Suddenly, it flashed across my mind that the store was a front hiding a much more important trade.

In fact, something about it puzzled me: the first time I had passed by it, I tried to open the door, but in vain. It was locked. I had never known before that they kept the doors of candy and ice cream stores closed all the time. They were supposed to be opened (during business hours) if their owners didn't mean to discourage prospective customers. Tony, Paul and company had a funny concept of trading.

A buzzer showed up. I pressed it. A female voice said harshly, "Who's it?"

"This is Peter," I answered.

"Peter who? Am I supposed to know you?"

Once more, someone didn't want to speak to me about myself. I believed that, after reaching a certain level of wealth, our sense of communication deteriorates and is gradually replaced by arrogance (and maybe a lack of memory).

A short moment of silence elapsed. Then I heard a voice saying, "Never mind!" A click occurred and, slowly, the door opened.

I stepped in cautiously and was ready to turn back quickly—if need be. To be truthful, I knew that it was against my better judgment to proceed any further. I looked round. I didn't see any sign of candies or ice cream boxes. "The candies and ice cream must be handled somewhere else," I thought, "This joint could be some kind of warehouse". I kept walking with measured steps and looking about the strange place. I saw a set-up which reminded me of a bank or check cashing place.

Tony showed his face through the window in front of me. "Well, Peter, this is our place of operation," he indicated with a suggestion of pride in his voice.

"Very nice," I only said.

He handed me a bundle of bank notes. "Sir, this is your wage," he stated.

After a pause, he added, "We must know you better before we can give you a position of trust. You'll do just fine. Keep a low profile."

I was on the point of turning around and leaving, but I remembered that I had wanted to urinate. I stopped short. I wondered if I should ask or not for the location of the *men's room*. I intuited that, beyond those windows, something unpleasant was going on. Again, I didn't have any fact to base my worries on, but that something awful, which I was unable to identify, had to be there. I had the certainty of it and I stopped being skeptical about my ability to foresee events. As a matter of fact, my instinct of self-preservation seemed to invite me to go away as quickly as I could. However, to the best of my recollection, there wasn't any other place in that neighborhood where I could go and urinate; unless I chose to do it on the pavement like a dog and take a chance on being arrested for disorderly conduct. So, I acted against my intuition and my instinct, which, I knew, I was about to regret.

"Do you have a bathroom?" I asked.

Tony didn't answer right away. He frowned and seemed, for a change, to indulge in serious reflections on the decision to be taken.

It was more than enough to warn me not to insist on asking for a bathroom. Why would Tony get involved in heavy thinking over a bathroom? If it was dirty I would understand, since it was a place of business, which had to allow promiscuity in the use of a toilet; but, once in while, I showed persistency in doing things. "Well, Tony, do you have a place where I can urinate?" I asked again.

"Sure, come on in," he finally answered. "You must be one of us by now."

I thought, "They are the funniest people in the world. They don't like others to use their bathroom, unless someone is one of theirs. What does he mean by that?"

But it was too late for me to decline the *membership privilege*, for, another buzzing sound occurred and a door flew open.

As before, I proceeded cautiously. The more I was heading towards the center of a dimly lit yard, the more a foul smell was offending my nostrils. It was unbearable. I promised myself to hold my breath while I was urinating and to leave as quickly as I could. They should be ashamed of themselves to maintain a place so dirty. And, like a flash of lightning, the truth leaped to my eyes!

Usually, whatever its nature, the truth hurts and makes us uncomfortable. However, at that specific moment, it made me dizzy and nauseous. It presented itself in the form of human distress, human beings reduced to the shadow of themselves.

They belonged to all races, ages and genders. They wore filthy blue-jeans pants, T-shirts and tennis shoes. The seen parts of their bodies were covered with deep infected ulcers and fresh needle holes. The men were long-haired and full-bearded; the women, for unknown reasons, showed relatively flat busts, which increased their resemblance to their male companions.

They were helping one another in their drug experiences.

Some played the role of *gurus*, acting as guides to *tyros* who were making their *first trips*.

Others were more experienced in the business of harming themselves. They prided themselves on it and performed *involved procedures* merely for show. They *acquitted themselves* well, doing the *flushing*. It consisted in drawing blood back into the syringe during an injection to be sure that a vein was tapped and that the elation would start immediately.

Many were going about hopelessly. They were drowsy, staggering, and talking nonsense.

I was standing speechless, facing this nightmare of which my description hardly gave an account.

How could human beings, with willpower, faculty of thinking and perceiving reality, allow themselves to reach such a low level of conduct? What could they gain from it? What were they aiming at? Were they the unlucky elements of the natural selection, to repeat after Yolanda? Then I remembered those masses that let sadistic leaders brainwash them to the point of welcoming death for no genuine cause at all. I asked myself if those leaders and their victims didn't deserve one another. But I was there. I was a human being, a true human being, with a sense of dignity, pride, transcendence, compassion, love and the positive qualities received from humanity. I was feeling the sufferings of those forgotten people, their nightmarish lives and their daily despair.

Meanwhile, my need to go to the "bathroom" had vanished and was replaced by a strong and uncontrollable feeling of anger.

My infuriation might have grown on me, gradually, steadily, but not too perceptibly; for, Tony, Paul, the *messenger*, the *giant* and other members of that deadly staff didn't show any sign of alarm. Wasn't I being received among the initiates?

They certainly hoped that I would get finally acquainted with that dreadful picture of a death factory, especially as my livelihood depended on it. Soon, I was about to have so much money that I would be able to drive fancy cars, to wear expensive suits, to brag and flaunt my wealth everywhere and to entertain half a dozen beautiful women. But I didn't feel that I was one of them. By nature and philosophy of life I was their enemy. I couldn't, for any reason in the world, identify myself with that kind of vile, criminal, animalistic attitude. No way. I rubbed my eyes, thinking that I was dreaming. Then, again, I scanned the crowd of addicts who were the shadow of humanity, but victims of the inhuman business I was a part of. I had no excuse. I should have walked away from Yolanda, once I discovered the abominable nature of her business. I couldn't find any light at the end of such tunnel.

I turned round to look Tony, Paul and their followers up and down. They were well-dressed and healthy-looking. They were easy going, casual, like true professional performing a worthwhile service to the public and mankind. Nobody should be surprised if they claimed social security benefits at the time of their old age or retirement.

Now they were being puzzled about my silent attitude.

I raised my hand to reach my jacket inside pocket. "Look out!" exclaimed Tony. "He's pulling a gun. That man is crazy. What's the matter with you, Peter?"

They calmed down a little when they saw the bundle of bank notes in my hand. "How could I be part of a bunch of vermin like you?" I yelled out, while I was throwing the bank notes at them. "You are just animals, lower animals! You have no heart, no emotion, not even one ounce of love! Really, you are purely and simply animals. You should be sent to the zoo or to the woods! Still, you would nauseate the wild beasts! Believe me. Anyway, you can't live with human beings, because you don't belong to their species."

These words were the only ones I could have thought of, but they were enough to persuade those ruffians of my dissenting position. They sprang to the attack.

My anger, however, had increased my strength and changed me from a quiet and submissive fellow to a dangerous fighting machine. Tony received a punch on his nose and screamed while drying his blood with his handkerchief. The giant tried to grab me, but I fell back and kicked his pelvic region. He collapsed like a stabbed bull and groaned in pain. As far as Paul was concerned, he tried some boxing feint, jumping about and attempting to catch me by surprise. He had a reputation for knowing all the tricks of the boxing trade. But, since I became bold and fierce, I stopped fighting according to the rules. I fell upon him and hit him on the nose. He dropped to the ground.

The whole gang launched an attack as one man. Some of the members pulled long knives, chains, guns, out of their pockets. I knew I was about to die. But I didn't care; I didn't care at all. I didn't see any reason for yearning for existence, once I found out that I had become the reverse image of my dream of becoming a respectable human being and that I had participated in harming and killing my fellowmen. It was a good opportunity for me to leave this valley of tears, where I had been experiencing so much humiliation, frustration and despair. Nevertheless, I did care about the way I would die as well as about the location of my death. I didn't wish to meet my fate in that filthy place, amid those dehumanized drug addicts.

I knew that, as soon as I would have been killed, the gang would take off, leaving behind their zombies and dreadful paraphernalia. When the Police discovered my body, the whole world would learn that I died of a drug overdose. It would be so much convenient and save lots of headaches.

Yet, as long as I was alive and had one minute to breathe and to be conscious of reality, I couldn't prevent myself from thinking about what they were going to say after my death, about the possible detraction from my reputation. Of course, I wouldn't like Aunt Emma and Yolanda to remember me as a waster. I wouldn't like my fellow students to picture me as a bastard. Above all, I wouldn't like Dr. Miles to exult over my death, claiming everywhere that he knew that I was "no good", (which would be a lie). I was good. I was yearning for a decent way of life. If I didn't succeed in having it, it wasn't for lack of trying.

Thus I had to die, but I would die happy, if I could reach the street. My death would look like plain murder, as it occurred daily in the world. People got killed by mistake, for thirty-five cents, during a shoot out, by cluster bombs, but not like rats among rats. I wanted to die away from those rats. It was the least I could do for myself. And I was about to do it. I would do it. Yet, the question, the inevitable question popped up: how could I do it?

I had to go through a human wall defended by angry knives, chains, fists, guns and two solid doors, before I could receive the type of death that would send me happy to the realm of nothingness I had been contemplating for days.

There was no other way.

I fell headlong into the melee, with the fury of despair. I fought with all myself: with my teeth, my fists, my feet, my head and my knees. I was amazed to find out how many weapons nature had provided me with. That Mother Nature! She anticipates all our needs. As a matter of fact, my fighting style was efficacious especially as my opponents, because of their great number, were in one another's way and were afraid of hurting one of theirs.

At last, I broke through the crowd, shattered the first door and was running for it. For a split second, I thought I was lucky enough to not only receive the kind of death I was contemplating, but also to save my skin. Unfortunately, I was few inches away from the front door when the first stab slashed my back wide open; then another one in the right foot; another one in the neck...I stopped counting them; I was unable to count them. They were coming steady. However, I didn't stop. I kept saying to myself, "You are going to do it. You have to die in the street. Witnesses must see that you are killed in the street, not like a rat, in a dirty shooting gallery, but like a decent man falling under criminals' misdeeds. You must do it..."

With all my might, I threw myself against the front door and landed, to my surprise, on the pavement.

I was covered with blood. I was standing there, a little groggy, but I was on the pavement. I felt the firmness of its reinforced concrete. I smiled. "I did it," I whispered. I immersed again in the stream of decent humanity: young and beautiful women, hard-working men coming from work, children playing, senior citizens with their compassionate eyes, policemen maintaining order, ambulance men...They were the ones who gave sense to life. Their children and their great-grandchildren, if they follow in their footsteps, will give meaning to this world.

Yes, those wonderful human beings were witnesses to my dying. I was conscious of that and was overjoyed. Yes, I was dying, but, first, they were present at my victory, at my return to the flow of pure humanity, the same one I had entered almost nineteen years before, through the womb of one of its decent representatives: my mother. I couldn't ask my destiny and my soul for a better lot. It had to be written in the great book of existence that my life would be ended at this early stage.

I felt my death coming slowly, but I was warmed up by the presence of such wonderful beholders.

Then everything went blank.

Part Two

10

Dreams, visions, events..., I couldn't tell. They certainly formed the *reality* contents I belonged to, which opened up on the most impressive waterfall I had ever seen. It was made of watery and pink rays interweaving into one another and falling endlessly, silently.

I then boarded a huge airplane on a trip to a distant country, *any distant country*. How could it be? It should have a name and a location. But there was no fixed destination, no schedule either. I was just about to fly away, like taking a plunge into the unknown. I burst into tears. There was no one available to comfort me, to wave me good-bye, to tell me anything at all. I was alone, the same way I had come into being. I was sitting in the airplane, ready to be carried away. I didn't see the pilot, but I imagined there was one somewhere, behind the panel in front of me; for, I heard the humming of the engine and saw the lights hanging from the ceiling, spreading on the floor and on the windows.

I was homesick by anticipation. I would long for the countryside I used to contemplate from my bedroom window. I would miss people, a lot of people I was unable to identify, except I remembered they were friendly and, once in while, they stopped to have chat with me. One of them was a pretty woman. Above all I would miss her. Definitely, I thought she was petite with an oval face, a cute mouth and shifty eyes. I imagined she used to wear a pair of high-hilled sandals which hadn't affected her slenderness.

A pretty woman! Why was I thinking about her, while I couldn't get a clear picture of her in my mind? Was she just a figment of my imagination or the image of an actual human being I used to be close to? What was going on?

Definitely, I couldn't remember her exactly, except that I *intuited* and was *certain* that she was small, sweet and pretty. Because of that woman unknown to me I wouldn't like to go on that one-way trip to a distant country, any distant country, located anywhere in the whole universe and other galaxies. It was a crazy idea which certainly didn't come from me. Who was responsible for this insane trip schedule?

Unfortunately, before I could make any protesting gesture, the airplane had taking off with a prodigious roar. I grabbed my seat arms while the aircraft was gaining altitude and reaching its cruising speed. It was an acceleration I could never imagine.

I had then a mixed feeling. Sometimes the idea of travelling in one direction only enraptured me; sometimes it disenchanted me.

While the airplane was climbing, I experienced a feeling of grandeur, taking myself for the *Creator of the Universe*. I thought that only the *Creator* of the world could be sitting alone in an aircraft with no pilot, going to any distant place. I was indeed experiencing the feeling of ubiquity. Why? I didn't know. It was so sweet to sit up, looking very important and reading a captivating story. I couldn't make out the title of the book and the name of its author. Nevertheless, I took no less delight in my reading. The scraps of thoughts I was able to pick up were sufficient to retain my attention. I was like a compact bell made of perfect alloy, which resounded at the slightest vibration. All the disjointed ideas, words, phrases, sentences, seemed to fall into the crucible of my mind, a source of coherence, harmony, meanings. From time to time, I looked through the window and got lost in the contemplation of a nebulous world I was flying over. It was a fluffy countryside in which everything was pure lightness and fragility.

Suddenly, my perception hypertrophied.

I was in my hotel room. It was snowing steadily. A biting cold made me crouched in my coffin serving as a bed. Why would I sleep in a coffin? I was an outcast, a savage, who was close to the thermostat without noticing it. All I had to do was to stretch my arm and set it to a warmer temperature. Then I realized that my lot was a blessing in comparison with what was going on outside. I had a look through to the window and I was petrified.

The *Armageddon* happened to be a fact!

I witnessed the progressive cooling down of earth caused by the sun extinction; which I was surprised at. The scientists, who had prophesied this kind of outcome, thought the apocalyptic vision would come about in millions years. Why this rushing? Why should this universal chaos better than people's wickedness?

The disastrous outcome spread like wild fire.

I saw human bodies being strewn all over the place. They were stiffened. Their mouths remained wide open in an attempt cut short to express surprise and disbelief. Their arms pointed at the ski, their ultimate vision and redemption. But it was too late for doing anything whatsoever. The sky kept a dead silence and seemed to indicate that it had never made any promise to mankind. It was a boundless blue-gray space. The idea of hope to come from above had always been in men's imagination. They should have known better and organized well their planet, their ultimate hope, something tangible, firm and full of almost anything good for humanity. It was a "gift" they should have cherished. Unfortunately, despite their knowledge, their philosophy, their world outlook, their pseudo fight for freedom and brotherhood, they had been going from stupidity to folly. They couldn't understand that the continuity of the species depended on their being together in all their endeavors. But it was too late to learn from the lessons of existence, from reason that was freely given, from wisdom accessible only by us, potential makers of civilization, fellowship and common ground. In our systematic disregard of that togetherness, we finally unleashed waves of hatred and miseries. I was the only witness in sight, with no claims on that entire messy outcome. In the middle of the ruin was the carcass of a cat. It was crushed flat, except its pink tongue attached to its flat head, which seemed to be put out at the world vanity.

The planet seemed to be completely purified, free from too much blood unnecessary wasted. It could be, from that point on, made ready by the *Creator* for a batch of new animal species. If that was the case, then there would have been some hope for the universe.

But an *inconsistent being* or *entity* took pleasure of confusing me and sending me back to the fluffy countryside made of lightness and fragility. Some point in time, the sun pierced the clouded mountains and revealed a city which had survived the disaster. How? I couldn't tell. It had to be pure luck or a whimsical decision of my *inconsistent being*; for that city didn't deserve a better treatment than the rest of the world.

That city, indeed, possessed everything: money, bread, light, love... Unfortunately, the money came from exploitation of men by men. Its bread was made of mud and blood. Its light emanated from a blinding source so much so that men, women, children, being at loss, were cannoning into one another. Its love sprang up out of a deceiving mirror concealing hatred instead. As a matter of fact, once in a while, people started all over their mutual killings, the exploitation of one another and the loss of purpose leading to their senseless cannoning into one another. And all this bred diseases, violence and despair.

A man came from nowhere. He was so tall that I felt dizzy looking at his face. He was, I thought, some kind of *soapbox orator*. His voice was deep, but sweet. He declared, "Men, women, children, stop for a moment and listen to me. I am going to use a plain language which can be understood by everybody. I am going to raise some questions which, I believe, have been in your mind for a long time. Hear me out. Can you understand why you have a housing problem? If there were no governments, no owners of apartment buildings, no engineers, and above all no legal prescriptions on housing, you would live in a house anyway. It would be one built with your bare hands and your limited resources. It's true your hand-made house wouldn't be as imposing and symmetrical as the one recommended by the law or designed by one of our skillful architects. It would certainly lack all the luxury of modern dwelling: cathedral ceiling, gorgeous master bedroom, foyer, fireplace..., but it would be your home anyway, a place to rest your old bones, to take shelter from the rain and the sun. Isn't it the primary purpose of shelter? We need shelter from the harshness of the elements. That should be all. Anything else is cheer luxury. Yet you can't even have these bare necessities of life!

"Now, the right to build and to own houses, being ensured by professionals and specialists, has brought you nothing but anguish, anxiety, fear of not having the rent money, fear of receiving the dispossess injunction, fear of foreclosing on a property that has never belonged to you, in the first place.

"Your whole life is controlled by professionals of all kinds, but your employment turns insecure. You spend months and often years vegetating. And, with all hopes gone, you swell the rank of the homeless. But if all depended on you, you would certainly make ends meet.

"My dear friends, don't believe that you are different from your ancestors. You are exactly the same kinds of beings as *Homo erectus* and *Homo faber*. They survived all the dark ages you can think of. Believe me, I've been an eyewitness to human history since day one, because I am older than mankind and its planet. Therefore, I know what I am talking about. When your ancestors were sick they managed to recover from their sickness, using whatever means available to them. If they didn't do it they wouldn't make it. If they didn't make it you wouldn't be here, would you? Think about it for a moment. You are the living proof of their ability to survive.

"I am telling you! I've been following you step by step in the unfolding of history.

"Your health is now at the mercy of professionals of different kinds: doctors, nurses, employees of Health Department, insurance brokers, drug producers. However, how many problems do you have, as soon as you have needed health care? It's pitiful to see so many people showing their rotten teeth, while dentistry has reached the acme of perfection. It's incomprehensible that so many people die from curable diseases because they can't afford the cost of medical treatments, while medicine is making astonishing progress.

"Human beings, in other words, used to solve their problems in the past, before the outcome of scientific development and modernization. But they have started to lose hope when the professionals have taken over and have suggested to them that they should trust them. Mankind has been simply betrayed, scoffed and debased..."

People stopped fighting and cannoning into one another. They were listening to this easy speaker. I imagined that his voice reverberated throughout the planet in as many idioms spoken by mankind. He showed no anger, no scorn; except I had the intuition that he was the center of grief, pity, charity, compassion. I suspected that he was the alpha and the omega of knowledge, but he was too concerned about people's sufferings to flaunt his omniscience. He was just talking the truth simply, plainly. The listeners seemed, for the first time, to have reached it and touched it like a tangible object.

Then the magnificent giant asked these simple questions, "What's the value of the greatest discoveries in the world if you, Josephine, Maurice, Andre and Bob, (I was astonished that he pointed at those he was calling by name), have been living in abandoned buildings with broken-down furniture, with no gas, no electricity, no running water? If you have the shivers from cold nights of winter? Tell me!"

Worries clouded his face. "Go home," he finally suggested. "Reflect on these words; and if you understand them, you will try to act accordingly. Take your future in your hands. Help one another, but don't impose your beliefs on others. You are all in the dark about the way to bring in happiness and brotherhood on Earth."

He came up to me. I had no fear of him. He was a *civilized being* whose presence brought me a feeling of security. He stopped a few inches away from me and smiled. I could sensate the warmth coming from his colossal body, the vibration of his chest; I could see his limpid eyes and his huge hands. With a fillip he could smash me (along with the surroundings), but I sensed that he had never been engaged in any act of violence and wouldn't condone any brutal action against mankind. He was the symbol of gentle force, a force guided, controlled by reason, love and compassion.

Then some point in time, he entered into conversation with me. I couldn't remember all the details of the ideas we had exchanged on philosophy, religion, politics, art and science, except that he concluded, while he was bursting out laughing, "You know my friend, people are just zombies. They must be awaked by slaps on their faces. They are so gullible that any impostor with a little imagination can throw dust into their eyes. So, a dynamic government should create a new civil service position: the *Office of National Slappers.*"

I split my sides with laughter.

The giant turned round, walked away and vanished on the horizon.

I was by myself, thinking of applying for one of the *national slapper's positions.*

I was immersed in a quasi-even state of mind and environment. It was a meaningless and undisturbed pink medium, which was spreading all over to such a par that I assumed a kind of pink personality from it. Time, continuity, space, past, present, future became blurred, then vanished or immersed into that pervading shade. Nothing seemed to be able to keep consistency. By the same token, I didn't experience any concern. I was living in a world where I didn't have to look for job, to worry about rent, to try to make sense to people's statements, to hurt and be hurt. I shed no tears; I felt no joy and had no fear of death. I was there, in a nondescript universe which was there, in its majestic overwhelming pinkness. I was at peace with the world and myself. I thought that I was in some kind of paradisiacal universe, a place one could enjoy undisturbed felicity, day in day out, for eternity.

How long did I revel in such heavenly life?

I didn't know, except that I started to notice that my pink medium was punctured by blue-gray patches or patchy beings.

They were, however, devoid of individualities. Not only they could be interpreted in any way I wanted to, but also they assumed all kinds of shapes, touched one another and sometimes blended into one another to give life to impossible creatures I had never imagined, seen or dreamed of in my life.

Suddenly, a painful experience happened to me in my serene existence: I began to remember or I thought so. Maybe the verb *remember* popped up in my mind, but there were no past events to recall. I didn't need to do so anyway, since I couldn't situate myself in some kind of clear present, nor could I forecast any future.

Fortunately, my remembrances were not coherent; they were rather flashes of images belonging to a distant past, so distant that, under normal circumstances, I wasn't supposed to remember them. I thought that my state of mind was abnormal, overexcited, and then I was experiencing a case of hypertrophy of memory. That's it! A case of hypertrophy of memory! Sometimes I was a small boy inquiring of a passer-by about my future. "You are going to be all right," he answered. "In fact, you are going to be the man of the hour." Once in a while, threatening faces jumped like jacks-in-the-boxes. Once, they hunted me. I tried to run, but to no avail: my motion was slowed down by the weed. I was hopeless and expected to be harmed by them any minute. I felt the intense heat coming from their mouth and smelt their foul breath.

Fortunately, I returned to my familiar environment made of those flashes of the past, alternated with the pink medium, punctured by blue-gray patches or patchy beings, intermingled, deformed, shrunk or blown out of proportion.

11

My environment was assuming more familiar configurations, or I believed they were. The pink medium insisted for a while, and then it lost its immaculate evenness, gradually but steadily. At last, it was replaced by a much firmer scenery: a car train.

Of course, the passengers in the car kept being transformed into various shapes and sizes. At first, they didn't distinguish themselves from the surroundings and their objects (mechanical objects). Then they assumed their human nature, but in a very unsettled fashion: now men, now women; now children, now a combination of all of them. They never stopped bumping into each other and fighting over a seat or some trifling reasons. Yet, I recognized these shadowy gestures as being human, full of meanings, leading to a life of purpose. But how could shadows behave purposefully? "Oh, I see!" I thought. "They have to be shadows of tangible beings."

The coherence of their behavior could also be an illusion responding to my mind or brain fundamental structure, which was able to convey meaning to what could be nothing but muddled, inane pieces of action. It appeared strange to me that I was able to come up with such sophisticated explanation. Did I use to be a person of learning? And what did I mean by coherent behavior? Had I ever been exposed to rationality some point in time?

The car was once silent, but crammed with riders. We reached a stop. A stocky young lady stepped on my foot and proceeded without apologizing. She was perfectly aware of her action: after she had stopped in the middle of the car, she looked back and made a face. I smiled. I forgave her from the bottom of my heart because it wasn't her fault. She was acted upon by drives. Thus she was unable to conceive of living in harmony with her fellowmen. She felt better in a context of crisis and animosity. It was some kind of drive, indeed, the same one which is induced by human combativeness causing bloody war between nations and turning any endeavor to international peace into a vain undertaking. We, human beings, are robots in a way, acting according to uncontrollable inner forces.

My *aggressive woman,* fortunately, had vanished. Another young lady dashed in. She wore blue jeans pants which suited her well and red flat-heeled shoes. A blue jacket shielded her bust from the biting cold of winter; a knitted scarf coiled round her neck; a large bag hung loose on her side. From time to time, she readjusted the strap to her shoulder.

In spite of her apparent sturdiness, she could hardly maintain her balance. She glued her body, like a parasite but lovely plant, to the door whenever it was closed for a new departure.

Quite the opposite was that heavy-set lady who freshly arrived. She walked straight while the train was speeding along the rail. She carried a baby muffled in a yellow woolen outfit. No sitting passenger had the decency to offer her a seat. Finally, a sleeper woke up with a start and invited her to sit down.

"Little Peter and you deserve my seat," he stated.

"Little Peter," I echoed him in my mind. How could that man know the name of the baby? It was obvious that the mother and her baby weren't acquainted with him. Oh, I understood. The baby's face looked like a Peter's, a future Peter's.

I didn't know what to make out of my deduction. I thought intuition had a great deal to do with associating that baby's face with the name of Peter, provided that there was certain morphology of the body or a certain facial crucible characterizing the face of anyone having such a name. I assume that my deduction was logical and unreasonable at the same time. Would it be possible that reality oscillates between these two poles? Then when did the truth start and the falsehood end? How could we have any firm belief?

By the mother and her baby was sitting a man in his fifties. He was reading a newspaper. Once in a while, he opened a little brown paper bag, pulled a paper cup out of it, removed the cap and had a sip of a steaming coffee, while closing his eyes voluptuously. Apparently, he had freed himself from worries or possessed whatever could make him the happiest man in the world. Next, he put the paper cup back into the little brown bag and saved it preciously behind his shoes, on the floor. He started reading again as if everything looked all right in the universe. I thought he was like me, experiencing no concern, shedding no tears, having no joy, no sadness and no fear of death. Could it be the proper attitude to adopt in this world I was living in? Then my aggressive female passenger had to suffer a severe case of abnormality. She should be reeducated.

Soon after, this profusion of mixed images or shadows of men, women, children, animals and objects, had just disappeared. I experienced nothing whatsoever in terms of sounds, colors, suggestions, concepts and configurations. I reentered my pink medium and stayed there for a long time. How long? I couldn't tell. When I became conscious again of other sets of events, different people were traveling in the car train.

The *dirty old man!* Why did I think he was a dirty old man? He should have a name. As a matter of fact, he responded, morphologically speaking, to the concept of a male. And all the males seem to have names.

Yes, for some unexplained reason, I thought I had seen him before. Yes, I remembered the state of excitement he was in, on our first acquaintance. He was in the same car, sitting by a corpulent lady. Judging by the resemblance between them, she could be his sister. But he didn't speak to her, because he was busy elsewhere, being unable to keep his eyes off a female student. She wore a short blouse and tight polyester pants. Her navel appeared whenever she raised her arm to grab the hand-rail.

That navel turned into an attraction point, a magnet to the *dirty old man*. Ah, that was the origin of his stain in my mind! I was amazed that such a small piece of meat could make that man in a frenzy state. He was making gestures expressing lascivious intentions.

Today, he was sitting quietly and wearing dirty clothes. He was the true image of the "dirty old man". With his finger nails, he tried to remove some stubborn stains from his pants. A pair of earrings scintillated in his ears. He certainly followed the trend for a *dirty old man*! His head was covered with a knitted cap.

He scanned the whole car and was perhaps setting out in the quest of an *attraction point*. But there were no young females in sight, with their navels on display.

A set of twins burst into the car. They carried each an impressive *AFRO*. Their heads were strangely round and macrocephalic. Their open mouths showed two rows of teeth in each gum. The incisors were sharp-pointed like those of Dracula.

Dracula!

The twins kept looking at me with an obvious animosity. Why? I didn't do any harm to them. I saw them for the first time in my life. I would remember having seen them before, because they looked odd and struck the imagination of anyone who laid eyes on them. I didn't know what I could do in case they should attack me. They looked strong and bellicose, and I was too weak to defend myself.

I shivered. I wondered if they were not evil beings coming from a distant galaxy. If not, nature happened to have made them up on a sudden impulse, on a stormy day. Could nature give birth, just like that, without a medium, without passing by the crucible of some pre-established forms and female wombs? It was a question I had no answer for. I promised to do some research about it. Where should I go for conducting my inquiry? I had no idea.

The pink medium, an oval object, a profusion of flowers, a dazzling explosion of lights, a waterfall made of watery illuminants...Humming devices...Then back to the pink medium...Back to the car train...

Why was I experiencing images or events which occurred in a car train? How could a car train be such a strong object of my reminiscence or something of that nature? Yet, these events were happening as if the world I was living in was made of accidents, variables, with no permanence, reference points to hold on to. I wondered if these ephemeral events were happening at all, as I was unable to have a clear description of the surroundings which kept on changing. Unless I was in a state of flux, in an ever-changing world, in which the concept of identity had the complexion of a blink. Was I also in a rapidly changing status and personality? I felt apprehensive about this kind of constant metamorphosis; for, some point in time, I could be changing to an undesirable being.

The car train was jammed full.

The *madwoman* arrived!

She made her way to the car center by means of her elbows. "Excuse me, excuse me!" she shouted. "I have something to tell you. Excuse me. This is something I want you to hear. Please, I am so sorry to disturb you."

I noticed that her face had shriveled up a little. Otherwise, she looked as firm as a rock. The first time I had seen her (the first time!), she was haranguing on the *Lord*. It was the worst verbal experience I had ever undergone. Her voice was shrill and testy. I remembered that my fellow-traveler had whispered, "This is the *madwoman*. Everybody knows her. She is harmless, except that, with her voice, she should be assigned to a society of indoctrination, in a concentration camp. The prisoners would beg to become converted to whatever they wanted them to, as long as they were free from her ear-splitting voice." I could have laughed heartily at the joke, but I couldn't exactly remember my reaction to it.

Now, that *mad woman's* voice had softened. She could have been wiser with time.

She was "lecturing" on something quite different from her previous topic about the *Lord* and much more down to earth: "I was dismissed from my job because they said I was depressed. However, I wasn't depressed; I was rather oppressed by my employer. We, the underdog, are being oppressed all the time. If they could stop abusing us and if they could confer a portion of their love for their pets and their properties upon us, they would solve all our problems, wouldn't they?"

I smiled. I remembered Adamo's song about the *presumed madman*. What did I mention a song by Adamo? Yes, I remembered it. When did I listen to it? I didn't know. Its lyrics should be in French. However, its English version was clear in my mind (at least the theme was):

Because the madman looked absent-minded,
They thought he was crazy.
But, instead, he was the one who pitied on his judges
And the world...

I thought the lesson drawn from that song was fit for my *insane lady* on the train and, eventually, I questioned the *healthy-minded passengers' assumption* of her craziness. Weren't her words the expressions of the *honest truth*? Were we sounder in mind to remain unmoved by injustice and inhumanity in order to be praised for our "good behavior", to depend on opinions and traditions before acting, to take a stand after the bloody outcome? Then, in the name of objectivity and fairness, we should commend that woman for being bold to tell the truth in plain terms, without concerning herself about the fact that truth offends and embarrasses. But even this simple act of commendation was a burden too heavy for us to carry.

As soon as my *insane lady* finished her speech, she kept silent and went nonchalantly but serenely to the next car where she would tell again the *truth*.

Pink medium; the oval object (the same one); the alternation of the oval object with the pink medium; persistence of the oval object...

A bed of jasmines appeared. Their flowers disturbed me to such a par that I composed a poem about them. Had I ever been a poet? But why didn't my poem express joy and an ode in praise of life? It went as follows:

My Stony Heart

There was beautiful Jasmine,
Who, one day, stole my heart.
I gave her love,
I gave her affection.
Heaven was on Earth:
Daily, in the land of joy,
I was carried away
By passion and devotion.
And then she set her conditions!
In a mellifluous tone,

She confirmed her love for me,

Her desire to be with me,

But she was also craving

For splendor, wealth and power,

She wanted to shine regardless.

Each of her wishes

Slashed my heart,

That was slowly filled of icy water.

And it froze and changed to stone,

Forever...Maybe...

If everything in my pink medium, punctured by images, shadows, patchy beings, was uncertain, devoid of permanent form, consistency and individuality, there was one object or being, however, which kept coming back to me, unaltered. It would resist to mixing up with anything else at all. As a matter of fact, it had never been part of the train car scenery. Although, at first, I couldn't identify it and grasp its meaning, it presented itself with a certain frequency in the middle of an abundant occurrence of appearances or happenings, like the beat of a symphony, which guarantees its rhythm.

Whenever it appeared, it overshadowed everything. I thought that its preeminence derived above all from the regularity of its outlines; but only later on I would be able to identify the shape: it was an oval one, like a giant egg. However, to the best of my recollection, I had never seen an egg of such magnitude before. Oh, I forgot; I was living in a world where everything had been strange and familiar to me at the same time.

Fortunately, this oval shape didn't frighten me at all. On the contrary, I experienced a feeling of security and warmth when it was there, to such a par that if it depended on me and my willpower, I would certainly have found great pleasure in reaching it, and caressing its smooth shell. So, I retired within myself in order to find enough strength allowing me to get to it. Unfortunately, I was totally devoid of the feeling of effort or willpower. My desire was remaining at the level of potentialities. Thus I had to be content with contemplating that oval object, silently, hopelessly. Yet I didn't feel any anger and frustration because of my being incapable of action, except that I was eaten up with my wish to possess the oval thing, my oval thing. Yes, it had to be mine since it made me feel so good.

I wasn't discouraged either. I knew that it was a matter of time before I could have the *privilege* of touching my guardian angel appearing in the form of a symmetrical and oval being. It could be some kind of god or goddess to which I was feeling an adoring reverence and homage, but I wasn't quite sure of my deduction. I didn't have recollection of my being bent on worshiping.

Then, one day, like a blinding glow, a face emerged! The oval being was a face! a human face!

Better still, my identifying it didn't change its symmetrical configuration; on the contrary, all parts were in their right place. And this new level of awareness brought me great joy, the more so as, at the same time, a crystal clear day appeared, indeed, flashed, like the *Fiat Lux of Creation.*

I smiled or I believed I smiled.

Why did I believe I smiled?

I should have known whether I smiled or not, shouldn't I? Smiling is not a concept, a deliberation or a philosophical discourse, which may raise doubt in our mind. Smiling is a facial expression which usually announces a state of pleasure (rarely a state of scorn or disgust). Therefore I had to be happy, being that I wasn't making fun of anyone.

I had to have good reason for smiling. Indeed, as sharp as the crystal clear day, the *Fiat Lux of Creation*, an explanation popped in my mind.

I had been experiencing images or events bathed in a pink medium, with no tangibility, no active and potential meanings, which, unfortunately, appeared to cannon into one another, like whimsical accordions. To be truthful, they didn't really affect me. I had never felt their tangibility, their concreteness, their ability to induce pleasure or pain into me. Then I had no reason, so far, to believe that my smile was actually happening, neither the human face nor the bursting daylight. In other words, I was in a context in which things were happening for no reason and purpose. I was a silent and insensitive witness to them.

Then I had a shock when the face had returned my smile! "Yes, the face smiles at me!" I thought. "I have no doubt about it."

Soon after, I tried to dismiss my claim, thinking that I was just dreaming or being engaged in a similar passive state of mind, to such a par that my attitude could be mere reflection of my own smiling face.

What kind of deduction was that? It didn't make any sense to me.

However, it was disturbing to see the face insisting on smiling for the sheer joy of seeing my own face shining with happiness. It couldn't be the reflection of my own smile; for, I would have needed a mirror for that. A mirror! What's that? So, if I was unclear about my smile because of my inability to prove it without a "mirror", I had no doubt about the existence of a smiling face other than mine. It was definitely a communication imparting interchange of feelings and signs. It was the purest, the most genuine and beautiful smile I had ever seen. It couldn't be mine. I had never had such refreshing and bewitching grin, as far as I could remember. It conveyed its sweetness and compelling optimism to my body, to the deepest part of my personality. It was definitely a caress, an ecstasy, a catalyst for persevering in existence. "A catalyst for persevering in existence," I echoed myself. Of course, I exist and want to keep on living."

"Welcome back, my angel," whispered the smooth lips which formed, with sparkled teeth, a *harmonious whole*. They completed each other; they couldn't be conceived of without each other.

"Don't worry if you can't return the compliment," the *harmonious whole* went on. "You open your eyes, and that's enough, my angel.

You smile, that's more than I can expect from you. You are going to be so much better."

I didn't utter these words. I had never spoken this way and had never called someone else "angel"

Was I in trouble or on the threshold of a new wonderful living adventure?

The face dissolved into tears. I didn't know what to think. Were they tears of joy or tears of sadness? Were they ceremonial acts of a welcoming ritual? I imagined that I did go on a trip and spend a long time on vacation, far away from where I was, otherwise, my return wouldn't cause any tearful emotion. Oh, I remembered now. I did board on an airplane, with no pilot in sight, to a distant place (any distant place). It was a one-way trip (at least it was supposed to be).I had questioned the rationality of that trip schedule. And before I had expressed my dissenting opinion about it, the aircraft took off with a mighty roar. On the way, I saw the fluffy countryside, the cooling off of the planet, the crushing of bodies, the cat with its flat head and pink tongue, like a movie replay in slow motions. Yes, I remembered! It was a long trip to a distant place (any distant place).Yet, I was unable to elucidate all those events or would-be events. I was awakening on a world which looked strange and familiar at the same time.

And the smiling face was still welcoming me. I couldn't fully understand its purpose, but I kept smiling at it and trusting its words. So, if it prophesied that I would have reason for rejoicing, it could be right.

Was I hallucinating?

No, I didn't think so. Hallucinating is, after all, experiencing something that doesn't exist outside the mind. I firmly believed that I was witnessing the smiling face, the tears of joy or sadness coming out of it. That face had to be real! Though I couldn't touch it, I felt it wasn't just the projection of my ego or my imagination playing tricks on me. Furthermore, it made articulate sounds that reverberated in my ears. No, I couldn't be so much mistaken.

Moreover, those tears compelled me to believe in the reality of the face: two drops of them coming from it had fallen down on my face. They were not imagined by me. Their warmth couldn't be just part of any realistic dream I might have. I wished they could remain there for a longer period of time; for, it was the first time, for eternity, I had felt something against my body, something other than my body, something we often call non-ego, which doesn't need us to exist. Non-ego! A sophisticated concept. Where did I learn to speak like that? And I defined it: *whatever is out there.*

Yes, I believed in the existence of those tears without any wish from me, regardless of my perceiving them or my experiencing their warmth against my skin. Therefore, their origin and the face they fell from had to enjoy autonomous existence.

However, the teardrops were dried with a piece of cloth. Again that piece of cloth was real. I felt its roughness against my skin. I didn't hold it, produce it and anticipate any need for it. As a matter of fact, I wished it didn't exist at all, to enjoy longer the warmth of the tearful drops against my skin. "What's going on?" I thought. "Why am I experiencing this chain of occurrences which reveal things existing without my participation? Furthermore, to make the comparison between those external occurrences and me, to recognize that there is a distinction between other things and me, I have to be alive. I am alive! What do I mean by being alive? Shouldn't I be? What's its purpose?"

Some point in time, my *one-way ticket* had been cancelled, and I was kicked out of the huge airplane bound for a distance place (any distance place). And I ended up in a firmer ambiance of which a welcoming smiling face was a part.

It was too much for me in one day. I went back to the alternation of the pink medium with flashes of the past, blue-gray patches or patchy beings, the car train and the oval being...

12

A tall and handsome physician was surrounded by medical students. He walked stately; a smile was playing on his lips. Along the way, he looked toward a pretty and suave-looking nurse, and inquired, "Fay, did you take Michael's temperature?"

"Yes, Dr. Colborne," she answered. "And everything seems normal."

The so-called Dr. Colborne stopped by the bed in which the patient, by the name of Michael, was lying on the back, with one foot and one arm attached to a string.

The medical instructor quickly explained the importance of body temperature to the students.

"Any major changes in the body temperature should hold the attention," his deep voice expressed assurance and contentment. "Most disease conditions are reflected in the changes above-mentioned. When a patient's body temperature rises above one hundred and six degrees or falls below ninety-five degrees, such a patient is considered to be in grave danger by the majority of health practitioners."

The medical group moved towards the next patient with a "gunshot wound to chest."

I didn't know when those patients were brought in the room. I didn't remember anything about my being hospitalized at all. What was wrong with me? Was I shot down by someone? Was I hit by a car? Did I fall down in front a train out of despair? I had no idea. However, from that point on, I was fully aware of what was going on around me and I was scanning the room and getting familiar with the surroundings.

Dr. Colborne stopped short and cast an amorous glance over the nurse. Then he smiled. He was clearly having nice, wonderful feelings to be close to the nurse known as Fay.

"Nurse," he recommended "make sure they run new tests on Michael. I mean a new *CBC* and *EKG*. Do it, otherwise, I'll wring your neck."

The nurse smiled back at the physician and kept working. It seemed that she was accustomed to his sense of humor and idle threats. I wondered if anyone would be sadistic enough to actually wring such a beautiful neck which looked like a fine piece of artwork.

Dr. Colborne took the *gunshot wounded patient's* bedside record and glanced at it. Afterwards, he drew the students' attention and summarized that patient's medical history, the surgical procedure which had been performed on him, as well as the medications and dietetic measures on which they had decided under such circumstances.

"We are going to give him a quick examination," he went on to say. "My guess is that a lot of progress has been made. Let's make sure of that."

He bent forward, peeped out under the patient's gown, scrutinized the suture indicating the recent operation he had mentioned earlier and showed an expression of satisfaction on his face.

He asked, "How do you feel Thomas?"

"Fine, considering," replied the patient in a rasping tone.

"You are doing fine, indeed. Thomas, if everything keeps on going smooth, you'll be out in no time."

"Thanks, Doc, for everything."

My turn came.

I was puzzled that Dr. Colborne, to present *my case* to the students, didn't use an approach as exuberant and friendly as the one he had used when it had been Michael's turn or Thomas'. He used derogatory terms which took away from his scientific and professional status. As a matter of fact, he no longer appeared self-confident and happy. He had to see me from a negative perspective. Why did my presence turn him sour? I had no idea. Yet prejudgment in a physician's activity should be limited to the minimum (if it can't be eliminated altogether); otherwise, it would trivialize the profession. That day, Dr.

Colborne's impartiality was so obvious that the students became perplexed and looked at each other.

"This scoundrel was brought here about five months ago," he bellowed. "He was stabbed repeatedly in the back, the neck and the feet. Who was the attacker? Nobody knows."

He took a deep breath and then continued, "To our knowledge, he had no history of injury prior to his present condition, also no history of chronic illness. Our data system has nothing on him. He came from nowhere and may not have seen any physician during his entire life. Most of the street people have no records whatsoever to go by. So, we were totally ignorant of him at his arrival on the emergency ward. And this means a lot; for, questions have to be asked with no answer. Is he allergic to some medications? Is he a diabetic? Does he have a heart condition? Has he contracted an infectious disease? All these issues had to be addressed and be forced. Mistakes and misdiagnoses were highly possible. Furthermore, we had to decide fast what to do about him. It was a race against the clock.

"Such situations are not rare in the medical profession, above all with the new breed of violent young tugs, with no morals and no respect for human life. They behave as if people are dolls they can change at leisure. And they can live dangerously for years.

"When that John Doe (that's his name, so far) arrived here, he was pronounced clinically dead. The medical team did wonders to revive him. His blood pressure was at the lowest point someone can expect to survive. His hydrogen ion concentration dropped to a fatal level.

They had to operate on him to assess the damages done to his heart, his kidney, his lung and other vital organs. And it wasn't easy, considering that the patient showed a dangerous case of hypothermia, a subnormal body temperature, caused by the multiple stab wounds inflicted on him, by his loss of blood and the length of time *EMS* made to reach our hospital with him.

"By the way, this is a Trauma Center," he proudly added. "We have seen a lot, the more so as this center is located in a poor neighborhood which breeds human tragedies."

He paused once more for breath and went on, "Well, this is what one can expect by being a punk.

"His life has been hanging by a thread. They have to call *777* on him on various occasions. Don't be alarmed! *777* is a medical jargon. It's like an *SOS* alerting a special unit and all the physicians in the vicinity, in case of cardiac arrest.

"You can imagine the number of hours of anguish and care he has cost the City and us. Above all Fay, that nurse you've just seen, who—for some unexplained reason—has devoted her spare time to attend him. She has been doing it against our better advice. But you know how stubborn women can be."

There was a burst of laughter.

"He has been showing some signs of recovery," he resumed in a sad tone. "I think Fay, in that respect, knows more than anyone else about his case. But, until further notice, his fate is in the lap of the gods."

Dr. Colborne thought that I was still in a semi coma state. He was too involved and too absorbed in his apparently unjustified bitterness to look at me objectively, with the trained eyes he had scrutinized Michael and Thomas. I was thinking about the difference of attitudes adopted by the same people placed under different perspectives. Emotions blur our objectivity to the point of being temporarily blind. Therefore we may not see an aspect of reality, even under our noses. Thus Fay seemed after all to be the only one who had noticed the big turn for the better I was taking, which was perfectly understandable, considering that she had been close to me for months. So, I knew the secret of Dr. Colborne's bitterness: he cared for Fay who had been spending too much time on me. Was I an important person? What was the nature of her special care? I couldn't tell. I had begun to understand my surroundings and to get re-acquainted with reality in general. But whatever it was, I thought that the physician and the nurse deserved each other: they were two professionals in the same field. Nevertheless, I wished this lovely nurse, by way of punishment, could keep showing indifference to that physician who had insulted me in my moment of distress. In fact, my wish could come true, for, although I was unable to understand all the intricacies of life, I had the feeling that physician's insults heaping on me didn't please that young lady at all. So, if he wanted to conquer her heart, he would better be nice to me.

Oh, she looked so pretty!

I was really hurt, not only because that physician called me a scoundrel, but also because I didn't expect verbal abuse from a physician surrounded by medical students. It was like setting a bad example to them. But I was too naive; in these days, insults are used frequently even by people who are supposed to be dignified.

I had believed before that a physician usually acted like an artist. He was supposed to be unaffected by elements of reality which often disturbed ordinary people's minds and perceptions. Like an artist, I had believed he should transcend his immediate and pragmatic impulses in order to find the joy and rapture of his profession. I expected him to treat a human being, to be eager to do so, because that was his goal in the first place, the meaning of his taking the Hippocratic Oath. His healing of a wound (any wound) should fill him with incommensurable and ineffable happiness, no matter whose body was hurt.

Why should we expect this kind of high standards from a physician? Because he has some positive knowledge, the most powerful tool in the world. In fact, a genuine intellectual seems to make (at least) a tacit vow to be a leader, to pave the way for higher conduct patterns. If his intention has been all along to give precedence of blind forces, drives, instincts over reason, objectivity and savoir-faire, then he would have wasted a valuable time in school; for, he doesn't need education to behave according to his primitive nature.

I understood that my piteous appearance on the day of my arrival at the hospital, unconscious, and the bloody event I was involved in, could lead someone to mistake me for a scoundrel, a punk. But was that enough to sit in judgment on me without knowing me?

Then I remembered that I had always been too naive. How many times my fellow students (my fellow students!) had laughed at my ingenuity, my everlasting idealism, my persistent naiveté ready to give the seal of integrity and decency to people of some knowledge and profession? They had often teased me for attaching too much importance to values and education as sine qua non conditions to understand goodness fully and make one behave accordingly. So, you can imagine that I had been in a constant state of shock whenever I had heard that a professional had misbehaved. "Oh! my God!" "I couldn't believe it!" "I didn't expect that from a policeman, a lawyer, a priest, a statesman, a judge..." These were my usual exclamations. And on each occasion, my fellow students cut me short, "Wake up Peter. You've been living in another galaxy. Why do you have to be surprised at this man's misbehavior, at that man's misdeed? After all, they are just human beings!" Yes, I knew they were human beings. I did also believe in degrees of humanity. I was so young, so idealistic! I didn't buy the fact that schooling only filled up our minds with inefficient theories with no applications in real life (apart from the spreading of gadgets); that they left us exactly the way we could have been or we were in the state of nature, with our deleterious drives, our spitefulness, our selfishness, our tendency to outsmart others for our own dooms. I thought that the lessons of greatness, love, bravery, honesty, objectivity learned from literary works, scientific disciplines and philosophic discourses, meant to impress, on our minds, the value, the importance of these transcendent attitudes, for life. I didn't believe that, once we passed our final exams and that we obtained our diplomas, we threw those values to the garbage can.

Suddenly, I remembered Dr. Miles' animosity towards me, his settled intention to humble me, to reduce me to the shadow of myself, to take position against whatever I said, just out of a systematic negation of my value as a person and a bright student, to try to pour into my mind the poison, the bitterness of hatred and animosity. Fortunately, that painful remembrance, instead of saddening me, brought me a consoling feeling. I thought that more than once meant several times, and that my fellow students might have been right in believing that human nature was the same wherever it manifested itself.

I had just realized how resilient I was. Having seen Dr. Colborne's provocation from its true perspective and having assigned Dr. Miles' deleterious idiosyncrasies to the past, where they belong, I was able to focus my thought on something else. Luckily, that something else was by far more pleasant. It was about Fay's personality.

For some unexplained reason, I was associating her whole image with smile and happiness. Was it because her smiling face was the first element of reality I was conscious of? I doubted it. It seemed that all around that nurse was smiling, radiating joy.

Her body was smiling from her smiling face, which I had met on my rebirth, to her shoes which, I imagined, hid *smiling toes*, not to mention her proportionate legs supporting a strong hip kept barely under control by her immaculate uniform.

The room was smiling along with her body. The walls were light-blue; they were adorned with flowered paintings. There were also vases of flowers with which the whole area was fragrant. All the aisles were free of objects of any kinds; and the beds and the cabinets were disposed in a symmetrical manner.

Fay's presence generated wonderful feelings in the room. The patients were smiling, so was I. How couldn't we be, since she treated everybody with kindness and respect, as if each and everyone was a king, as far as she was concerned? She had to be of a *heavenly* nature. Her voice was so soft that, in the event that she could forget her manners and start to use abusive words, she wouldn't offend anyone. Yet, to the best of my knowledge (at least ever since my awareness of reality), she had never uttered abusive remarks. It seemed she was perfectly aware of the inner damages insulting utterances are capable of. She rather used tuneful modulations to make everybody at home. "Handsome, what do you want today?" "Gracious, you are doing so much better today!" "The only way, my angel, you can have an extra cup of ice cream is if you behave yourself." Those were the sentences among a thousand she was using on her daily dealing with us.

Her hands were velvety. They had the power to administer injections and bitter pills without causing the slightest pain and discomfort.

I was qualified to talk about it.

I was (and I am still) afraid of injections. The simple idea of a needle entering my skin made me in a very uneasy state of mind. I could never be a drug addict. I could never lose consciousness of the pinching of a needle, the sight of the blood coming out of my vein and my being vulnerable, at the mercy of the phlebotomist. I had a reputation for staying away from doctors and nurses because I associated them with injections and needles. But, whenever Fay had finished giving me an injection, I asked myself whether she had "really" done so. And, to be honest, I would be willing to be injected by her again and again.

On her days off, our room wallowed in a gloomy mood. The other nurses—except the so-called Maude—would seize the first opportunity to make us yearn after Fay's return. They addressed foul remarks to us, they found faults at anything we were doing and often showed no kind of compassion or gentleness in treating us. As a matter of fact, one day, a nurse who had relieved Fay, gave me an injection. My skin popped like a ball. Although she had desperately tried to conceal the damage, using gauze pads one after the other, blood was oozing through them. Finally, she resorted to verbal abuse "You, punk," she stated, "you have tough skin! I shouldn't expect anything different from you, being a street person, a drug runner, a bad apple."

I didn't believe her. If I could speak I would let her know that I wasn't a *street person*, a *drug runner* or whatever she meant; and that Fay didn't share her negative opinion about my skin. No she didn't at all. In fact, she had nothing but praise for my whole body. "Your skin is flawless," she affirmed on various occasions, being fully aware that I could understand her. She even called me once: "black velvet". Therefore, that nurse who "stabbed" me with her bloody needle just mishandled my "velvety" skin and was looking for an excuse.

Fay's body was a source of ambrosial delight. I didn't mean a strong perfume that could, in the long run, give someone vertigo because of its pungency. No, it was a much subtler but persistent scent. Ah! The scent of jasmines! *Once, my beautiful Jasmine!* Everything was so clear to me. In other words, Fay tried, through her smell, to show, in another way, that she did care about people. She knew that she had to rub shoulders with members of the staff on a daily basis, and to make her patients feel good. One of the best ways to achieve her goal was through the smell emanating from her *divine* personality. Thus, she was the first person who made me understand clearly that we can show generosity and love, or arrogance and carelessness, in the way we carry ourselves in terms of presentation. Didn't someone say to a reporter who was commenting on the odd aspect of his outfits that he was wearing a *leave-me-alone* suit? I believed someone did say that. When? I couldn't tell.

13

"Angel, you make me so happy," Fay whispered. "I am telling you the truth. I have never given up on you. I have always believed that you will recover to the fullest. You can imagine that, after I've been taking care of you for so long, I feel that I am very close to you. You are like a member of my family. I feel your pain; I have the intuition of your thoughts, your unexpressed thoughts. I sense that you are clever, generous and respectful. I believe strongly that you would like to reach me. Everything could have been different if I knew your name. That's true; I don't know your name. They've been calling you John Doe. That's so degrading. You must have a name, haven't you? I wish I could know it. I wish you could talk. Come on, say something."

She looked so sad that I felt sorry for her. "I feel sorry for her!" I thought. "What a paradox! I should beg her for her compassion and understanding instead. I was the one who was emerging from unconsciousness. I was the one who should be grateful to her. Then why did

I feel sorry for her? I had to do something to dispel this confusing situation. But what can I do to please her and bring a smile back on her face?"

I did my utmost to raise my hand to let her know about my willingness to be in communion with her in any respect. Did I really raise my hand or was I possessed by an impossible wish? I couldn't tell. However, if it was a wish, I would be so happy that it materialized for my own sake, for my sanity and my serenity. Hadn't I been yearning for that *beautiful being* since my *rebirth, for* reaching my *oval object*, the *human presence*, the *guardian angel*, the *smiling* and *weeping face*, I was awoken on? Fay had been standing all along behind those comforting symbols! How many days she had been trying to communicate with me? How painful and frustrating it had been to her! Above all when her colleagues, doctors, administrative staff members let her know that she was *sick* in her mind to insist on helping a would-be *destitute man*, a *mentally deranged person*, a *serial killer*, a *homeless*, a *slovenly bastard*! Still, she didn't give up. She had faith in me. She thought I was an important person who deserves respect. Then her magnanimity deserved a reward.

Henceforth, I thought that I couldn't let her down. What kind of man would I be? She would have her victory. I had to speak, especially as the speech patterns kept spinning in my mind, and that all kinds of thoughts had been crisscrossing my head. They were latent, but they were there; otherwise, I wouldn't be conscious of them and try to keep them in check. All that was left to do was for me to unlock those thoughts and throw them out, in the form of articulate sounds.

I huddled up within myself and became the witness to my own handicap, to the dilemma I was caught in, the dilemma of my incapability of expressing my thoughts which were just occurring to me... I was cheering myself on taking up the challenge for breaking down the barrier standing between the object of happiness and me, between that wonderful woman and me, between the return journey of the *distant traveler* and the warm welcome of the *princess*.

Finally, like a revelation, my first name burst out from my mind, as clear as daylight. Subsequently, being invigorated by a surge of optimism and joy, I grumbled, "Peter".

It wasn't just a thought. There was an articulate sound, for, the nurse turned suddenly and looked at me. And to convince herself that she had heard me "loud and clear", she repeated, "Peter?"

I nodded consent.

"Peter, that's a beginning!" she exclaimed. "Thanks God! It's Peter! Peter! He said Peter!"

As if the first articulate sound had opened the path to my speech power, I voluntarily growled my last name.

She lost all composure. "Peter Young!" she yelled. "Peter Young! Peter Young!"

Her voice echoed throughout the floor. In a flash, the room was filled with doctors, nurses, technicians, housekeepers, patients, visitors...Fay kept telling them the *good news* she had been waiting for months. "Yes, my friends," she shouted, "his name is Peter Young! He said it himself."

Everybody looked at her in admiration, as a true heroine who had just covered herself with glory.

Next, she held my hand tight and squeezed it, while she was repeating, "Peter Young! Peter Young! Peter Young!"

Then she grabbed my bedside card and crossed out my admitting name: "Unknown black male or John Doe" and proudly wrote my real one. With a pair of scissors, she cut the arm band around my wrist and replaced it by another one with my name inscribed on it.

Soon after, she left the room. I had a quick feeling of panic, believing that she was going away for good; since *her mission* had been accomplished. And that I would be again at the mercy of the unknown. Fortunately, she returned a few minutes after with the heavyset nurse called Maude.

This one asked me for my name. Again I was able to say it in a clearer tone of voice.

She turned round and looked at Fay. She burst out crying. Fay patted her on the back to appease her. Finally, she regained her composure and said, "My child, you did it all by yourself. I am glad I didn't discourage you. You were the only one who believed in his return journey. No one else did. Your optimism has paid off. Your compassion has no limits. My child, you are an angel. You make me so proud of you."

Fay kissed her on the cheek. "Thanks, Maude!" she said feelingly. "I needed your compliments. They are the only ones which count around here, because you are sincere. As a matter of fact, you have always meant whatever you have said to me. You are like my very mother. And what I like the most with you is that you have always great respect for my judgment and the way I feel."

Maude hugged her as if she were trying to smother her. She looked as strong as a sumo fighter, but, later on, I would learn that she had the heart of an angel. "I will always care about you," she promised. "You know that I will always be there for you, no matter what. Now, as the time goes by, I am certain that you will find more and more about Mr. Peter Young. I do believe he has friends and relatives who've been worried about his disappearance. But don't rush him. Let him pull himself together at his own pace."

She had a pause. Then grabbed her colleague by the sleeves and went on, "I meant to tell you not to care what they say. This young man's recovery shows that you've never been a fruit cake (as they've been calling you); you are full of wisdom and compassion: two rare pearls in this pragmatic world.

"And, as long as you do your job well, nothing else matters. Likewise, what you do with your free time is your own concern. You feel happy to help this young man in distress, do it. What's the meaning of life if one can't do what makes one feel happy? if one can't express the deepest feeling he is actuated by? if one has no worthy purpose in life?"

She took another pause before adding, "There is something else I want to say. You know, Fay, my child, I notice that true happiness and morality often go together. Evil can bring us some pleasures, but its aftertaste always turns sour. On the contrary, happiness, as well as morality, brings us a certain lasting serenity, a blissful feeling, a high self-image."

Fay, with a gentle twist of her body, freed herself from her friend's *suffocating hug*. Then, after catching her breath, she said, "Maude, does anyone have ever told you that you are also an angel?"

"No, never," answered her coworker smilingly.

"Then allow me to say that you are one."

"Thank you."

"And Peter agrees with me. Right, Peter?"

Both nurses looked at me.

I nodded.

I was happy to see that these two nurses love each other. It was better that way. I wouldn't like to see Fay at the mercy of Doctor Colborne. I didn't trust him at all.

As the time went by, my recovery was making headway. My speech power had also tremendously improved; to such a par that, some point in time, I was able to express my feelings in any way I wanted to, to exchange ideas with people and to find them, by the same token, less frightening. I was so lucky to come out of this nightmare without a profound or severe mental and physical handicap. I wouldn't need any reeducation, speech therapy or other long-term follow-up treatments. My brain and my soul remained safe and sound. The latter had certainly heard my prayer and had chosen to keep on living in my body.

My communication power went so well that my mind started playing tricks on me: I had fancied Fay was *especially* kind to me, which I began to contemplate with a great deal of reservation and discretion. For one thing, Fay, as I said again and again, was naturally kind to everybody; therefore I could be terribly mistaken and put myself in a very embarrassing position.

Again, my imagination is one of my most precocious faculties, which has never stopped being vivid. Since childhood, I've been forming mental images which I haven't actually experienced, and which have never stopped being sharp. I've been capable of recombining my sensory data to bring about new possible mental structures of the same data and making them more appealing to me. So, my precocious imagination has led me to build castles in Spain and end up in happy fancies, to picture a more humane world, without too many sufferings and negativisms.

I remembered, when I was maybe four, I idolized a beautiful woman who could have been my grandmother. Yet, she was radiant with grace and youthfulness. In my fanciful little world, I disregarded the age difference between us and *strongly believed* that she shared my feelings. When she spoke to me and touched me, I was filled with an indescribable joy. The funny thing is that, until today, I haven't been able to absolutely obliterate that woman's image from my mind. I know she belongs to the past. She may be dead. Certainly, she can no longer possess her pristine beauty of yesterday (provided that she is still alive); but my memory of her keeps picturing the attractive woman she used to be.

Could it be possible that Fay, in her dealing with me, happened to be much kinder than she had been accustomed to, and to add a little extra pinch of *spices* to her treating me? Or could I be again a victim of my own imagination?

I thought that all the male patients, who had been in that nurse's care, could have experienced the same emotion, the same impression, as I did. For, there was nothing equal to her touch. But I wasn't interested in other men's reactions to her heavenly touch, her melodious voice, her angelic smile. Those men were free to grant more or less importance to her kindness. Indeed, they would have to belong to some kinds of cold-blooded animals to remain unmoved by her. What I really cared about was my experiencing her gentleness. It became part of my reality. I was the only one who could speak absolutely about it, the same way I would talk about the pink elephant, the cheese on the moon, the diamonds in the sky, the fortune dreamed of, I might be fantasizing. Better still, that woman's sweetness was even more real than the objects of my possible hallucination, because it did occur, I did feel it, and it was more vivid, being a combination of my sensation and my fancy.

Someone inquired, "Mr. Peter Young?" I was far away in the land of imagination.

I opened my eyes and saw a middle-aged man. I thought he was a physician since he was surrounded by the same students who had accompanied Dr. Colborne a few days before. However, he was wearing a three-piece gray suit, not the usual white lab coat doctors carry on duty.

All in all, I preferred his approach to Dr. Colborne's. He called me "Mr. Peter Young". That was the proper way to address a *gentleman*. And, for some unexplained reason, I strongly believed I was a good person, that I had nothing to be ashamed of; otherwise, I would also have remembered my immoral orientation, along with myriad of impressions, ideas and images which kept rushing back to my mind where they belonged.

"Yes, I am," I replied in a nice and civilized manner in harmony with my *gentlemanly manner.*

After a short pause, I inquired, "May I find out whom I am speaking to?"

"Forgive me," the physician quickly replied. "My name is Doctor Glenn. I am a dermatology professor at the State Medical School. I am initiating my students into the procedures and treatments involved in the field of dermatology. Eventually, whenever I happen to be here, I advise the medical staff on therapeutic matters."

"I see. Welcome to our room, Doctor Gleen."

He breathed deeply before proceeding, "Mr. Young, I must tell you that I don't believe in the incompatibility of the various branches of medicine."

I had to be a true gentleman or look like one; otherwise this man of science wouldn't feel any reason for giving me a glimpse at his personal thought about his profession.

He went on, "All of them deal with the same human elements. In other words, we visualize the whole person, not parts of him. Thus, before my students and I start considering the type of treatment we could think of, which will get rid of your scars, we would be so pleased to talk about the miracle which happened here in this hospital, five months ago. Yes, Mr. Young, it has to be a miracle! I must confess in my students' presence that I had doubt about your leaving this hospital alive. A very thin veil, in your case, was between life and death.

"By the way, Mr. Young, I took the liberty to go through your chart and I must say that you have a strong personality."

"Thank you, Dr. Gleen," I replied. "I wasn't ready to take this one-way trip to nothingness."

Everybody burst out laughing.

I proceeded, "For, if I took that trip, I wouldn't have the privilege to meet a gentleman like you."

"You are simply amazing, Mr. Young," asserted the professor in tones of emotions.

Then he turned round, signed to Fay to come near us and stated, "Nurse, I was talking with some of my colleagues, nurses and administrative staff members, and they told me what you've done for Mr. Young. This kind of dedication should be known to anyone who wishes to enter the health profession. As far as I am concerned, I will repeat it from generation to generation of students, so they will understand the true meaning of their future vocation.

"Now, would you tell us what induced you to help a semi comatose patient and made you believe that your action could make a difference?"

At first, she looked puzzled. Then she stared in the distance, smiled and finally explained, "Well, to start with, my heart was bleeding when I saw this young man lying in bed hopelessly. First, I am a human being; then I am a professional. So I pictured myself in the same predicament as Mr. Young and, chances are, nobody would like to go out of his way to help me. Then I convinced myself of the fact that one shouldn't hesitate over accomplishing a good deed. It's a chance to contribute something positive to humanity one shouldn't let go.

"I knew that our medical staff (one of the finest in the country) had done its best for him; the proof being that they pulled him from the claws of death; but, not having anyone to visit him and bring him a personal comfort, this young man could have taken a long time over his recovery. So, I volunteered to bring him that personal comfort.

"Furthermore, although I am not a psychiatrist, a psychologist and a specialist of the human brain, I am aware of a growing belief that prenatal impressions exist. If that's true, conveying impressions to a semi comatose patient could be even more feasible. Such a patient could be susceptible to notice others' presence and try to communicate with them.

"In fact, during Mr. Young's semi comatose state, I hadn't missed an opportunity to address him as if he could communicate with me. Maybe, in a way, he did respond to my verbal stimuli, though he couldn't be fully conscious of it.

"I hope my explanation has elucidated partly, not fully, the drive behind my action."

I was so proud of Fay! She was the focus of many intelligent eyes! And her handling of the English language and her diction! My impression about her *angelic nature* had been reinforced. For one thing, her magnanimity seemed to be boundless. I didn't detect any sign of tiredness and disgust on her face.

"Nurse, you are a wonderful person and a professional full of insight and compassion," Doctor Glenn admitted. "Your approach of the semi comatose state deserves consideration, since it has led to Mr. Young's recovery.

"Now you can resume your regular duty. But don't stay too far; I may have to talk with you about the way to get rid of the dead skin on Peter's scars."

Fay nodded to the physician and walked away.

Dr. Glenn touched my scars with his bare hand like a curious child. "Well, you are doing find," he remarked. "I didn't expect your wounds to heal so fast. In fact, as I said, I didn't expect you to survive your wounds. That's amazing. You must have, as they say, a tremendous hold on life. Yes! You said it! You wanted to meet a gentleman like me."

The students, the patients and their visitors gave a loud hearty laugh.

"The only thing now left to do is to remove these dead skin and crust," said the professor.

Then he turned on his heels and gave his students a searching look. "Mr. Young has been kind to let me examine him in front of you," he pointed out. "He is a true gentleman like me (laughter). You have seen the dead skin and the crust on his back, his neck and his feet. What can be done about them?"

The students looked excited. I bet their young minds were bubbled over with answers.

A female student motioned to the professor and shyly asserted, "I think we can apply a dermal abrasion procedure."

The professor smiled. Then he acknowledged, "This is one of the procedures to contemplate. I am very proud of you. It's clear, based on your answer, that you have made progress in your studies and training. You are on the verge of becoming a fine doctor.

"Are there any other suggestions?"

A male student, who wasn't sure of the professor's reaction to his advice, bit his finger before asking (maybe against his will), "How about chemical abrasion?"

"That's very good, Jason" acknowledged Doctor Glenn, "very good indeed. Your advice is worthy of consideration."

With a large motion of the hands, he drew the students' attention and gave his opinion on the matter, "Well, my friends, I think you have both mentioned two current methods used in skin trouble. I have to tell you I am glad to notice that you've done your homework. However, I believe we should use, in the case under consideration, a much milder method. I am going to tell you why.

"Dermal abrasion is a surgical removal of the frozen epidermis and as much of the dermis as necessary, by mechanical means (low or high-speed wire brushes, emery paper cylinder etc.

"Chemical abrasion, on the other hand, is the application of a cautery, such as phenol or trichloracetic acid, to the skin for the purpose of causing superficial destruction of the epidermis and upper layers of the dermis.

"Now the procedure I alluded to a while ago partakes of dermal abrasion and chemical abrasion, but it is much closer to the latter than the former. More likely Mr. Young needs to take about half a dozen sponge baths made of a weak solution of alkaline carbonates."

I thought that professor Glenn was a *born diplomat*. He didn't want to take any side, yet he managed to make all the students feel good. His attitude was in harmony with the new trend in pedagogy, which favors praise over constant blame and strengthens the personality of students, future bearers of the social torch.

Having terminated their discussion, he and his students took leave of me. The former stopped on his way to speak with Fay.

I saw them gesticulating while looking at me. I definitely was the object of their discussion. But I didn't mind: they were both two wonderful persons who wanted the best for me.

Fay came up to me. She was all smiling. "Peter, this is just between you and me," she joyfully announced.

I was puzzled over her statement; but before I could have inquired about the meaning of it, she took me by the arm and uttered, "Let's go, Peter. It's time for your first bath."

"My first bath!"I echoed her.

"Yes, it is."

"Do you want to know how you've been kept clean?"

"No, I don't want to know. I will be too embarrassed."

"Then, follow me without a murmur; otherwise I will give you a quick rundown of your care, while you were unconscious."

"Fay, please. I am willing to follow you. No need for blackmailing me."

"Then follow me."

The first steps I made were very painful. I had just remembered not having walked for close to five months. I might have to learn again how to ambulate properly. Fortunately, as I was proceeding, my muscles became more flexible. I was glad Fay didn't want to use a wheelchair.

We left my room and walked through a long hall. Hampers, full of soiled laundry, were waiting to be rolled away by housekeepers. At times, nurses and doctors passed by hurriedly. They waved at Fay who waved back at them or found some nice words to greet them. At the end of the hall, we entered another one, on our left. A large metallic door showed up about three yards away. Fay opened it.

Suddenly, like a spark, gleamed the famous "bathroom" everybody was talking about.

It was equipped with a variety of tubs, pools and other devices for showers, hydro-pneumatic massages, hydrotherapy and other types of follow-up treatments.

The sweet-smelling scent of deodorizers pervaded all over and exhilarated me. I felt that I was in paradise.

Fay asked me to get rid of my gown.

"Not in front of you!" I exclaimed.

She blindfolded herself with her hands, like a child playing hide-and-seek. "You see, Peter, I close my eyes," she assured while giggling.

"No, that's not enough," I protested. "You still can take a 'peek' at my body through your parted fingers. You must turn your back on me while I am getting into that funny-looking solution. I'll tell you when to turn."

"Be my guest."

With great pain, I strode over the bathtub edge and slid into the special bath. I felt good. I then suggested, "You may turn around now."

She stared down at me and giggled.

I looked all around me to see whether any intimate part of my body could be seen by her. Not having noticed anything unusual, I inquired, "What's the matter now?"

"You know, I feel just like pulling the stopper and draining off the tub," she replied. "You would be lying there like a naked fish."

I panicked. My body, full of scars and wounds, wasn't a positive image to offer to such a beautiful woman's eyes. "You wouldn't do that, would you?" I asked imploringly.

Furthermore, the whole idea of being seen naked by her disquieted me. Apparently, when I was unconscious she might certainly have a "peek" at my body. And, as they say, what you can't see shouldn't hurt you. However, to my knowledge, I had never deliberately exposed myself nude to anyone, except when I was a baby (and I had not been conscious of that).

Fortunately, Fay understood my apprehension. "No, I wouldn't," she avowed. "I am just joking. My intention is not to harm you, but to help you getting back on your feet. Don't ever forget that. I am not a witch."

"I know that," I said, having regained my quietude.

Because of our closeness, we became silent. We had to mind the least gestures we could make in order to avoid any regrettable confusion.

Meanwhile, wearing surgical gloves, she was engaged into motion, and with a sponge, exploring and rubbing all my scars the location of which she seemed to know by heart. I felt her warm breath against my neck and my face, and I smelt her ambrosial body. I wished I could be fondled by her eternally. Suddenly, I had the insane desire to grab her and pull her against me, into the giant bathtub. But I realized in time that I belonged to a society and that it possessed sacred rules which couldn't be violated without endangering its very existence. "What would Fay think about my misbehavior?" I wondered. "She could be an angel, she could devote herself to helping me, and, perhaps, she was fond of me. But, acting in accordance with my insane desire, would probably mortify her, frustrate her, and disgust her—to say the least; because she would be the laughing stock of her colleagues and patients who were attending the 'famous bathroom'. She would be subject to disciplinary action or dismissal, as they would think that she was devoid of professional ethic and decorum."

Gradually, my reason was re-conquering its influence over my behavior, and I was rediscovering my spiritual sanity. To put an end to any surge of uncontrollable emotions in me, in that garden of temptation, I said anxiously, "Are you finished, mother?"

"Yes, my son," she replied in the same joking manner.

"In that case, we have to go through the same process. You are going to turn your back, so I can get out."

"I believe I should."

She turned her back again on me to allow me to get out of the bathtub and resume my gown.

While taking my arm, she suggested, "Don't you think I should let you come back here by yourself? I'll mix the bath solution for you. But I must let you do things on your own. You are getting stronger and better."

"I think you should," I replied unconvincingly.

I presumed she was afraid, like me, of something unexpressed.

14

I went back to bed. My heart was pondering with excitement. I tried in vain to shy away from my reality, my true feeling about Fay, by raising all kinds of imaginary fronts, walls and excuses, but I was also conscious of my being untruthful to myself. I should have known better, since I kept comparing her with the middle-aged lady I had a crush on, while I hadn't even reached my years of discretion. However, Fay belonged to my generation; my feelings towards her couldn't be that silly love of a little boy for a grown-up lady. I had to be very much in love with Fay! There was no doubt about it.

They admit that, usually, the discovery and acceptance of one's true feelings bring him certain serenity. Not to me, at that time, above all with an almost certain belief that I stood no chance to conquer the heart of that self-possessed woman. Therefore, it would be so much better for everybody if I didn't fall in love with her at all. I would be the first person to rejoice over my lack of interest in her. For one thing, I wouldn't make a fool of myself. Indeed, I wouldn't even think that I could be loved in return by her or by any respectable woman. No way! Of course, Fay might like me, have pity on me, but she wouldn't love me. The odds were against me. I was pictured as a street criminal who had received exactly what he deserved. Both Dr. Colborne and the insensitive nurse who had "stabbed" me with her bloody needle, had described the kind of person I appeared to be: a scoundrel, a punk, an unknown, with a tough skin popping like a balloon, on receiving an injection. And I was almost certain they were not the only ones who had been holding me in low esteem.

At least, *my version* of *the story* hadn't been heard yet. I knew the truth of it. It was far away from the image others had made up, which was the exact consequence of their total ignorance of the fact. Unfortunately, ignorance, for unexplained reason, sometimes captivates the mind. Would they ever make an effort to listen to another version of my story? Even if they allowed me to present my case, would it be too late? People hold as true whatever they want to believe in, above all they tend to trust the *first version* of a story, which is kind of *spicy* and *freshly concocted*. It doesn't require too much cerebration and criticism. It was the story of a punk. I was in a pool of my own blood. I was unconscious and couldn't give that first version of the events I was involved in. The authorities assumed the right to be my *official spokespersons* and they *buried me alive*. In their report attached to my chart, the policemen "present at the scene of the crime" stated:

This John Doe is found unconscious on the pavement. People believe that they have seen him before and that he could be a drug dealer. However, we have no record on him. He is a perfect stranger. The best explanation we may come up with is that, he is victim of his own lifestyle, a lifestyle of betrayal, heartlessness and total disregard for human life.

Thus a woman who fell in love with me, a dirty John Doe, a drug dealer, a heartless guy, carried on a stretcher, covered with blood, would simply attempt suicide. Not only her life could have been in a state of constant danger, but also, at once, she would be treated with contempt by her own peers.

It was true that I had regained my true identity, but my apparent social status remained unchanged. So, I had no right to even think of letting Fay unravel my feelings towards her by my attitude. For, she could be so disgusted that she would decide that, from now on, she would behave like the majority of doctors, nurses and other employees at the hospital, who treated patients with contempt and little consideration. And that would be my fault.

In fact, I wouldn't blame her if she loathed me for the remaining of her life. I had nothing positive to offer her, except my life full of problems, devoid of any dreams and ideals. "She belongs to Dr. Colborne," I whispered regretfully.

Coming from nowhere, she inquired, "How do you feel my love?"

I started. I was so absorbed in my *foolish thoughts* that I didn't see her arriving with two Policemen.

I felt uncomfortable as if I was betrayed by the woman I was in love with. But it was one-way love. She couldn't be made responsible for my feelings (at least she wasn't deliberately).

"Peter, this is Officer Warren and his partner," she went on. "They belong to the *Narcotic Division*. They have been trying to speak to you for quite a while, but, the medical staff has opposed to that, since you were in no condition to be interviewed. It's up to you now."

"Excuse me," the so-called Officer Warren interjected, "Nurse, I think it's no longer your business. We are trying to lead a criminal investigation. You've done your medical part, you've to step aside."

I looked up and had the feeling that I had seen that policeman somewhere. His face looked very familiar to me. But he had no right to speak to that lovely nurse the way he did.

I raised my hand to inform him that I wanted to say something and stated, "Officer, there is no need to treat her harshly. This is her job to protect her patients. Imagine your reaction to someone who yells at you at your station..."

"Listen!" he shouted,

"Would you please just let me finish!" I yelled back. "You are not God, are you? You can't anticipate the conclusion of my thoughts I've just started. Am not I entitled even to finish my thoughts? Although the police report has wrongly presented me as a scoundrel,

I've never stopped being a thinking being. So, let me conclude my statement, for Christ's sake!"

I realized that I had regained my speech power to the fullest.

The atmosphere was tensed. I noticed that Fay barely controlled herself and that she looked lovelier when she was mad. It seemed her beauty was made for all occasions and moods.

I also got the impression that policemen all over the world seem to create around them a confrontational atmosphere, worsened by an authoritarian tone of voice, the wearing of uniforms and the carrying of deadly weapons.

The unnamed officer said, "What's the matter with this guy anyway? Doesn't he know that he isn't in any position to bargain?"

"Who says so?" I shouted.

"I do," he replied provocatively.

"You've made a big mistake. Not only I can bargain, but also I can refuse to do so. Now, if I refuse to bargain (or whatever you call it) what are you going to do? Are you going to torture me? to break my legs and my arms? I am not a criminal. I am the victim of a crime, not the other way around. Don't forget it. Let's leave the equation the way it has been. If really you want to do your job and are interested in catching the ones who almost killed me, then look for them. Don't come and harass me. What harm can I do while I am incapacitated?"

Officer Warren stepped forward and asked, "Ok! I believe that we've started off on the wrong foot. But how can we find them if you don't help? Your silence indicates that you don't want to betray your dear friends and partners in crime."

"They are not my friends and partners in crime," I pointed out harshly. "Let me repeat it: I haven't committed any crime. How can you jump to such conclusion? What kinds of friends would they be, after stabbing me repeatedly? I don't see any rationale to what you've just said."

Human justice sometimes works in a strange way. I was the victim of crime and I was the one put under pressure! I bet Tony, Paul and their friends were still operating in that house, in Queens, and having the time of their lives. They were still wearing three-piece suits, driving fancy cars, going to expensive hotels and restaurants, living in mansions, dating beautiful young women. They didn't get scared, above all since they knew they had "executed" me, the "traitor". Usually, they didn't keep up with the course of events. All they were interested in was to spread death and despair all over, and to make big money so they would acquire all the good things in life. Therefore, they might not even realize that my *one-way ticket* to *any distant country* or *any place* throughout the planet or the galaxy had been cancelled.

In other words, the police stayed away from trouble and felt comfortable with me, the innocent victim.

"This is just weird," I said loud.

Officer Warren asked, "What's so weird?"

"Don't bother!" I replied. "You are not here to help me, but to harass me. That's all.

"The explanation is simple," the unnamed officer stated, who sounded as if he stumbled on the greatest discovery of the century. "You wanted to double-cross your friends and partners in crime; they were mad and tried to kill you."

"Didn't I tell you?" I said annoyingly. "You don't intend to help me. Why are you here? And, Sir, I don't have the faintest idea of what you are talking about. Apparently, we are not communicating with each other."

"Don't play games now!"

"Oh, boy!" I exclaimed. "Now you believe this is a game. What else can I tell you in order to make you believe me? The simple words become too meaningful to you. I've been repeating for the last hour or so that I am not a criminal, I am the victim of a crime. Is it possible that you can't believe in anyone? Are you the only righteous person in the world? It seems that you don't want to understand the meaning of such simple words. Then I think a new language must be created to accommodate and persuade you."

"Just a minute, punk!" he screamed, while he was coming up to me with threatening fists.

It was the first time I had the absolute confirmation that we belong to the animal kingdom. The aggressive policeman's appearance could be confused with any large beast, any prehistoric beast on a rampage.

His eyes were bulging out, his nostrils dilated; his teeth showed up and looked frightening.

"Go ahead! Hit me," I shouted. "You are no better than the ones who had tried to kill me. Go ahead! There are witnesses who will tell what happened: a police officer beating on a very sick patient. This time, your will use your abusive authority not against a drug dealer, a punk, a sexual deviant; it's just...Go ahead!"

Officer Warren grabbed his angry partner, held him tight and yelled out, "Bill, what do you think your doing? You have to control yourself. Mr. Young is right. He is a victim of a crime committed by thugs. So take it easy. You are a police officer. Remember."

Gradually, Officer Bill calmed down. Only then Officer Warren let go of him.

"Officer Warren," I advanced quickly to ease the situation, "you may have my entire cooperation under two conditions."

"Such as?" he replied angrily.

"First, you must apologize to the nurse. Second, I must speak in her presence."

There was a moment of dead silence. The atmosphere was turning pleasant again. Fay was smiling; Officer Warren and his hot-tempered partner, less tense.

"Ms., I don't know what's going on around here," Officer Warren finally stated, "but I think you have won all hearts in this neighborhood. Wherever I go, you are kept in high esteem.

"This is supposed to be a substitute for saying: I am sorry. Mr. Young is right. I didn't mean to yell at you. The situation just happens to be so confusing and discouraging. We are going nowhere with this investigation we've started for quite a while. We know that awful events have occurred, but we have no clue to what's going on. But I am sorry. I learn my lesson. It won't happen again. And Mr. Young is here to remind me if I forget."

After a short moment, he went on, "Mr. Peter Young, contrary to what you've said, I am here to help you. My partner Bill has no other alternative but to carry out his duties as police officer, a representative the law. It can't be otherwise.

"However, I am not still following the second request made by you: you want the nurse to be present during our questioning you. Why?"

Fay shrugged her shoulders.

"I want her to hear from me what happened," I explained. "She may have heard the *official version*. In fact, she must be familiar with the police report on the event, since she has been going through my chart. But I would like her to hear my own version. I want her to know that I am not a criminal, a bum, a homeless; that I have done my best to avoid trouble; that I have only been unlucky to find myself in this predicament. She didn't save the life of a useless fellowman. This is what I would like her to believe."

There was another dead silence. I scanned the room and caught my roommates and their visitors eavesdropping. But I didn't mind. I had nothing to hide. The more people who were going to hear *my version*, the better off it would be. For one thing, it would spread. But, above all Fay had to know it or I wouldn't *cooperate* at all.

Officer Bill asked, "Why?"

I looked at him; his animosity against me had mellowed. Apparently, he had read Officer Warren's remark about his duties as a warning.

"Because, besides Aunt Emma," I answered, "Fay is the only person I don't want to look down on me."

"You said Aunt Emma, didn't you?" Fay inquired, with a shade of anxiety mingled with hope.

"Yes, I did. Her name and image have appeared suddenly from my mind. She has been taking care of me since my parents died a few years ago."

Officer Warren cut in, "Ok! In that case, we don't have any choice. Let's go ahead with the investigation."

Someone shouted, "What's ok? What investigation?"

We all cast a glance at the door. Dr. Colborne came along. He looked furious. "Nurse," he thundered, "you have other patients who are waiting for your care! Your colleagues have been complaining about your unjustified disappearance. This man is not the only one who needs your care. Remember."

"I can't go now," she pointed out,

"What! You don't want me to report you to the Board of Directors, do you? Everybody said you've disappeared for more than one hour. You have to fulfill your obligation like anyone else. "

"I know my obligation, as a nurse, Dr. Colborne. I don't need you to remind me of it. However, everybody has to wait. I get stuck with Peter for a while."

The physician's eyes were bulging out of their sockets. He was breathing heavily and pursing his lips. I wouldn't be surprised at seeing another reminder of our bestial origin. Fortunately, the *angry doctor* was content with screaming, "This is just out of this world! I didn't expect this kind of behavior from you. What's happening to you? Are you going to mess up your career over a bum? That's beyond me."

Officer Warren intervened and asked him to step aside. Then he explained to him the reason for retaining Fay. "We need her as a witness to our meeting with the patient," he added, "so they wouldn't accuse us for overstepping our authority. She will resume her duty as soon as we will have finished with her. Our investigation has to go on. So, it isn't the nurse's fault. It's quite the contrary. Her presence will facilitate the on-going process."

The physician walked away. He was awesome-looking with his clenched hands.

Officer Warren came back to us. He looked a little concerned and whispered, "That investigation baffles me. I've never been exposed to so much human oddness. What could be responsible for Dr. Colborne's nervousness? Someone should tell me something."

Fay didn't say a word, being in complete darkness like anyone else. However, she was deeply disturbed: she was the first time she had been threatened by that chief of staff who had usually been playful with her.

She only shrugged her shoulders to Officer Warren's question.

The latter went on, "We can proceed now with the investigation."

I drew a long breath, looked back in my memory in order to become my *whole past* and asked, "Should I start from the beginning? I mean what caused my indirect involvement in criminal activities?"

"Yes, we have plenty of time," Officer Warren replied. "Don't forget that you have to convince us. Furthermore, I had the angry blessing of Dr. Colborne."

I then started my "story" at its very "beginning". I briefly related my misfortune at the City College, which had robbed me of my sense of dignity and effort. "I dropped out, contemplated suicide and, finally, went to live with Yolanda," I proceeded. "At that time, it seemed it was the only positive thing to do. Soon after, I suspected that she was involved (maybe unknowingly) in some kind of illicit enterprise. But I couldn't tell what it was. Anyway, my suspicion came too late: she was pregnant. I couldn't abandon her. I couldn't either betray her or inform the police on what I thought was going on in her apartment. I would feel bad for the remaining of my life. The best alternative I conceived of was that I had to free her from the deleterious environment she was exposed to. I sent an anonymous letter to her parents, asking them to come and take their daughter away. Of course, our son had to follow his mother: I wasn't in any condition to take care of a baby."

Suddenly, Officer Bill asked, "Where do Yolanda's parents live?"

I saw the implications his question might entail. Giving their address to the police would sound like a betrayal. I couldn't to that at all. Therefore, I answered quickly, "No, I don't."

"But, come on!" the police officer pointed out. "Is it what you call cooperation?"

"But, Officer Bill, how would I know?" I answered. "I've been confined in a hospital room for the last five months or so. I was unconscious. I imagine that a lot of changes in people's lives have occurred since. In fact, that's not the type of question I was expecting from you."

"What do you mean?"

"I was expecting you to ask me how I managed to send my anonymous letter to Yolanda's parents."

Officer Warren, who seemed a little annoyed about his partner's irascibility, urged, "You can go on, Peter. Tell us everything. We will draw the appropriate conclusions. Your cooperation seems to clarify a lot of loose ends."

I invented a story that Yolanda had told me that her parents were in town, looking for her. After having conducted my own inquiry, I knew which hotel they stayed at: it was *The Clinton Hotel*. How did I know the name of the hotel? That was my secret. In reality, it was mentioned by Mr. and Mrs. Clinton when they came to pick up their daughter and grandson.

In other words, a previous event *properly* postdated enabled me to add coherence to *my story* without compromising Yolanda and my son. I deliberately lied, to some extent, but for a worthwhile cause.

I went on, "The rest of the story is easy to understand. I met a *naughty little* boy in the neighborhood of the hotel and asked him to deliver the anonymous letter to Yolanda's parents. They went to their daughter's apartment, as soon as they had received that letter, and insisted that she should follow them. Since she was only seventeen, she had no other alternative but to comply. You should know that Mr. Clinton is a wealthy and powerful man."

Officer Bill was still being suspicious of my intentions and inquired, "How did you get caught in the middle of this illegal enterprise?"

From that point on, my story was the expression of the truth. "Simple," I replied. "The gang thought I knew more about their activities, and that I betrayed Yolanda so I could either take over her *storekeeper's position* or seize upon the 'loot'—as they called their stuff—and disappear. It's also possible that they believed I was a government agent planted in their organization to gather information. They jumped to the wrong conclusion; for, I had never posed a threat to their insane activities. I was more interested in seizing the first opportunity to move far away from them. That's all."

A relatively long moment of silence had elapsed. I wondered if the policemen had bought the *untruthful part* of *my version*. Nevertheless, I had to lie to save Yolanda and our child unnecessary trouble. I really did it not only because of our close relationships, but also because of my firm belief that both mother and baby weren't consciously responsible for harming others, and that she had never gone beyond the limits of her position as a *storekeeper*.

Suddenly, I realized that Officer Warren had to "approve of my invention" and shared my feeling about Yolanda's innocence, otherwise, he would have insisted upon my giving him more specific information on her. He was the officer who had called me "my son" when Yolanda's parents went to pick her up from her apartment and that Mr. Clinton assaulted me! Yes he was the same one! Oh, I was so much grateful to him for keeping his irascible partner in ignorance of all that.

He asked, "Peter, do you believe that those criminals are still operating over there, in Queens, at the given address?"

"Why shouldn't they?" I replied. "The way I see it, they believe I am dead. Although I managed to get out of that rat hole and fall unconscious on the pavement, they may think that nobody would link my alleged death to their activities."

"Are you willing, Peter, to go all the way to testify against them?"

"Yes, I am. Why not? They are criminals, and I am not."

"Well, you know sometimes things can go wrong, cases can be thrown out of courts for legal technicalities. A judge may influence the jury which may vote in favor of the criminals. Who knows? Therefore, criminals can go back home, free like birds, and they try to get rid of undesirable witnesses. It would be unfortunate to expose you again to great danger."

I thought for a while about the policeman's indirect warning. I wondered how worst could those criminals treat me if they hadn't done so.

Furthermore, what did I have to live for? Maybe for Aunt Emma's sake? Maybe for...? No, I didn't want to say it, because I didn't have any claim on Fay.

"Officer Warren, I am all yours," I declared. "I will make myself at the entire disposal of the Justice Department. If really you care about people, you will do your best to protect me from harm, at least until you can put those beasts behind bars for the remaining of their rotten lives. They will be having plenty of time to think about the sufferings they have been spreading around. I..."

I couldn't finish the sentence. I started to cry. I didn't think about myself; not at all. As I said before, I had been exposed to all kinds of values, transcendent values too long to become a prey to those hoodlums. I cried because the whole past had suddenly caught up with me and I remembered the nightmarish situation which was going on in that Queens Hell house.

Officer Warren put his hand on my shoulder and, with the same sweet tone of voice he had spoken to me the last time, at Yolanda's apartment, he declared, "My son, I fully understand your situation now. Everything will be fine. I will do whatever in my power to protect you. And my partner will help me. Nothing will happen to you, not now, not ever. You've suffered too much. I mean it. I am not a politician. I am not lying to you to get your vote. I do have now a complete picture of the case under scrutiny. I am very grateful to you for your assistance. I've never stopped believing in you. Remember?"

He looked me straight in the eyes to convey his *message* full of innuendo.

"I will come back to you—if need be," he went on. "Meanwhile, my partner, other guys from the Narcotic Division and I are going to zero in on that Hell house in Queens. I strongly hope your deduction is correct and that those criminals are still operating over there.

"I am also going to inquire about Dr. Miles hurtful idiosyncrasy. No one should be allowed in our pluralistic society to prevent others from improving their existence and broadening their intellectual horizons. What that man did to you is unacceptable. You may not be his first victim. I don't like any child to be subject to this kind of treatment. Furthermore, what kind of teacher is that man? A teacher is supposed to open up the mind of his students, to instill optimistic feelings into them, so they may become later on well-balanced and productive adults. Through teaching, society passes on a whole generation's experiences to another generation with the hope the new one may carry the torch of social continuity and dynamism. I will see what I can do, in that respect. I happen to know powerful people who think like me."

I was very impressed by Officer Warren. He had certainly missed his profession. He could have been an excellent leader to many.

Both policemen walked away directly afterward.

I looked at Fay. She smiled. I felt embarrassed. "I am sorry, but I shouldn't show my emotion in your presence" I whispered. "Now you may think I am too sensitive for a man. And I am also sorry for getting you into trouble with Dr. Colborne."

She cast a tender glance at me. It made me shudder. It was the concentration of all that a human being could express through the eyes in terms of compassion and love.

"Don't worry about Dr. Colborne's threat," she said softly. "I am at peace with myself. I happen to have a very demanding profession: I may be a good nurse in any health care institution. But nobody can force me to act against my conscience."

She paused for a short while and then went on, "Peter, you are so wonderful!"

"I am, am I not?" I replied

"I don't know how, but I suspected that you were," she insinuated. "Although you were unconscious, you were able to appear to me like a noble warrior. I am telling you how I felt about you, from day one. I had never confused you with the rotten image they had associated you with. But today, your own version of what happened nearly more than five months ago has come to confirm my intuition. I want, as a token of my consideration, to give you something."

She bent and kissed me on my cheek.

She caught me by surprise. I didn't know what to think. Did she kiss me on a spur of the moment, being actuated by a burst of enthusiasm, or did she mean something deeper?

"Peter, I know you are a little puzzled and even confused," she mentioned, in an attempt to clarify the situation. "But again before I found out what really happened to you, I had thought that it could be a little bold on my part to kiss you on the cheek (she giggled). That doesn't mean I didn't want to do so. But, now, I feel a relief since you are worthy of love and respect.

"What's the meaning of my kiss? I don't know and I don't care, except that I gave you one. We've been so close for month! So, Peter, you should be content with my kiss. It could be the first and the last one you'll ever receive from me. Nobody can foretell the future.

"By the way, I am going to see that wonderful Aunt Emma of yours. Apparently, she has made a good impression on you to have her name and her image appearing from your mind. I will tell her what happened to you. I must set her mind at ease. Give me her address if you still can remember it."

She wrote the address while I was saying it piecemeal. Then I kept silent. I didn't know what else to say and to do. I didn't know if I should shout for joy, like a madman, or if I should feel sorrow and regret, since the kiss I had just received from *my angel* could be the "first" and the "last" I could have? Should I proclaim victory on the vicissitudes of life which seemed to start showing a brighter perspective? But whatever the turn my intention could have been taken, it would have been too late, because Fay had walked away.

15

Our room was so divinely cheerful, bright and peaceful (at the same time). The sun, subdued by the curtains, changed the surroundings into a crystalline little universe, a place I would like to stay forever. My roommates and I were imbued with such enchanting atmosphere, so much so that we felt closer to each other; indeed, we struck up a genuine brotherhood for the occasion. We told each other our "little secrets", as well as our "plans" for the future. We all hoped that things would be looking better.

Michael put his arm around my neck and pointed out in a low pitch of voice, so no one else would overhear him, "You are a lucky bird. Happiness seems to follow you wherever you go."

I didn't have the faintest idea of what he was talking about. For one thing, I would hardly call a victim of deadly use of force causing him to spend months of hospitalization a manifestation of good luck. It could be that Michael's medication had made him a little confused or delirious. As a matter of fact, to prove me right, he mistook me for a *lucky bird*. For one thing, I had to be a clumsy one since I was unable to fly on my own. And I wondered if I could ever find my way around, in the unfolding of reality. I assumed then Michael's mental unbalance would be short-lived: the side effect of whatever they had given him would soon disappear.

"Why do you say that?" I asked him for conscience's sake. "You know what I've been through."

"First of all, you are smart and educated," he explained. "The way you express yourself indicates that you are a man of learning. This is more than someone can dream of."

"Well, Michael, that's a good point," I conceded, "however, without a piece of good luck, your point means nothing."

"I was about to mention your luck also," he said, while rumbling conspiratorially.

"Luck!" I exclaimed.

My reaction was logical, all things being equal. If someone was looking for a hapless fellow I was the one.

"Come on, my dear friend, don't play stupid!" he insisted. "You know I am right."

"Frankly, I don't know, Michael, what you are talking about."

"That..."

He stopped short: Fay came in. She was supposed to start working at nine o'clock, but, for some reason, she had come a little early. She certainly came in time for rescuing me from Michael's *overwhelming optimism.*

"Sorry, Michael," I said. "We will finish this conversation later on. You've aroused my curiosity. I may have a gold mine under my very nose and can't see it.

Then I put myself at Fay's entire disposal. "You are so early!" I observed. "You are the most dedicated nurse I have ever seen."

I paused for a short while before insinuating, "I understand your punctuality: after yesterday's incident, you want to put all the odds on your side.

"And I am glad that you are playing it safe; for, I don't know what would become of me in this hospital without your care. So, for my sake, do your best to be on your best behavior."

"No, your guess isn't quite accurate," she replied. "I am ready to defend my behavior everywhere. As I said yesterday, Dr. Colborne is free to denounce me to the Medical Board. I have a clear conscience. Having said that, I come early to see you."

"Oh!" I uttered.

She smiled while staring at me in a strange and disturbing manner.

Now I felt uneasy. I couldn't guess the reason behind that look. Unknowingly, I could be guilty of something. But, whatever it was, it signaled not too good news. Was sadness waiting for me around the corner?

"So all the reasons you've put forth are unnecessary," she maintained. "I've been a punctual employee since day one. I've also been playing safe here at this hospital and elsewhere. I've been doing my best to be a wise person, not to please Dr. Colborne and company, but to please my own inner self. And to accuse someone of wrongdoing one has to prove it. I am very curious to find out what Dr. Colborne and company get on me."

She paused for breath and then went on, "Again, I came early so I could discuss something with you."

"Fay, did I do something wrong?" I uttered.

And then I sighed with relief; since, according to her last statement, it was just something to discuss. She could be willing to just "chit-chat". There is nothing wrong with a good conversation.

"Am I in trouble?" I added.

"It depends," she replied.

"By the way, I saw Aunt Emma," she went on quickly, "she is a lovely lady. She will come to see you later on."

Then she kept silent, while she was still looking at me. I sensed a suggestion of challenge in her eyes. "Oh! What could be wrong?" I thought. I don't want to lose that woman's friendship."

I mentally retraced the nature of our relationship for the last two days or so and couldn't remember, not even once, having tried to hurt her deliberately.

"Peter, I appreciate your willingness to speak to the policemen in my presence," she said in one go. "And, as I told you, having learned from you what happened had eased my mind; the proof being that I gave you a kiss on the cheek, which you richly deserve (she giggled). All goes well, except that I was puzzled over something (and, to tell you the truth, I am still)."

I thought hard, trying to remember the different stages of my meeting with the policemen in her presence, but I was unable to put my finger on what could be bothering her.

"What is it?" I inquired. "If I hurt you unknowingly, I ask you to forgive me."

She drew a long breath. She was simply lovely! "I have decided to clear up any misunderstanding between us," she insinuated. "I notice that you had deliberately covered up for Yolanda."

"I had, hadn't I?" I answered.

"But you know you did. The policemen and I thought that you hadn't told the whole story about her. Did you love her so much? Maybe, you are still in love with her..."

I didn't say a word. I had no idea of the type of answer which could please her. I didn't intend to hurt her feeling and scare her away. I was hoping that she wouldn't insist on my answer. But she asked in a pressing manner, "Peter, did you hear me?"

I nodded.

"Peter, try to understand me. For the last five months or so, you were a black hole. Now I found out that you were living with a woman. I don't want to remain too close to you to avoid trouble and unnecessary confusion. Let suppose I kept being dedicated to you, being close to you, and that, one day, Yolanda shows up. What am I supposed to do? And she may be your legal wife. I have no business to be too close to a married man. I do have moral principals to go by. Do you understand me?"

We kept quiet. She looked at me inquisitively. Her bust rose up; her breath became shorter.

I had the intuition that she was about to raise a puzzling question. Truly enough she said, "I know, you don't want to talk about it. You did love her. She was your first love and maybe your wife. In fact, that's not my business."

I was in a state of panic. My silence seemed to be an implicit assent to what she had implied.

"Fay...," I finally said.

With a shade of anger in her voice, she asked, "What?"

"I want to make it your business."

"Why?"

"I want you to know all about me."

"Your behavior makes me believe differently from what you've just said. In fact, if you are still keeping her image in your heart there won't be any point to continue this conversation. You are quite right to keep your mouth closed. I have nothing to do with your love life and your marital status. Don't worry! I am not going to pass censure on you. Do as you please. In fact, let me go about my business. Sorry to give you cause for concern. As a nurse, I've gone too far. I am not supposed to put confusion into a patient's mind. There is nothing wrong with loving someone. Let me go. See you soon."

To suit the action to the word, she stood up and was getting ready to leave precipitately. I grasped hold of her hand and pulled her gently. "Please, Fay, listen to me," I said imploringly. "I do really want you to know everything about me. I mean it. I have so much respect for you. You are the embodiment of so many positive things I aim at. However, I am so afraid that you might not believe what I have to say, which would certainly hurt me a lot."

"Why do you think I won't believe you?"

"Well, you know, Fay, people have been lying in order to embellish their images and get people's high esteem."

She calmed down. "Try me," she recommended, "and let me be the judge of what you have to say."

I looked at the ceiling as if it could pull me from my dilemma. Suddenly, I felt up to telling her what was in my mind, no matter what. "Yolanda is a wonderful person and she means a lot to me," I confessed. "For one thing, I am very grateful to her. In my moment of distress she welcomed me to her home, she fell in love with me and she had done her utmost to keep me away from her illicit activity. In return, while we were together, I did whatever in my power to protect her. As a matter of fact, I did keep her away from harm.

"But we are not legally married. And you should also know that I couldn't love her because, between us, there was an incompatibility of ideals or plans for the future, or whatever that was. Love presupposes compromise and sacrifice. This is the commerce of what is dear and precious between two persons. This aspect of love, Yolanda refused adamantly to accept. So, we couldn't reach this kind of harmonization. Our respective ethical values happened to be irreconcilable, though we didn't have any big fight."

After a short moment of silence, I added, "I hope I make some sense."

Fay's face brightened up. "Yes, Peter, you do," she admitted, "you certainly do. And thank you for insisting on making me listen to you. I was too judgmental. I am so sorry. From now on, I promised to be wiser."

She sat down on the edge of my bed and invited me to do the same. She whispered, "By the way, is she beautiful?"

"Yes, she is," I answered hesitantly.

"Is she more beautiful than I?"

She giggled.

I thought that women can never stop completely behaving in a childlike manner. Their eternal youthfulness is what makes them so curious, *dangerously* curious (and beautiful too). "No Fay," I finally replied. "She is as beautiful as you. She reminds me of an indolent female cat with all the grace and caprice of the feline beast, while you remind me of an agile gazelle with a hind's eyes."

She kissed me on the forehead and walked away swiftly, as if she was being chased by someone. "I must sign in," she pointed out, while going sideways. "I'll come back during my lunch hour."

It was too much for me; I was exhausted and fell asleep.

Something heavy fell down on me. I woke up with a start and asked myself what it could be. Could it be the ceiling? And, before I could realize what was going on, I was squeezed, kissed, blindfolded by Aunt Emma.

"Peter, Peter, Peter, Peter, my son, my only son, my flesh and blood," she said, while sobbing. "What have they done to you? How could they hurt a sweet little boy like you? Oh! God! This world is falling apart! Oh, all this time, without my sweet Peter! No news, nothing. I thought I was finally alone in this world. God is so good! He won't let that happen!"

Then Aunt Emma stood up and stepped back to evaluate me from the distance. "Thanks God, You are in one piece," she went on. "You are going to be fine."

I was also carried away with delight. I opened my arms, she fell in them. "You know," I whispered, "when the bird thinks it can fend for itself and almost breaks its neck! This is what happens to me by leaving you.

"I am sorry to put you in so much anguish. You don't deserve to be treated so badly, the way I did. You have always done your best to make me feel happy. Sorry.

"But, Aunt Emma, you are the third person who has said that I would have a brighter future. I am beginning to believe you."

Indeed my profound pessimism started to fade away. The proof being that I saw Officer Warren's *grim account of justice* from a different perspective.

Although I would never back out of my promise to help the police and the whole society with getting rid of one of the criminal groups plaguing the country, I would also like to cling to life. I had just realized that I had two wonderful persons to live for: Aunt Emma and Fay.

Aunt Emma had said it herself: I was her only *flesh* and *blood*. I knew that she had some cousins who lived in Delaware and other relatives who had settled in New England. But, for some unknown reason, she had never taken an interest in them. She mentioned their names once every three years. I had never met them and I was unable to remember their names. I could go pass them in the street and I wouldn't recognize them. Aunt Emma's entire fondness was concentrating on me. To the best of my recollection, living in her house happened to be the securest and sweetest moments in my life. I was grateful to her. Thus, endangering my life couldn't be the proper way to thank her, to pay her back. I was hoping that Officer Warren was a man of his words and would protect me.

Now I had Fay. However, my feeling of "having" her was vague, kind of *illegitimate*. I still refused to believe that she would prefer me to Dr. Colborne. I had received a kiss from her. So what did that mean? For quite a few women, a kiss is an act of greeting, like handshaking for men. Was Fay's kissing me a substitute for handshaking? or could I claim victory? But what kind of victory could it be? I wasn't in any competition with anyone, certainly not with Dr. Colborne, a chief of staff, a professional, a well-paid physician, known to the scientific community, a distinguished member of professional associations. All those questions were gamboling in my mind. Whatever I did to get rid of them had failed. They were there, harassing, nagging, repelling and attracting each other. I was entirely possessed by Fay or by thoughts about her. Better still, for some reason, I believed all this was just enough to live for, as people live and die for ideals, for founded or unfounded doctrines.

In any case, something exciting occurred to me ever since I had been kissed by Fay: I was regaining a great deal of my self-confidence. Once in a while, I whispered, "You never can tell."

Of course, I was still aware of my tremendous limitations and the aimlessness of my life. I knew I had, so far, nothing to offer in terms of material security. I only possessed my body and my dreams (and maybe the potentialities lying behind these, which had no guarantee to be actualized). But I also firmly believed that there were values other than those of money and power, and people who could appreciate them. I mean integrity, self-respect, compassion, craving for tran-scendence, loyalty—to name a few.

While I was recovering slowly but steadily, I kept thinking about such values and I was almost certain that I might possess them (or I would over time), since I had been craving for them for years. Thus, if I possessed them, they would be the only assets I had to offer. Would they be sufficient?

I also had the feeling that Fay belonged to the category of people who craved for these values, which I suspected that I might have. The funny thing was that I couldn't define them clearly, grasp their full meaning, submit them to reference for comparison. Anyway, Fay had to be able to appreciate them. I couldn't explain otherwise her reason for doing nothing to dissipate my "illusion" about her, to forbid me to entertain the hope of loving her, to remind me that I belonged to a class of citizens who were not independent (materially speaking), who couldn't function.

I reached the conclusion that she was not a snobbish person; she wasn't a slave of opinions and traditions. She could reach a high degree of objectivity and go beyond the appearance of reality. She seemed to be able to unearth latent inner strengths in people, as well as their potential drawbacks. She had a gift for understanding the inexpressible, and it was a special stamp of her intelligence. Since I couldn't express my feelings through verbal means, while I was unconscious, I imagined that, with the help of her acumen and her gift, she managed to grasp and appreciate my strengths (and also my weaknesses) which were oozing out of me—so to speak—; even though she and I couldn't be fully conscious of them.

Well, the key question remains to be answered: how could she have gained access to those *values of mine,* while I was unconscious?

The answer to this question may never be found, apart from her presumed *special stamp of intelligence* and her acumen. Would that be sufficient? Quite a few of us have these qualities to some extent (although they might be more intensified in her). Yet how many of us are capable of guessing right when it comes to read others' character, inner strengths, and drawbacks I had evoked earlier? Let me only suggest a few unconvincing guesses. A French old saying goes: «Le visage est le reflet de l'âme. [One's face is the reflection of one's soul]". It might have been possible for a person like Fay, imbued with love, understanding, compassion and acumen, to experience the *Bergsonian intuition*, to enter my very nature through such means, to communicate with me and discover the *inexpressible* in me.

As I told you, my explanation wouldn't be convincing, but it holds water. I was referring to the kind of knowledge with no identifiable methodology. Indeed Fay believed that she was holding some kind of truth, an intuitive truth about me, to such a par that she had been consistent in caring about me in a special and personal manner, from the onset of my tragedy, from the first minute she saw me, when I was a picture of hell.

Once, I tried to challenge my "illusion", arguing that she was naturally kind to everybody.

It's true that she was assigned to the male ward and that she was treating each patient as if he was a *king*. I was fully aware of her kindness, her willingness to make an extra effort to please the most crabbed personality. As a matter of fact, once in a while, some patients behaved so badly that I got the impression they were sent by a *whimsical being* to test that nurse's patience. But she never lost her cool and humaneness. So, I didn't think she had just made up her mind to learn kindness overnight, after she had met me under special circumstances. It had to be in her blood; it had to come natural to her, in order to focus it on a particular person with a remarkable ease. Still, as far as I could remember, I had never seen her kissing a male patient on the cheek, crying over one, looking at one with so much sweetness, so much tenderness, the way she was doing to me.

It could certainly be the work of my vivid imagination I had mentioned earlier, an imagination working like a magnifier, giving a disproportionate, unreal meaning to whatever it touched on.

Then Aunt Emma came, whose presence had upset all my equation and brought more confusion in my mind.

I rediscovered my deep love for her. I wondered how I would reconcile my distinct, indeed different, but equally important fondness for her and Fay. I couldn't give myself up to the latter without lessening my love for the former. That eventuality could be a very trying position. I would be miserable all my life. I could mystify myself about a lot of things if I so desired, except about my love for Aunt Emma. If I abandoned her, I would never be at peace with myself. I would have to live permanently in bad faith, trying to repress a feeling of guilt.

But could I love them both with the same intensity? What should I do?

I didn't have to answer my own question: Fay and Aunt Emma were coming hand in hand, like two longtime friends. After all, their spontaneous and mutual understanding shouldn't surprise me: they were good-natured people who didn't need too much to start getting along with each other.

"Peter, I am leaving for the day," Fay said. "I am so glad that Aunt Emma can keep you company. I will see you tomorrow."

She was so ravishing. She was wearing a purple blouse with white ruffles to the sleeves. A black silk skirt fitted her from the waist downward, setting off her lovely legs.

"You know, when my Peter is back on his feet," Aunt Emma stated after kissing me on the forehead, "you will make a fine couple."

"Aunt Emma!" I exclaimed unconvincingly.

There was a moment of silence around my bed. Fortunately, my roommates and their visitors were busy talking and didn't notice anything happening *on our side*.

Fay put her arm around Aunt Emma's neck and kissed her on the cheek. "Aunt Emma," she said in a sweet tone, "no one knows what the future keeps in its safe for us. But I would like to be very close to you, like your daughter. In fact, I would like to live with you. You are so cheerful, so sweet!"

Aunt Emma, truly elated, replied "Oh, it's so thoughtful of you to treat me so warmly! It's the kind of tenderness I haven't—if ever—experienced for years. I love you, my child, I love you very much."

"Thank you, Aunt Emma."

Fay took her leave from us hurriedly afterward. I had the impression she was afraid to have said more than she should.

"This is a fine young woman," Aunt Emma mentioned, who kept waiving at her until she disappeared behind the wall, in the lobby.

Then, all smiles, she showed me a rectangular box. "Guess what I've brought you," she insinuated mischievously.

"Aunt Emma, don't tell me!" I answered.

I mentioned all kinds of objects I could think of: shirts, pants, books. However, all my guesses proved unavailing.

"I give up," I conceded.

"I made this bread pudding just for you," she triumphantly revealed.

"Of course, a portion is missing on the way," she whispered shortly after. "You know these puddings sometime get a mind of their own."

"Aunt Emma, this time you've gone too far," I stated, feigning anger. "I don't know any pudding imbued with a mind. You've helped that pudding in its decision.

"Now, what did really happen to that missing portion?"

"I gave it to someone."

"I knew it! Who is it?"

"Fay."

"You are an angel, Aunt Emma."

I kissed her on the forehead.

For the first time, I realized that she was romantic (in her own discreet fashion). I wondered why she had never got married or had children. Those would have enjoyed one of the best mothers in the world. But it was her secret, not to get involved in any love affair, which secret I may never know (and I wouldn't dare attempt to decipher).

Now that Fay and Aunt Emma were fond of each other on first acquaintance, I breathed freely. It was so silly of me to worry about the way to reconcile my love for both of them.

"Aunt Emma, women have ways with lots of things," I remarked abruptly.

"Indeed, Peter, indeed," she only uttered.

She was a woman of few words, but behind them one felt the vibration of powerful unexpressed ideas which kept reverberating long after in one's consciousness.

Soon after, she stood up, kissed me goodbye. "The streets are not safe at night," she asserted, "I have to reach home before dark. I won't be able to defend myself against the new breed of criminals. I am too old."

"Yes, Aunt Emma, you should go," I acquiesced. "I need you alive."

I couldn't complain, since she left me with something I love so much, and which was made by her: my big portion of bread pudding shared by Fay. "Nothing else I could ask for," I whispered.

Without any ceremony, I started to cut up my portion of pudding. I was on the point of having a mouthful of it when Michael and Thomas cleared their throat in unison in order to remind me of their *presence*.

I gave each of them a *modest piece*. "That's all you are going to get," I said.

"How could you be so stingy?" Michael jokingly mentioned.

"I am indeed when it comes to Aunt Emma's bread pudding, the most delicious in the world."

We stopped short: Officer Warren, his partner and other policemen arrived behind Tony, Paul, the messenger, the *giant*, a young woman and a bunch of other criminals. Their presence took me back to the nightmarish atmosphere I had found myself few months earlier. But what was strange, I didn't hate them. I felt sorry for them instead. I wondered how they could choose a way of life in total contradiction with the laws of the land, the normal sets of values and the kind of existence bringing serenity, absence of constant fear and the feeling to be part of a viable community.

"Peter, don't worry," advised Officer Warren. "We've used the service elevator to avoid troubling the staff. We want a positive identification from you," Officer Warren said. "Are they the ones who attacked you?"

"Yes," I answered without any hesitation.

"Good," the officer went on. "That house was taken by surprise by the police. A number of teenagers have been left in their parents' care or entrusted to the city reformatory schools. They will also attend detoxification therapy.

"Now, are you willing to affirm these people are the same ones who were storing drugs in Yolanda's apartment?"

"Yes, they are the same ones," I replied.

"Could you also tell us more about their places of delivery?"

I told him about the different locations I used to go to receive the "parcels". I also informed him that the "goods" came from all over the world.

"That's all Peter," the officer said. "If we need further information, we will contact you. But, thanks!"

Tony struggled with a police officer who had gripped him by his belt, from behind. He tried to break loose so he could jump up and hit me.

He was slapped on the face repeatedly and pulled away.

"Peter! You are a dead man!" he shouted "I'll come back for you. That's a promise. What do you think you've done? Absolutely nothing, man, nothing. We have connection in high places and good lawyers. So, when we are out, we'll come back to get you! When we finish with you, you won't be good enough to be fed to our dogs! We'll reduce you to dust!"

A cruel grin twisted his mouth.

I wasn't scared; not at all, except that I thought that he finally lost his mind.

The other criminals were quieter, except after each of Tony's invectives, they kept repeating like a chorus, "That's right, man! That's right, man! That's right, man..."

Gradually, the hospital returned to its peaceful atmosphere.

16

The intuition of the *smiling face* about my coming happy days and Aunt Emma's exhortation materialized, and more so than I could have imagined. From a *villain's status*, I passed to a *conquering hero's*; at least, according to a reporter's announcement on an independent television station:

A major criminal group, having international connections, was neutralized by the police. Not only the most influential members of that gang were arrested and might face fifty years to life, if convicted, but also their centers of operation and delivery were discovered and closed down. Several million dollars, sophisticated weapons and ammunition, as well as several bags of pure cocaine were found on the premises and confiscated. More people were also indicted, some of them happen to be high-paid employees in the administration. All that was made possible thanks to the moral strength and the integrity of a teenager called Peter Young.

However, he didn't have any recognition until now. He was an A student at one of our colleges. The prejudicial action of one of his professors against him made him drop out. Looking for a job, he found himself in a situation in which he had either to go along with the criminal group they have just neutralized or to oppose it and take a chance of being harmed or killed in the process. He then opted for the second choice and was at loggerheads with the gangsters. As a result, he was stabbed repeatedly and was taken to the City trauma center. His life hung in the balance for several months.

You must realize how many youngsters' lives that man has saved by his heroic action. He deserves all our love and respect. He reminds us that it's never too early to act wisely, purposefully, meaningfully.

I was flabbergasted by the televised remarks about me. It was exciting and scary at the same time to hear someone speaking in high terms of you (in public). I couldn't believe it. I was certainly dreaming. I had so often been loathed by people that I had lost hope of being somebody one of these days.

One hour after, I perceived an approaching clamor and I wondered what could be going on. All of a sudden, our room was filled with people: members of the administration, employees belonging to different services and coming from different floors of the medical center, community leaders, patients, their relatives and their children. They didn't know they had "such a remarkable guest as a patient for so long." I received hugs, kisses, flowers.

The reporter, who had commented on my "heroic action", came along. He asked me if I didn't want to "say anything at all".

"I can try," I responded, "but I am going to be so gauche. I have never had the opportunity to make a public speech."

"Listen, Peter," he cut in, "you are doing just fine. You are already on the air."

I was shocked and relieved at the same time. I could have made a fool of myself, and yet it was simple to be on television. I declared:

Well, it's better to be alive to experience my being treated like a hero (laughter). *I owe the gift of life to those fine policemen and the emergency people who took me right away to the trauma center; to the medical staff who did wonders in reviving me. I also thank the police officer called Warren for being a man of his word and a dedicated civil servant. Of course, I give my thanks to the most wonderful nurse I have ever met. I am talking about Ms. Fay. Even though I was brought here unconscious, dirty, bloody—the very picture of a street punk—, she treated me like somebody, like a human being. Now, being conscious of the transcendence of her action, this has given me heart to live. Again I thank her from the bottom of my heart.*

To conclude, I would like to say that prejudice and greed are among the worst human ills. They are enough to reduce the world to shambles. I pray that mankind may keep them under control all the time...Thanks!

There was a moment of silence. Then the hospital was returning slowly to its calm.

My roommates approached me and shook hands with me.

"Man, what you did was great," Michael said. "You have a strong personality."

As far as Thomas was concerned, he kept slightly pondering me on the chest with his fist. "I knew, the minute I saw you that you were special," he finally acknowledged. "I sensed it."

"Thank you, my friends," I only uttered,

Ms. Joseph came along. She was about forty years of age. She was the *Head Nurse* at the Medical Center and ran it with love, under-standing and discipline. Though she was heavy, she rather looked lusty and charming. A man in her life would have changed her to a ravishing, robust and sensuous woman. Likewise, her large smiling face made her more prepossessing than feared. As the time went by, we became very fond of each other. Accordingly, she showered on me kindness and often brought me an *extra cup of ice cream.*

However, not having seen her coming that day with a *little treat* in her hand, I said to myself that something of the highest moment was going on. I wondered if our *honeymoon* was over—although I didn't remember having done anything to displease her.

She pulled a chair by my bed, sat down and looked at me in the eyes. Her face was not smiling nor gloomy, but concerned. Then she came right to the point, "Peter, I have never been married. Twenty years ago, I had a fiancé, but I had to drop him like a bag of potatoes. He was a jerk who could have driven me to madness. Later on, other men tried to get fresh with me, but I didn't trust them because once bitten twice shy.

"It's difficult for a serious-minded woman to find the man of her dream. Believe me, I know what I am talking about. So I stay away from unnecessary aggravations and I've been living happily ever after."

She paused for a moment.

As for me, I was at a loss for words, since I couldn't understand the reason why she was confiding in me. She was a nice person, showing respect and affection for me. However, I didn't think that we had reached such a degree of intimacy making me deserve her trust. Could it be possible that her usual cheerfulness was a façade, hiding a deep sadness? "Oh, human nature," I thought, "it can never be entirely inventoried and grasped. It is always a challenge to meet."

"My only child is Fay," She went on. "I met her at the City Nursing School where I've been teaching for a long time. She has been one of my brightest and most lovable students. I have ever since considered her as my only daughter and friend. If I die, all my possessions should go to her."

Oh, my Lord! What was she driving at? Was she going to reveal to me some unpleasant aspects of Fay's character? Wouldn't *my idol* be exactly the way she appeared to me, my sweet Fay, the smiling face, the self-possessed woman, the apparently virtuous lady? "No, destiny," I said imploringly to myself, "don't do that to me! Please. Make Fay exactly the way she appears to me. Please."

"I want her to be happy," Ms. Joseph resumed. "Therefore, I wouldn't like anyone to hurt her."

"Oh, God!" I thought. "Who is going to hurt my lovely Fay? I want to know, so I'll do all in my power to prevent harm to come to my beautiful nurse."

Maude took another pause and looked at me intensely as if she wanted me to grasp the full meaning of what she had just alluded to and what would follow.

"No one has told me anything," she continued accusingly. "For the first time, Fay has been hiding behind a disturbing silence. Now you must understand my concern. Usually, we talk about everything. Once a month, she spends a night with me, just to confine in me and vice versa. Believe me, it's one the best therapies to have a trustworthy friend to talk things over with.

"Yes, no one has said anything to me. But I am not blind, you know! Fay falls in love with you. You know, this is the first time I've seen that happening.

"She has been living a simple life, far away from the excitement of social life, to such a par that I was afraid she could emulate me and shy away from romance. Once in a while, I've blamed myself for offering her such unexciting example.

"My concern is the way you may feel about her. If you don't care enough for her, I will beg you, after you are released from here, to go away and try to never see her again. Because, if you hurt her, you will destroy her happiness and optimism in life for good, and you will also deal me a heavy blow. Of course, I know you are not the kind of person who would like that to happen to anyone. Please, don't hurt her, she is my only child."

Forgetting all decorum, I grabbed Ms .Joseph's hands and squeezed them with excitement. "Maude," I said, "this is the sweetest thing I have ever heard, that Fay may fall in love with me! If that happened to be the case, I would be the happiest man in the world. But, I don't know and don't want to keep my hope too high. Maude, I do love her."

Then, releasing Ms. Joseph's hands, I went on, "I must tell you that I won't do Fay any harm. I've never and will never hurt a woman deliberately. All the sweetness of life I've known comes from women. My mother loved me so much! Even when I was eleven years of age she used to make me sit by her while she was sewing, just to look and smile at me. Once in a while, she stopped everything to rub my hair and ask me whether I was feeling comfortable. Then tragedy came: she was killed along with my father by a drunk driver. I thought that my moments of happiness were over, at the tender age of eleven. But Aunt Emma came along to the rescue. The only difference between her and my deceased mother is that the latter gave birth to me. However, in terms of love, tenderness and concern, the difference hasn't been noticeable."

I stopped in order to catch my breath and proceeded, "Finally, in my moment of despair, I found another woman who devoted to me spontaneously. I meant Fay.

"So, as you can see, whatever the course of action, I can't hurt her or any other women. As a matter of fact, if I hurt Fay I would hurt myself in the process. I would self-contradict myself, showing no respect for generosity, compassion, love; these are all values I revere and yearn for. Do you want to know something? Here is my belief: a genuine woman is the greatest gift a man can ever receive from Nature or God (depending on the perspective one looks from). By genuine women I mean the ones who are not competing with men and emulating their usual selfishness, greed and love of power. Fay is one of them."

Ms. Joseph stood up and kissed me on the cheek.

"Hum, hum!" someone uttered.

We looked round. It was Fay.

"Well, I arrive in time to break an affair," she observed jokingly. "Maude, you are a sneaky creature. You want to steal Peter away from me."

Ms. Joseph gave her a gentle shove and stated, "I was just leaving to avoid a crime of passion."

"Don't move so fast, Maude! For a corpulent lady, you are too light-footed."

"What is it now?"

"You know that I am off..."

"So!"

"Can I stay for a while with Peter? I have nothing special to do at home. And..."

Ms. Joseph gagged her with her large palm. "Say no more, Little Angel," she assured. "You can stay as long as you want to. As I told you before, what you do with your free time is nobody else's concern."

At these words, she walked away, while she was waiving and smiling at us. She appeared much lighter and younger to me. And Fay was right: she was light-footed.

Fay was sitting on a chair; I was lying in bed. We looked at each other, finding nothing positive to talk about, although our closeness seemed to keep us aware of each other's presence. We were nervous. It was the first time our being together had absolutely nothing to do with *business*. Therefore, we knew that we were not going to spend all that time elaborating on my wounds and my recovery progress, my past, my present and my future, my philosophy of life, my idea of women.

She inquired, "How do you feel now?"

I thought that she just tried to break the ice; but we both were fully conscious of the fact that I was getting better and that I would be soon released from the hospital.

Then we started talking about cats and dogs. The world was full with exciting events, some rotten to the point of disgust, some pregnant with a sense of hope. But speaking about them in a relaxing manner was refreshing, and we felt that our mutual harmony was growing firmer.

"I wish I could unravel what's going on in your big brain," she insinuated.

I smiled, but I didn't make any comment. All I wished to do was to kiss her. However, I wasn't bold enough to do so. I was settling instead for a simple eulogistic observation, "Fay, you are so pretty."

She looked intensely at me. She was perspiring just where the hair began; her nostrils and her eyes dilated. She asked in a childlike manner, "Do you think so?"

"Yes, I do. And you are so lucky!"

"Why do you say that?"

"It seems that you are perfect."

"I am perfect! That's heavy. I am conscious of the fact that I may have some qualities; but I've never dreamed of being perfect."

"But yes, you are in the context of humanity."

"Why do you believe that I am perfect in the context of humanity? I am perfect, well, I must do my best to keep up with the depth of your thoughts."

"You are pretty, kind and intelligent."

"Well, if you think this is what they should call being lucky, then I believe you."

"Yes, Fay, you are lucky. You are the embodiment of the viable aspects of the cosmos."

"Really! Go on. I welcome this kind of compliment. It makes me a replica of the universe in miniature. This is the first time I've been told to be such a meaningful symbol."

"You happen to be the focus of the driving forces on which rests the world. Your prettiness corresponds to symmetry and order in the cosmos. Your kindness partakes of free creativity which is responsible for the multiplicity of beings pervading the world. Your intelligence springs from a purpose in the world. Whenever those three forces are absent from someone or a community, we experience corruption, inhumanity, disorder, chaos."

She laughed. It was the most crystalline laugh she had ever had since I had been conscious of her *buoyant* existence. "Listen, Peter," she said, "I didn't know I was the sanctuary of so many good things. You wouldn't fool me, would you?"

"No, Fay, I wouldn't," I replied. "In fact, I have the feeling I have only touched on the tip of the ice, as far as you are concerned. Your potential in terms of goodness, purpose and creativity may be boundless. You are a spring of wealth and hope."

"Peter, you are too much."

And, after a short pause, she added, "But I enjoy being with you. You keep my mind in a state of youthfulness and optimism—not to mention alertness. You don't let any room for mundane, idle talks, or negative gossips. I like your company very much. And yet, I don't feel I am being exposed to any danger or something I could regret later on. Well, in that sense, you too are a living source of wealth."

"Fay, I mean every word I've said."

"I know you do. I don't even have a shadow of suspicion about your sincerity; none whatsoever."

"Your presence brings me wonderful thoughts and a renewed will to keep on living. You are not an angel, are you? I could be dead and be in paradise. You are the angel assigned to my new life setting. You may not be visible to others' eyes but mine."

"No, Peter, you are not dead. Soon you will have to face the reality out there. And I am not an angel. I am made of flesh and blood, like anyone else."

"As far as I am concerned, you are the embodiment of a celestial entity."

She nodded to me, and the dead silence returned. I felt that it was, nonetheless, the presage of more important topics we were about to discuss. As a matter of fact, I inquired in spite of myself, "Do you have a boyfriend?"

She shrugged her shoulders before asking, "Why do you ask?"

"Oh, I may have been a little too abrupt. Don't answer my question. It's uncalled-for."

"Don't tell me that, Peter. You have to get a good reason for asking this question. Remember, one of the qualities you've just given me is intelligence."

My approach was clearly too abrupt and clumsy. In fact, I had always been clumsy when I had to let a woman know my feeling about her. But, as far as Fay was concerned, I didn't want her to be offended, in case her kindness to me shouldn't aim at anything I had in mind. Not that I had been actuated by bad intentions about her; not at all. I would rather have her as my wife, my right hand, my angel. These wishes rather expressed a craving for mutual completeness.

In reality, apart from my clumsiness (my diffidence included), I thought there was a legitimate reason which inhibited me from opening my heart to her. Not that I feared she would be angry at me over my *eventual boldness* or she would express her pleasure of my being in love with her. I was quite certain, if she wasn't interested in me and didn't want to encourage me, she would find some of her sweet words such as, "Angel," "Handsome", "Honey," "I don't intend to go that far in our friendship." And those words would be enough to cool me off and put me in my place. The reason for my backwardness was nothing but fear of failure. It was something I had learned the hard way, when it was unpredictable, unnecessary, unprovoked. I had learned it from college, a center of learning, which presupposed to develop self-confidence in me, to open up my mind and make me understand better the intricacies of reality, to optimize my power of communication. It had done the contrary of all these. From that point on, I was fighting shy of any undertaking, dreading the idea of meeting with a failure when I least expected it.

Being fully conscious of my dilemma, I had one alternative: I could succumb under its weight and become a victim of my own self-pity; or I could use it as a stepping stone to recreate a new self-image and act accordingly.

I had just expressed my own perspective, standing beside myself to analyze my position. Now, putting myself in Fay's shoes, the prospect wasn't any brighter. My rejection by her was almost ineluctable for reasons I had stated many times. I knew we were on friendly terms, and, at times, our hearts seemed to work in unison. That was sufficient to make me act accordingly, boldly. Still I kept thinking of her as being so far-reaching, so accomplished, that, in my mind's eye, she stood like the Mount Everest I couldn't climb up and conquer without incurring the risk of breaking my neck.

I got up and then sat down on the edge of the bed. We looked at each other like two fighters on the point of entering the ring for a decisive battle.

"What I mean, Fay," I tried to explained, "I wish you couldn't be engaged or something like that."

She kept pressing the issue, "Why, Peter? You are not going to tell me that I shouldn't. I am going to be twenty years of age very soon."

"I know, Fay. I am just expressing a wish."

"Again, can you tell me why?"

I thought that she was acting like a mischievous little girl. Couldn't she notice that I was on tenterhooks?

"Well, Fay, I want you to have the best things in life," I stammered. "You deserve to be happy. Your kindness needs to be rewarded. I wish you would make the right choice when you decide to be engaged."

She looked at me and smiled with a suggestion of perplexity. "This is an ambiguous kind of talk, Peter," She pointed out.

"Yes, Fay, it is," I conceded. "I have so much to say that my mind gets confused."

"I am sure of that, Peter. But I have no complaint. I enjoy your company, which is understandable. As you know, everybody looks for pleasure and tries to avoid pain. With you, I experience great feelings, feelings of joy and serenity, at the same time."

At these words, she stood up. "Let's go to the open window to contemplate the sunset," she suggested. "Can you stand up? Try. You need to move around and have some exercise."

I stood up. She put her arm under mine. We went and leaned on the window frame. We looked outside and witnessed a profusion of colors and motions. The sky was pink with green and blue large stripes. A big reddish sun, like a curious eye, was sliding into the river undulating over yonder. Down in the street moved on a multitude of vehicles and pedestrians. It was the proper atmosphere for me to give a specific meaning to what I had started to tell her.

Unfortunately, I could only say, "What I meant, Fay..."

I was unable to finish my thought: an animated debate over God and the universe broke out, so to speak, among my roommates and their visitors.

Fay and I couldn't prevent ourselves from listening to arguments for and against the world as a *divine purpose.*

My mind sprang across the swarm of galaxies: those I was acquainted with through my readings and those which were too far to be properly described. I asked myself if we knew really the past, the present and the future. "We don't even know what is happening exhaustively," I whispered. "There are so many elements of the present we are ignorant of! We use a euphemism to name them: margins of error. Couldn't they be the most important ingredients of reality, the sands on which rest truth, knowledge and foresight? Could it be possible that our ignorance of them prevents us from acting wisely, from discovering the panacea for life all-pervading unhappiness, from stopping to be a fright to others and ourselves? We, human beings, are walking in a daze, blindly, in the context of history, which is nothing but the registry of our own limited endeavors.

"Even history has to be accepted with a grain of salt. What portion of it describes the truth? If we difficultly know what's happening now, how about what we know through documents, written and oral statements made by witnesses who have been long gone? Among us, for prestige, prejudice, personal gains and power, falsifiers are rampant. How could we be sure of the number of falsifiers in the past? Some of them could have been taking for great figures. Their layers of untruths have been piling up one on the top of the other and become part of the cognitive landscape. Then, how much do we really know about reality of the past, the mass of events which could be diversely interpreted, the true feeling driving history makers to action, the anachronism of social atmosphere?

"Then, beyond history, we must only be content with our likely and 'coherent' stories, which will take all kinds of complexions, depending on the power of our imagination.

"What will happen? Again we don't know. We act and hope that something meaningful to us will occur, instead of the grim picture of people dying from starvation and violence.

"So the arguers in our hospital room and their likes, the ones before them and the ones coming after, have been and will be talking about things they don't and won't have the faintest idea of, just for fun, for love, for hatred...Mankind is too young to know in depth."

I felt so insignificant, so lonely, in this incommensurable and incomprehensible cosmos I was a drop of, that, in spite of myself, I put my arm around Fay's waist.

Perhaps she looked at me and saw that I was lost in space, but I couldn't tell.

We were staying there, at the open window, like two statues, my hand round her waist, until I came back to my senses.

I moved aside quickly. "Oh, I am sorry!" I said. "You see what these debaters made me do? I was miles away in the cosmos, holding on to you for support and companionship."

Fay squeezed my arm repeatedly. "Don't worry about that," she whispered. "No harm done. I am still in one piece, am I not? Furthermore, I was also miles away and glad to have a fellow traveler."

The room returned to its quietness. The debate had ended, and my roommates' visitors had left a while earlier. Fay turned to look at me. I shivered. "The answer to your question is no, I am not engaged," she murmured. "I am waiting for a man I really love, who deserves my love and who will make me proud of being loved by him. Thus, as soon as I find him, I will give myself up to his mercy. These are my only conditions I have set out to impose on reality. I will not deviate from them."

I was troubled and speechless.

While giggling, she asked, "Any more questions, Peter?"

"I don't think so," I answered pitifully. "And I would be afraid of having more, because they may get me into deeper trouble."

She inquired worriedly, "What's the matter? I get the feeling you are no longer happy. Are you afraid of not being able to live up to the image of the man I am looking for?"

"Fay, please..."

She put her arm under mine and breathed deeply. "Let's go back to your bed," she advised. "You shouldn't be on your feet that long. It's my fault."

"By the way, I would like to tell you that I took the liberty to make a decision concerning you."

She breathed deeply and then heavily exhaled. Next she went on, as we were heading for my hospital bed, "I said to myself that you would kill me. But it was a chance I had to take."

She appeared more and more complex to me. Her smiling face and her natural kindness shouldn't be taken for granted. She was a rare combination of heart and brain. I thought, "But what was she up to? Whatever it is, it will express her good nature and generosity. So, Peter, there is no cause for worry. You are going to be happily surprised."

"Peter, lie down and listen to me," she went on. "No interruption until I finish telling you something."

I obeyed as if she were my mother.

"I know that you are a proud man. How do I know that? Well, if you weren't, you would prefer making big money to being injured, wouldn't you? It's a great feeling to be able to acquire expensive cars, to get the most beautiful women in the world (not a simple beauty like me), to wear fancy clothes, to eat at the best restaurant, to be able to travel wherever, whenever. Of course, it's a great feeling, but it isn't a lasting one. You have shied away from it because of your high standard values. God knows that I would be happy to give you a helping hand. Likewise, you have never asked me for anything at all. However, what I am going to say doesn't express my intention to humble you. Oh, no! There's many a slip' twixt the cup and the lip! (She giggled.). I finally said it right! Helping another human being should fill anyone with joy, because it appears to be a natural thing to do. We belong to the same species, we live in the same world, and we may communicate as one person to another person (if this is what we desire). This being said, you are not losing your self-esteem by accepting help from someone who is willing to do so. In fact, as I said, I feel happy to help you."

"But Fay, you've already done so much for me," I argued unconvincingly; "I don't want to impose on you any more. You've done your best to put me back on the road, it's up to me to capitalize on this impetus and become fully functional."

"Of course, Peter, you will become fully functional with or without me. You are too smart to wallow in nonsense. Yet, what I've done for you, I've been doing it for anyone who happens to be a patient here. Of course (she giggled), a little more 'spice' is added to the care I've provided you with, but it has been professional care, what I get paid for. I am a conscientious employee. I want to be proud to deserve my paychecks. The other kind of care I am talking about is something like an imperative imposed on me by the deepest part of myself. If you allow me to do it, I will have a feeling of inner completion and of reaching the acme of perfection (in the context of humanity), as you've put it so lovely; you will make me the happiest woman in the world. Don't you want me to be the happiest woman in the world?"

"Yes, I do," I promptly acquiesced. "I will do anything in my power to make you happy. Tell me what you've done for me without my knowledge, and I will agree with you. I strongly believe that you can't conceive of anything harmful to me."

"I want you to go back to school," she declared bluntly.

I stiffened and frowned.

"You look so innocent when you frown," she remarked.

As she didn't have any answer from me, she insisted, "Peter, did you hear me? I want you to go back to school!"

I couldn't remain silent without being rude. "Fay, I don't want to be abused again by a maniac," I finally replied.

"No, you won't," she assured. "First of all, Dr. Miles was suspended and won't be allowed to teach for a while. They found out that other black students were messed up by that man. Everybody concerned with your other cases and yours has reached the conclusion that Dr. Miles, for the time being, can't properly function as an instructor in a multiracial society. His racism has reached a pathological state and made him a danger to society.

"Second of all, you are going to attend a college in the West Coast. My Uncle is the dean over there. He happens to love me very much and he is willing to help you because of me. I told him about your ordeal and he agreed that you could go and pursue studies over there as if nothing had ever occurred. You will start from where you have dropped out. Peter, please, for my sake, do it."

She stood up and kissed me quickly on the cheek. "I must go. Here is my uncle's answer to my letter. Here are the forms to fill out for registration and fellowship. Tomorrow, I will take them back and mail them to him.

"Bye and have pleasant dreams!"

She left swiftly like a naughty girl who tried to stay away from the *trouble* she had caused.

17

Fay wanted it all: intrinsic values and some kind of material security. Her warmth and kindness to me seemed to testify to her willingness to trust her intuition and acknowledge the former in me. She didn't want, however, to delude herself with respect to the lack of the latter in me. She didn't have to tell me; my self-assessment depicted a somber image of me: I had been confined in a hospital room for over five months, as the result of bloody events I was involved in, either as an actor or as a victim. Yet nobody should be blamed for having some doubt about my possible shady lifestyle. Additionally, to the best of my knowledge, I didn't have any gainful employment, I didn't hold any college degree, nor had I been practicing any profession before my confinement. I was too young to have made a career. I didn't come from a wealthy family. As a responsible person, I had to pinpoint these drawbacks of my existence. Otherwise, I would fool myself.

Evidently, that woman granted precedence of intrinsic values over material security; otherwise, she would have "given herself up" to Dr. Colborne long time ago. Yet she would lose nothing by being careful in life.

Anyway, she had alluded to the sine qua non condition under which she would consider to belong to me; therefore, it depended on me to do something about the whole matter. If I was sincerely interested in her (and I was strongly) I would have to price high my prospective undertaking. I had to transcend my pitiful condition, my diffidence and my pessimism to become someone full of craving for what is good in life, in terms of promoting further spiritual, intellectual and material self-improvement.

But what could I do? And how could I do it?

At first, I didn't have the faintest idea of the course of action to be taken. My future was wide-open, like a black hole. Whatever the alternative contemplated, it was cancelled out by a stronger argument. All I was sure of, it had to be something I hankered after in the first place. Indeed Fay's suggestion that I should pursue studies was compatible with my ideals, with all that I had been craving for. As I said again and again, I believed in the value of education and in its power to raise us up in the hierarchy of beings (without mentioning its possibility to improve our living conditions).

So, thanks to Fay, I rediscovered my goal which was so bloodily interrupted: I was going back to college. This goal belonged to a wholesale promise I was about to endeavor to keep. It would be a ceiling to reach, to live up to.

Once re-engaged in the learning process, I wouldn't have any other choice but to go on and develop again a thirst for knowledge.

My decision brought me serenity, lucidity and an unbounded flush of optimism. I was feeling again like a genuine potential person, a person a la Nietzsche or a la Toussaint Louverture, a bridge which would close the gap between my past falling through in the end, my present which bubbled over with ambitions and ideals, and my future which would be striving for perfection in order to draw near to that ceiling (my ceiling) imposed on myself.

Yet my decision would lack something if it was caused only by my desire for self-perfection, requiring sustained dedication. How long then would last the intensity of such desire? Couldn't it be only a flash in the pan, while I was in bed, having nothing else to do but dream? There was no guarantee that my elevation of the soul wouldn't fade away as soon as I would have left my hospital room to be in contact with the outside world, a deceiving world. I knew the kind of emotion a confined place can arouse in people. I was thinking about the time I used to go to the movies and that I identified myself with the hero of the story, who was capable of making a big difference in a society rotten to the core. I felt his emotion and was pervaded by the elevated intentions he was the embodiment of. But, once out of the movie house, I would return to my routine life, with no *incentive to change the world*

Nonetheless my desire would become endlessly intense (or at least sustainable) if it was caused, not only by my craving for self-perfection, but also by the idea of being challenged by Fay.

Yes, she implicitly issued a challenge, a kind of summons to engage in types of actions which are conducive to an existence of greatness. It was as if she completely changed into a precious golden statue which could be possessed under specific conditions. Then, as soon as they would have been fulfilled, she would be mine, she would become my wife.

In my imagination, I pictured her being pregnant and taking a maternity leave. She would be very beautiful and fragile too. She would be happy like an angel and sluggish like a cat. Daily, I would return home from work, with either a little present in my hand or a sweet word on my lips for her. She would wait for me in the living room, making knitwear for the unborn or reading a captivating book on maternity. As soon as she would have seen me, she would stop whatever she would be doing and would cover me with welcome back kisses. I would feel her stomach and inquire about the "little angel inside". She would surprise me, by cooking my favorite dishes anyway. Later on, I would sit on the sofa, and she would lie down on it, her head heavily resting on my lap. I would whisper honeyed words in her ear; she would ask me to "stop it", in a tone of voice which would mean *not to stop it*.

Someone said, "Mr. Young?"

I looked up and saw a nurse. "Yes, I am." I replied.

"Fay is on the phone," she informed, after having eyed me suspiciously. "She wants to speak to you."

Since I hesitated for a second, she went on harshly, "Are you coming or what? I don't have time for foolishness. And I can't be your messenger."

I remembered her! She was the one who *massacred* me with her bloody needle! "I had to comply fast to avoid another assault coming from this Amazon warrior," I said to myself. I thought that her character should have been improved by then. Unfortunately, her unfriendly look and tone of voice let me believe that she was impervious to reason and compunction.

To fall into step with that merciless female giant, I walked as fast as my recovering body allowed me to. When I arrived at the *Nurses' Station*, I noticed the presence of a great deal of people, Dr. Colborne included. Usually, most of them could have been anywhere else except at the *Nurses' Station*. Therefore, I assumed they wouldn't go away until they found out the nature of Fay's call.

"Peter, honey!" she whispered on the line.

I looked round, as I had feared that the "noisy" people nearby could overhear her. I smiled afterward at my *being silly*.

"Yes, Fay," I responded.

"I left a letter with you by mistake. My uncle has sent it to me along with your application forms."

"Oh!" I exclaimed. "But you deliberately gave it to me."

"Certainly, I didn't know what I was doing. Have you read it?"

"No. I haven't."

"Peter!" she shouted,

"Honest. I had the intuition that it was addressed to you and that you were the only one who should read it. I respect people's privacy."

"Peter, you wouldn't lie to me, would you?"

"No, I wouldn't. I have been doing my best to eschew lie and deceit."

"I don't believe you."

"Why do you say that?"

"You wouldn't tell the truth in a nice sweet voice!"

"I don't see why I have to use a high vocal pitch to tell the truth. This won't make it any more genuine."

"Come on, Peter, one who possesses the truth has the tendency to shout it."

"You said 'one'. I am not 'one', I am Peter. So, if they let me do it, I will tell the truth in a sweet tone. Is it against the law to tell the truth in a civilized manner?"

"Of course not. There is no such law I am aware of."

"Good. We agree on something."

I pause for a short while, just to look inquiringly at the people present at the *Nurses' Station*. They were the pictures of attention.

"But, seriously, I did tell you the truth," I went on. "I was about to read the fellowship and registration instruction forms when I was told that you were calling me. I value too much your friendship to do anything which could jeopardize it. I wouldn't do it for all the gold in the world."

"Oh, Angel, listen, I trust you," she affirmed joyfully, while emitting a sigh of relief. "You can read the first two pages of the letter if you want to. They deal with your admission to the college. Then stop right there. Don't go any further. Please. Otherwise, you will never see me again. I'll have to look for a nursing position somewhere else. I'll be too embarrassed to look you in the eyes. My uncle says things to me, which I wouldn't like you to read (at least for now)."

"Fay, don't worry, I give you my word. I want to see you again and again. It's a small sacrifice I have to make to keep seeing you."

"Not that my uncle says anything about you and me; you know...Listen, well, he is teasing me about my 'losing my cool' ...It's the first time he has seen me in a state of excitement. I get no idea what he's talking about. As far as I know, I've been acting in a normal fashion. Of course, I may have been a warm, enthusiastic champion of your case; for, I had to convince my uncle of your worthiness. You understand, don't you?"

"I see. In other words, what he says is personal, between uncle and niece."

"You are extremely clever. Do you know that you are smart?"

"Fay, since you said it, I believe it. You wouldn't fool me deliberately."

"Of course, not."

"Again, Fay, I give you my word. I won't read the letter at all."

"But you may read the first two pages."

"No. I won't. I may be tempted to have a peek at the rest of the letter. You know how curious human mind may be. Once it's aware of the cookie jar existence, it won't stop until it revels in these delicious sweets."

"Well, Peter, you have a very poetic way to talk about my worry. So stay away from the cocky jar altogether. Too many sweet things are not good for your health anyway."

"Fay, you definitely make your uncle's letter sound like a forbidden fruit. Again, as a human being, I can be tempted by its fragrance. The best thing to do is to stay away from it (she laughed heartily at the end of the line). I may read the first two pages in your presence—if it is necessary"

"I know I can count on you, Honey. And you promise!"

"Yes, I do."

"Bye!"

"Bye, Fay."

I laid down the receiver and got ready to return to my room when Dr. Colborne behaved in a very disgusting manner. "This is staggering," he stated loud enough to let me overhear his remark. "Fay falls in love with this bum! I can't believe it. That's mind-boggling. And, the funny thing is that she still trusts him after he's stolen something from her. Women! I can never understand many of them. They have to do the wrong things. I no longer have any respect and sympathy for that nurse. She should get what she deserves."

"I can't believe that either," added the nurse who had informed me of the phone call. "What could Fay expect from that thing? Yes, this is a thing, not a man. She is going to ruin her career. But, Henry, I must make a correction to your statement. Not all women are without any vision, any sense of responsibility, any pride. Some of us are very choosy about men they want to be close to. So, Henry, don't put all women in the same bag. Between that thing and you, I wouldn't have the slightest hesitation in choosing you. You have a great deal of clout; you are a professional highly respected by society. That thing is nobody. No I wouldn't have any hesitation in choosing you over this thing."

"You are quite right, Angelica," another nurse observed, "but I agree with Henry, that there are women, like Fay, who take pleasure in falling in love with slovenly men. As far as I am concerned, I wouldn't touch this one with a ten foot pole."

A female clerk exclaimed, "Boy, boy, boy! How naive can you be! Women like Fay are in search of degenerate men to boss around. This is another way to say those women enjoy service at home. Who could give it to them? The answer is clear: those desperate unskilled men who, because of their stupidity, can never find their way out by themselves. This is the only reason for Fay to put herself at risk. This is something I learned a long time ago."

"But, I feel sorry for Fay," Angelica said. "She is a sweet woman deserving a better lot in life. But what can we do. This is her life. She can do whatever she wants with it."

I couldn't take it any more; I walked away fast, returning to my room. I felt very depressed. "Why do they treat me like that?" I wondered. "I am not a dog or a thing; I am a decent human being. Above all I am not slovenly. It's a lie. I've been trained to be clean by my parents and Aunt Emma. Why can't they be patient? I'll leave *their hospital* one of these days. I am just recovering from wounds I didn't inflict to myself. Oh, I wish I could be somebody! I'll be somebody!"

They brought me supper. I took only a carton of milk and waved the other stuff away. I couldn't swallow any food, with that lump on my stomach, my state of anger and frustration. "I am not hungry," I said to the lady pushing a huge food cart.

"That's your business," she remarked, while going away to other patients.

"I know that, but thanks anyway for your offer," I retorted.

I wasn't quite conscious of what happened afterward, except that I remembered promising myself to ask Fay the day after whether I was a dog. The prospect of seeing her again made me feel relaxed a little bit and I slept until that following morning.

I felt better when I woke up, though Dr. Colborne and his friends' hostility toward me was still making me a little uneasy.

Another lady, who looked more agreeable to me, was serving out breakfast. "Good morning, Peter," she greeted in a congenial fashion.

"Good morning, lady," I echoed her.

"Oh, don't be so formal. Call me Margaret."

"I promise to do so."

"Here is your breakfast. I want you to eat it to the last piece. You must be hungry, since you didn't accept your supper last night."

She stopped short and looked at me. She then smiled. "I learned about what happened last night and that you didn't eat," she added. "These people should be ashamed of themselves. They certainly didn't behave like true professionals. We have no business mistreating our patients, above all a patient like you who deserves love and respect. What you did could have saved my son's life if he was in the same predicament as the youngsters in that Queens Hell house. But, fortunately, all of us are not like your disparagers. Some of us love you. I would be so proud to be your mother."

"Thank you, Margaret. You have made my day. From now on, I will be happy, knowing that some of you love me. Thank you."

"Oh, I meant to tell you that my late mother used to remind me again and again: to give love you have to love yourself. Your disparagers are incapable of loving themselves and others."

"Margaret, you are wisdom in action."

"Thank you, Peter."

I received my portion from that *wise female Buddha* and started to eat it immediately: I was starving. Then I went to the bathroom and had a long shower. More than ever I had to be clean in order to make sure I wasn't slovenly, as my disparagers tried to delude others into believing that I was. With the help of the cool water pouring over my body and Margaret's wisdom, I partially regained my joviality. I even mumbled a pretty song I had heard several times, but I didn't know its lyrics. I thought that it was a German arietta "a German arietta!" I thought "I am definitely a man of culture".

I returned to my room, sat down and started to read the application forms sent by Fay's uncle. A female hand interposed between the printed materials and my vision. I knew right away it belonged to Fay: it was symmetric and clean.

"Hello, Fay! Is that you?" I said.

It was surely comforting for me to realize that she too was still on my side. So, like a child obsessed with curiosity, I was waiting for an opportunity to ask her whether I was a *dog*.

Suddenly, my head was filled with the unpleasant remarks Dr. Colborne and company had heaped on me the night before. More than ever, my willingness to know her feeling about me couldn't suffer any delay. It had to be satisfied immediately. I tried in vain to be *philosophical* about it, which was understandable: those people had belittled me so much that I couldn't prevent myself from wondering if she wasn't making a fool of me, pretending to be fond of me.

"Fay, you keep calling me angel," I stated with a suggestion of bitterness in my voice. "Why?"

Her eyes opened wide with surprise. "But...but, because you are!" she stammered

It was the first time I saw her being at a loss for words. Ordinarily, she could talk forever and ever without losing her smoothness of elocution. Then I knew that I had made a blunder and rubbed her the wrong way: she was no longer smiling.

Yet, I pressed on, which was an indication that I was consumed with anger, "If I am an angel, a handsome, why was I treated like a *dog* last night? Are you making fun of me? You wouldn't do that, would you? Is it your civilized way to belittle me? Fay, give me the bitter pill today."

She drew nearer to me and put her hands on my shoulders. "Peter, don't ever make me pay for somebody else's misdeed," she remarked. "You know that you've hurt me too. Yes, you have!"

She paused to breathe, then she went on, "I resent that, Peter, I resent it. I thought I was special to you. I am innocent of any wrongdoing against you. I trust you, Peter; I believe in you; I respect you. You are a genuine human being, with your hope, your fear and your idea of transcendence. I've never thought of you otherwise."

She burst out crying. I was worried and ashamed. It was so inconsiderate of me to hurt "my little Fay". I should have known better than that. She had given me the gift of life. She was my *mother* in a way. And a *good mother* would never harm her child deliberately.

"Fay, I am so sorry," I implored. "You are perfectly right. You can never hurt someone the way those people hurt me last night."

She calmed down and breathed heavily. "That's ok, Peter," she assured. "No matter what we do, we can't prevent sadness to be also part of existence; once in while, it has to show up. But it's something I haven't expected now. I have taken for granted that we've been living in harmony. To the best of my recollection, I've never mistreated you. After what you've been through, I wouldn't play with your feelings (unless I was struck by madness)."

She remained silent, trying to make a sense out of the whole situation. Then she patted me on the back and sat down on the bed. "Peter, I am so sorry that some of us treat you so bad," she whispered. "As far as their animosity is concerned, I have no explanation. Like you, I am in complete darkness. I didn't ask them to protect me from you. If this is what they are doing, then they are serving the wrong cause. As a matter of fact, if I felt that you were a threat to me, I would have avoided your company."

Then, she asked abruptly, "Was Dr. Colborne among your detractors?"

I nodded.

"I am beginning to understand what's going on. Since Dr. Colborne is the chief of service, the others were trying to please him. Most people are snobs. They want to be part of the greater number or the more powerful. Only individuals with integrity and character don't behave according to general opinion and belief.

"I know that you understand what I am talking about, don't you? You, with your big brain and your all-embracing frame of mind! Even tragedy couldn't hamper you acumen. In a way, you are gifted."

Another moment of silence occurred. I wondered if I didn't go too far, by getting Fay involved in this ungracious situation. But, in a way, I was glad to have one great confirmation: her generosity and inner strength are boundless. Those qualities were in her veins and on my side.

For conscience's sake, she inquired, "Peter, what really happened last night?"

Her question took me by surprise. "Oh!" I exclaimed. "While I was talking to you on the phone, at the Nurses' Station, Dr. Colborne and his friends made insulting remarks about me. They thought I was a bum, a slovenly bum, a degenerate person, a dog. A female nurse even compared me with a thing. She said, and I quote, 'Henry, if I had to choose between that thing and you, I wouldn't have the slightest hesitation in choosing you over that thing."

"That's incredible!" exclaimed Fay.

I went on, "They were also puzzled over the fact that you could fall in love with me and that you would ruin your career and your life. Where did they get their deduction from? I have no idea. As far as I can remember, we were talking about this and that in such a playful manner, but we didn't say anything about love.

"Not that I wouldn't like to be loved by you, but our relationships have been, so far, the most innocent ones in the world. Furthermore, you are so important to me that I wouldn't like to see you being disparaged for any reason whatsoever. And if that happened, I would feel responsible for it (in a way). I should have had a normal and lawful existence which would prevent me from being assaulted by thugs and finding myself in your way. You would have never known me, gotten closer to me and felt so much compassion for me. So, Fay, I've caused you so many headaches."

"Please, Peter, don't speak like that. No, you are wrong to feel responsible for my being loathed by my colleagues. And you should never stop believing in your innocence and straightforwardness. It's not your fault if you find yourself in this predicament. Again don't speak like that, if you don't want to hurt me."

"No, I don't intend to hurt more than I've already done."

"Peter, you have to stop believing that you are hurting me. It's quite the contrary. As far as I am concerned, you are above reproach."

Then, shortly after, I asserted, "Thanks you, Fay, for believing in me. I won't misbehave deliberately, so I will always respond to the positive image of me you've in mind.

"However, as far as these people are concerned, I've given up on them. Since they haven't changed their opinion on me by now, after having heard my own version of the bloody events I was involved in, they would never accept me for someone with a sense of pride and dignity. They are incapable of transcending their hatred of me."

" ...Then, Peter, you thought I was making fun of you!" she interjected. "You believed that I was doing the same as these widows, but in a more subtle fashion! Peter, I thought you knew me better than that. I will never, for any reason, behave like that. It's totally against my nature and my philosophy of life."

I was shocked by her deduction which was absolutely right as far as my state of mind was concerned.

She remained silent for a short time. I sensed some inner tension overtaking her. I thought that it wasn't wise of me to let her know about my problems. Fortunately, she was able to keep her anger under control.

All of a sudden, she asked, "Peter, how do dogs perceive reality?"

I was puzzled. I wondered if her sense of humor wasn't uncalled-for. I was hoping she wouldn't take the word *dog* literally.

"Peter," she insisted, "my question may seem trivial, pointless, but I am serious. I would like to hear your answer."

I still didn't answer, not knowing what was in her mind. Finally, I replied, "Well, Fay, I can't tell you. I've never been a dog, to the best of my recollection. I've been Peter Young, looking at the world through my mind filled with preconceived ideas from mankind and my own."

"You've given me the right answer," she agreed. "But let me go one step further. I believe dogs perceive reality in their *doggy manners*. Don't you think?"

I smiled. I fully understood that her question was pregnant with meanings.

She paused to breathe and allow me to realize she wasn't talking nonsense.

"My answer to your question is that you are not a dog," her voice turned didactic. "You don't look like a *dog*; you don't react like a dog. Your stand against crime doesn't describe the ways of dog. The depth of your thoughts has evidenced that you are a man of learning;

for you are recapturing your physical health, as well as your inner life, as they were before the brutal assault. So you were exposed to positive knowledge. There is no doubt about that. If my reasoning has been correct so far, then its contrary must also be correct. I mean that Dr. Colborne and his friends are seeing you like a dog because they are looking at you, they are perceiving you, in their *doggy manners*."

She drew a long breath to calm down. "Dr. Colborne is just a *dog*." she continued. "That's true! He is a big *dog*. He has nothing in mind beside having sex. He goes to bed with almost everybody and anywhere: with nurses, housekeepers, patients, in motels, in the hospital bathrooms, in doctors' lounges, maybe in the streets at night, in dark alleys. I wouldn't be surprised at learning that some of your last night female disparagers are among his mistresses. Rumor has it that I am supposed to be the woman he really loves, and who could appease his insatiable sexual hunger and make him come to his senses. He would settle down and have a family. Am I a kind of tamer of wild animals? Tell me!

"To tell you the truth, I believe that doctors and nurses are not worthy of too much consideration when they are devoid of self-respect, respect for others and dedication. What else do they have to offer without these qualities? Indeed, without them, they could be nothing but mechanics of human machines. As a matter fact, many are repeating automatic gestures routinely, blindly, with a systematic lack of compassion for their patients. I don't want to be specific and blow the whistle on people. I am not an informer. But I must tell you that negligence and irrational behavior are rampant in this hospital and other health centers. What they are reporting on the news is real, not fabricated; it's going on. Patients have died in hospitals from infection, negligence and visible mistakes."

She looked less tensed as if she had eased her mind of a heavy load. "Peter, you have so much to offer," she proceeded. "You don't know it or you are not showing off. Believe it or not, Dr. Colborne will never overshadow you, as far as I am concerned. The reason is simple: I feel soiled in my body and soul whenever I had to work by him, while I feel purified, wonderful, at ease, whenever I am with you."

She stood up. It was nine o'clock. She had to sign in. She said hesitantly, "Have I covered all the grounds? And, please, don't ever hurt me like that again. I will never look down on you. This has never been in my mind. It can't be since I know what you stand for. And what do you say for yourself?"

Her face glowed once more with happiness.

"Fay, I am sorry," I reassured. "I made you sad. I had to be a fool to do so. Again, I am sorry."

She patted me on the shoulder. "I must go now," she insisted. "But let me tell you something: you will have a big surprise very soon. As they say, it will blow your mind."

"Is that so?" I inquired. "Will it be a pleasant one?"

She made an affirmative sign with the hands and rushed headlong towards the lobby.

As far as I was concerned, I had regained my sense of value and my self-confidence I had almost lost the night before, thanks to her. She was definitely my *fairy godmother* and knew the secret of putting me in a state of mind not far from *Alice's in Wonderland*. In my case, to keep up with my gender I would have been *Alex in wonderland.*

In other words, Fay had a talent for putting things in their places: she made them simple. "I love her so much," I whispered. "I will do all in my power to deserve her love in return."

I thought then Earth could be wonderful if people were not trying to make things so complicated. "Simplicity seems to be the key to the essence of reality," I murmured. "It could also be the challenge to our complex minds with tendencies to build up sophisticate theories. Because, all things considered, life, for example, is simple. We are born, grow up, breathe fresh air, drink water, eat and perform various activities, which don't require too much. Whatever we need springs from nature free of charge. The price tag attached to things happens to be our own doing. Even our artifacts are originated from nature. We don't create anything from scratch, because we can't be above or below nature. We are absolutely in its bosom. We are the results of cosmic history the origin of which is lost in the mists of time. Therefore, everything should be working properly, since nature is a generous provider. Again, only our crooked minds have made up difficulties by raising *gods* and *barriers.*

"These gods and barriers come in all shapes: superstition, more and more sophisticated machines, sophisms, envies, greed... We must always interpose something unnecessary between the simplicity of life and us. We can't take reality as it is. There are so many channels we must pass through before the construction of a simple road. We believe it's too simple to sit around a table to discuss our problems. People are suffering all over the world and need relief now. But taking relief to people in need is too simple. We must make plans to do something in the next two months or so. By that time, death would have cut down many of them. Why? We must stand behind our ideologies: Capitalism, Socialism, Liberalism, Conservatism, Fascism, Anarchism, Individualism—to say the least. They dictate the structure of our interpersonal relationships. They make us decide who shall eat and who shall not, how to eat and how not to eat, how to harm and to be harmed, who shall get access to education and who shall not. This labyrinth of permissions and inhibitions supersedes our perception of things, our communion with the goodness of life. We make ourselves miserable beings which know nothing but what should be done in order to continue to spread unhappiness. In the name of our *gods* and *barriers*, we fail to recognize that we have now enough of everything to make the world happy. We cannot even stop deliberately, for a moment, from engaging in costly and unnecessary activities in order to focus our endeavors on the manners in which the overabundance of goods mankind possesses now could be used wisely, rationally, humanely. Why do we believe that anything else matters? that we could help better if we postponing indefinitely to help now? that we may be engaged in all kinds of detours, including the ones that lead us to other planets and galaxies, and once returned to earth, we will solve all our problems?"

I smiled. I realized that I was in my usual meditative mood, the one I used to experience before the attempt on my life (above all when I was alone in Aunt Emma's attic). I was so happy to have my mind intact, untouched and ready to welcome a life of transcendence and positive attitude.

18

The day of my release from the hospital finally arrived. I was completely recovered. I had never felt so strong and young before. I was like a machine thoroughly overhauled and tuned up. Then how could I explain my unhappiness? Why did I feel uncomfortable? For one thing, I had no money and no place to go. Of course, Aunt Emma would be delighted to welcome me back, more especially as I wouldn't have to stay too long in New York before starting for my new college in the West Coast. However, I didn't want to go back to her house. I would rather she led a peaceful and serene life, and that she became accustomed to the idea of my living apart from her.

I didn't know what to do anyway. I had a plane ticket to reach my school, and nothing else. No new clothes, no money, nothing. I decided then to wander about the city, like a vagrant. I could be lucky enough to find me a temporary job. But could I really work? To start with, in spite of my recovered strength, I wasn't in any condition to perform onerous duties. I had never done so, therefore, the perspective of getting a job had to be disregarded. Still I was against the idea of staying for a day or two with Aunt Emma. At least, I would reconsider this option by the end of the day, after I would have been near to collapsing from hunger and exhaustion.

But, all this wasn't enough to make me so depressed. If worst came to worst, I wouldn't hesitate in going to my aunt's house. This prospect would have been enough to prevent my gloominess, since it was one of the possible, feasible courses of action I could take. I was depressed, drained of energy, desire, incentive to go on struggling for life, because Fay was off that day! Her absence was enough to change the world into a kind of cold tomb (as far as I was concerned). It hurt me so much to leave without seeing her, kissing her, at least on her cheek, doing anything at all to show her my gratitude to, my fondness of and my interest in her. But all this was just a façade hiding my mental sufferings. Definitely, her absence, on my discharge day, triggered in me a feeling of self-deceit and lack of acumen, and seemed to betray my foolishness and total absence of common sense and realism. All these times, I'd been deceiving myself by thinking that I meant something to her, that I was the wonderful "prince" she had been waiting for. It was silly of me to have entertained these ideas. Still they were mine, they enlivened my existence. Fay shouldn't ruin them in one day by her absence. She just made a fool of me! She was cruel, wasn't she?

On the other hand, she couldn't be made responsible for my naivety. It was up to me not to have believed too much in her, not to have thought she was different from anyone else. In fact, she was admirable enough to let me foster some hope. Her congeniality was enough to fill my head with castles in the air. Unfortunately, they were my own, imaginary castles with no foundation, no tangible materials. They have never existed. That woman, finally, resumed her human nature fashioned after public opinions; she finally accepted my disparagers' advice to say away from, a center of possible tragedy and despair; she finally discovered that I was a danger to her livelihood and her future.

I felt small, dirty and repulsive. I had to do my best to leave the hospital at once even in pajama before losing my human dignity, my only asset in life. I wouldn't be able to suffer the agony of being looked at by Dr. Colborne and his friends in a way that would proclaim their triumph over me. Yes, I had to leave with the remaining pride I had.

Now I blamed myself for sitting in judgment on Fay. I had no right to be in doubt about her sincerity. Didn't she pull me from the claw of death? She had to have very important reasons for being absent that day. Whatever these reasons might be, I had no right to heap abusive words on her. She wouldn't deliberately miss my departure. Only my anger and fear of the unknown made me see her through the distorted prism of hasty conclusions.

I wished she could appease my anger by any means possible. An explanation from her would be largely sufficient. She could have even told me, "Darling, my work is over. I've done my best. I've devoted myself to you for five months. I've eschewed the pleasures of going shopping, visiting friends, relaxing at home. I've even lost friends in the process. Now you are on your own. I wish you the best. You are smart; you will know what to do to be going in the right direction". I would have understood this kind of farewell speech. I wouldn't have asked for the impossible; I wouldn't have asked her to cut off her relationships with her friends, coworkers, relatives, because of a perfect stranger, the bearer of possible deadly secrets, the center of disturbing, twisted drives. I would have understood that, at the last minute, she realized she was too careless to get so close to a perfect stranger passing by.

But where could she be? Perhaps it was her day off.

Suddenly, I realized how much I had ignored about her. How could it be otherwise? She was a human being. She didn't know herself completely. I bet that, daily, she was making a new discovery of her character. Then I was simply presumptuous to believe I knew her well.

I could look up her address in the telephone book. It was a chance I could take if she had a listed number. But even if she did, I couldn't go to her house, uninvited. She would have a legitimate motive for cursing me and asking me to go away and try to never see her again. I would deserve to be verbally abused by her and brought disgrace upon myself. I had to leave her alone, to let her breathe and regain her life she had neglected for taking care of a *semi-comatose patient*. She had done her utmost and paid her dues. Nothing else should have been required from her. I had to recognize that she was one of the greatest human beings on earth, that, once, such a precious and wonderful woman took care of me, that I had the distinctive privilege to be close to her and that I had learned from her that magnanimity was possible. In terms of human experience, I had to feel lucky to have been part of all this and proud to have been a protégé of such a great human being.

In fact, I didn't know her at all, besides her angelic smile, her oval face, her dazzling beauty, her velvety touch, her ambrosial body and, above all, her melodious voice which reached the deepest layer of my soul when it said, "Angel, darling."

Well, she was the one who had *masterminded* my returning to school. She knew the college address. If she wanted to write to me, she could do so. I still kept my pride and I would prefer wandering like a gypsy to begging. In fact, whom was I supposed to beg? A woman I thought I was loved by. No way.

Perhaps I was magnifying the situation for no good reason. It was possible that Fay needed some time to think things over. After all, she was a woman and had to be careful. She couldn't just set her heart upon a stranger (above all when her life had been so well organized). I had no right to expect the impossible from her. No right at all.

Ms. Joseph, the head nurse (Fay's closest friend and "adoptive mother"), brought me a parcel. Usually, she was smiling, but, that day, I noticed some sadness in her eyes. She stood by me for a while and kept silent. Finally, she said in a slightly tremulous tone, "Peter, from the bottom of my heart, I want to tell you that I am going to miss you. I am going to miss your wit, your genuine sense of seriousness, that little spice you have brought to the hospital. I am going to miss you. You know something? I am willing to adopt you as my second child. I love you so much. However, we can't keep a healthy young man like you forever and ever. You must go and conquer the world. Above all, follow my daughter's advice: go back to school and get as many degrees as possible. Then, you will see, the world will be offering all kinds of opportunities. I know it will be hard for you, but you have the brain and the energy to carry out this plan of action."

She took a pause and breathed deeply to keep her emotions in check. "Oh, yes, Peter! You are going to be fine," she proceeded. "There is nothing but goodness and intelligence in you. I know you are not going to deviate from your philosophy of life. Wisdom seems to be ingrained in you. I know that, and I feel it. I have never experienced any negative vibes on approaching you. Believe me; you are going to be fine."

She sobbed for a while. I hugged her and patted on her back. Finally, she calmed down. She stood up as if she wanted to evaluate me one last time. She nodded satisfaction.

Then, having noticed my being puzzled, she asked, "What's the matter?"

"Nothing," I replied. "Except that I believe that you have made a mistake by giving me somebody else's belonging."

I held up the parcel and went on, "Although I didn't know how I arrived here, I am almost certain that I didn't have a parcel on entering this hospital. I didn't have time to pick up anything, except my soul, my stubborn soul and its will to live."

I kept silent for a short while; I was remembering the ordeal I was involved in, the pains I suffered from the first stabbing and my joy of being in the street, bloody but comforted by decent people's presence until everything went blank.

Maude might have the intuition of what was going on in me and cared not to disturb me. She sort of joined me in my moment of silence. Finally, I pull myself together and went on, "Come to think of it, you can do me a big favor by calling my aunt and telling her that I am being released."

"I wish I could," she replied quickly, "but I don't know your aunt's telephone number. Fay may still have it. I bet that the parcel is from your dear Aunt Emma. She loves you so much.

"Indeed she does."

"The parcel was delivered to me this morning."

As I kept looking at her *suspiciously*, she shook her fist at me, simulated anger by frowning. Then she asked, "Peter, you are not going to give me a hard time, are you?"

"No, of course not," I replied, while holding up my hands feigning dread.

"Don't make yourself liable to spankings on your last day of confinement."

"I will do my best to avoid such harsh punishment."

She pointed at the parcel and said, "Look at the name on the label."

I looked. She was right. The parcel was addressed to me.

She pressed on, "What do you see?"

"My name," I answered.

"So?"

"In that case, Ms. Joseph, I keep it. It may be full of goodies."

"I certainly hope so. And call me Maude and don't forget to come and give me my goodbye kiss."

"I won't for any reason in the world."

"And I expect to see more of you from now on."

"Yes, Maude."

She walked away.

I turned over the parcel, squeezed it and weighed it on the palm of my hand, with the hope of identifying the objects inside, but in vain. It could be anything: a gift of goodbye from Maude herself or anyone else. I smelt it, put it close to my ear and slightly tapped on it with my middle finger. I didn't have a faintest idea of what it could be. Finally, I opened it briskly, like a child who has received a Christmas gift wrapped in crispy designed paper. I saw a brand-new sky blue shirt, a pair of matching pants, white underwear, a pair of navy blue socks and one of black shoes.

In one of these was a folded piece of paper. I opened it. It was a note from Fay!

Peter, my angel,

A big surprise, isn't it? Don't be ashamed. This is not charity. This is a manner of expressing my joy to have known you. I believe that Aunt Emma would have done the same. By the way, I told her I would take care of everything. Furthermore, it makes me feel good to do it. So, I want you to accept these gifts because they are the concretion of my inner feeling. You wouldn't give a cold shoulder to the concretion of my inner thought, would you? Remember that it belongs to my wholeness. They can't be appraised separately.
Fay.

I was looking at the note, aghast. I was happy and ashamed at the same time. "My angel" didn't forget my release from the hospital. I erred in my judgment on her. I wished she could be here in this hospital room to receive my apology and ask her if nature had set all the conditions of generosity in her or if her goodness had been a consequence of her philosophy of life? I lay down with the open parcel on my stomach; I was lost in my thoughts.

Still, my happiness was unable to fill the gap left by her physical absence. As a matter of fact, it would make me later on more miserable since it gave me a taste of the *promise land*, the *missing one*.

I was ready to leave. My new clothes fit me well. I suspected that, somehow, Fay had an accurate account of my measurements. Still, in spite of her generosity and her kind note, I couldn't get rid of that pinch in my heart caused by her absence. I whispered, "Why is the human soul so demanding? It should be content with these precious gifts and relieve me of all worries." I had no answer, except that I was inconsolable. I would like so much to tease that *beautiful woman* and do all kinds of *silly things* to her: kissing her, squeezing her shoulders, playing with her, looking at her in a funny way, before leaving the hospital. I would then have the impression that she belonged to me in a way. So, the memories of that imaginary last hour encounter would have stayed with me forever and ever. But, like a graceful bird avoiding my approach, she "weaned" me at the last minute and flew away to the top of *Mount Everest* where she belonged.

In spite of my evanescent happiness brought by her gift, in spite of my recent effort to forgive her, I started to think again how cruel she was to make me fond of her and drop me later on like a bag of potatoes. It was definitely wrong of her to behave that way. Maybe she didn't know, but she was playing the love game with someone whose heart was like an ultra sensitive machine. I couldn't be hurt again. She shouldn't have spoilt me so much if she didn't intend to keep on spoiling me for the remaining of my life. I was hurt and would always be hurt by the blow dealt by her. It was worse than the stab wounds I had received from Paul, Tony and their friends. "Why does she act like this?" I whispered. But, I had no answer.

I took leave of Michael. He hugged me and wished me well. He observed, "You are a decent human being. You have inspired me, and I promise myself that I will become a better person to deserve your friendship. I hope to see you again."

I hugged him back and said, "Of course, you'll see me again. And since you promise to follow in 'my footsteps', then we are going to be good friends."

We both laughed.

Michael had been my only roommate ever since Thomas' release a few days before. He looked sad. But I knew he would get over it: he was such a resilient old fellow. Additionally, I wouldn't hear the last of him, since he wished to extend our friendship beyond our confined hospital room.

I went to the Nurses' Station. The day shift employees were busy, attending their various duties. They used to treating me well. I kissed Ms. Joseph who hugged me exuberantly while she was crying. I also kissed other female employees and shook hands with the male ones. Finally, I walked alongside the hall, towards the exit. Here came Dr. Colborne!

I stopped instinctively and tried to reach his hand. He brushed me aside. "Just drop dead!" he yelled out, "or put your head under one of the trucks wheels passing by!"

I didn't know what to think. It appeared odd to me that a grown-up man behaved so childishly. What for? I didn't steal Fay from him. I was turned away by her. Like him, I was a *loser*. Yet it seemed I was showing more decorum than he. In fact, I didn't nurse any grudge against him. In a way, he was not responsible for his behavior. His miscalculation to which was added a strong dose of self-assurance got the better of him, which I understood perfectly. He might have been really in love with Fay and wished to marry her and get settled. The wild in him—as she would say—could eventually be tamed and change him to a pussycat. As far as I was concerned, I couldn't tell how I would react if I were he. Being a physician, having a decent salary, being imbued with feelings of self-complacency (not to say superiority), I wouldn't be happy to see a wonderful nurse, preferring the company of a *nobody* to mine, although I wouldn't agree with him on his bad opinion of me. I was somebody. I knew I was one, and I couldn't be totally wrong, for, the first sign of human character must come from the self-awareness of it, not from an external source. I felt that I was a seed full of potentialities, ready to be actualized, in the proper environment.

Yet, in spite of Dr. Colborne's abusing me verbally on various occasions, I happened to be grateful to him. Although he couldn't have foreseen, while I was unconscious, that I was about to put a stopper on his dream of happiness, and in spite of his *doggy nature*, to quote Fay, I was lucky that he had behaved after all like a professional. My life was at his mercy. During my recovery, he could have easily substituted a deadly poison for my medications. In the event that such homicide would have taken place, it would have been highly possible that nobody would find out what would have happened to me. I was pronounced dead; then, I was hanging between life and death. So my being poisoned would be taken for the fatal outcome of my wounds.

Anyway, I took leave of him, whether he wanted to shake hands with me or not. I would be no more a target for his jokes and his sneers, for the unjustified animosity of his friends and coworkers, for being *stabbed* by Angelica's *bloody needle*. I was finally out of the hospital. I landed on the pavement. It was as firm as the one I had stood on when I had thought I was about to die over five months earlier. It was my reintroduction to the stream of humanity, the genuine one, the one which made sense and gave reason for hope. It was so good to breathe deeply the outside air for the first time in months, so good to bathe in the sun, so good to be alive, so good to start struggling for life. Yes, I felt good to be able to do all that, far away from Paul and Tony's gang, and from my detractors at the hospital. The only person I wouldn't like to be away from was unfortunately missing. But what else could I do? I was unable to win them all.

I turned into the street, on the first corner to my right. A shock! The crowd was growing up instantly. Hundreds of men, women and children were brushing against one another, going to and coming from everywhere. They betrayed a variety of morphologic particularities. The majority of them were obviously going to work or to some kinds of business meetings. Others were wandering alone or with their family members. Among them could be visitors from other States or distant countries: they were pointing their cameras at almost anything at all.

I plunged into that human flow with renewed self-confidence: I felt well, rejuvenated, carried away by such emotional warmth, full of affinity or even of a rich, pleasant, peaceful diversity, the very stamp of reality, as well as its dynamism.

It was a *peaceful* day in *New York style*, which I tried to poetize in my mind as follows:

A PEACEFUL DAY IN NEW YORK CITY

This morning,
A refreshing breeze,
A crystalline mist veil,
Drift across New York.

People,
Pervaded by a joyful impulse,
Move leisurely;
But each of them
Has a way of being happy.

That woman,
While breathing in deeply,

Revels

Into gobbling down big slices of watermelon

And striding along.

This man,

More serene,

Is lost

In a past full of exhilarating emotions.

This adolescent,

A ravishing expression of innocence

On the face,

Smiles at existence.

This woman,

While casting a searching look

To the surroundings,

Distorts her face

With her charming fingers.

This taxi driver,

Contemplating the horizon,

Is peacefully waiting

For the clearing of the street corner

By nonchalant pedestrians.

A day of pleasure, of joy, of optimism,
In New York.

I was so happy to immerse in that ocean of moving emotions that I surprised myself feeling love for all these perfect strangers. But such love was also for my own sake, because I was identifying myself with these strangers, I was relating to their desires, their joy and their pains. The only difference, I thought, existing between them and me was that they were going somewhere, they had plans and purposes; they weren't released from hospitals, after close to five months of confinement, between life and death. By the end of the week, they would get rewarded; they would go to their favorite shopping centers and had a ball. They would organize family reunions and exchange good feelings and gifts. I had no fixed destination; I was walking at random. I had no place of work to go to, no one to reach for friendship and love. I felt lonely and scared.

I was about to step across and walk at random when a small beautiful orange car practically brushed me and stopped. There was no doubt about the driver's *antagonistic behavior* towards me. I said to myself that the adversity of life shouldn't strike me at my first step on the pavement, after months of confinement. Could it be Paul and Tony who came just on time to finish their job? I wouldn't be surprised if one of my disparagers at the hospital went one step further in their badness and informed the criminals on my being released. But, after quick critical thinking, I had to dismiss such idea. "No, my disparagers could be anything but criminals' informants," I said to myself. Moreover, those drug dealers were supposed to be in jail.

I bent forward and looked inside the car to see who was that *trouble-maker* at the wheel and give him a piece of my mind. I was still a little weak, but my tongue could be *sharp* if need be.

Here was Fay!

I was standing there speechless. Other vehicles were waiting for her car to move. Then, all of a sudden, the deafening cacophony of horns started, going from soprano to baritone. I still didn't move. In fact, I couldn't make the slightest gesture. I felt as if I were drained dry. Any harm could have happened to me, including being crushed by a foolish and angry automobilist.

Finally, Fay got off her car, hugged me, squeezed me and kissed me. She opened the passenger's door and pushed me gently into the vehicle, as if I was a precious statue. Then she resumed her seat behind the wheel. The exasperated drivers gave her a last wild symphony of horn blowing. She waved them goodbye and drove away.

19

I was unable to understand the direction taken by the course of events, but, judging by the way I was feeling, I wouldn't have any dissenting opinion about it: reality seemed to be smiling at me. Moreover, Fay was, in way, *my leader*, a *good* and *sensitive leader*. I knew that she was opening up a *road* of *greatness* for me. I bet she was heading to Queens and was about to drop me at Aunt Emma's home. I wouldn't be surprised at learning that she had visited her and had enjoyed one of her home-made puddings, apple pies, carrot cakes or any of her delicious recipes. For some unexplained raison, Aunt Emma's dishes could flatter the most delicate palate in the world.

I finally accepted the idea of spending some time at her home if she and Fay wanted it this way. It seemed it could be part of a whole-sale plan these *two wonderful women* had in their bags for me. Thus I was sitting quietly, my head leant on the head-rest, and my eyes closed. I was at Fay's entire mercy. In fact, she was doing all the talking, which her over-excitement and mixed feeling of freedom and guilt made inexhaustible and spicy.

"Peter, honey, nobody but Maude knew what I had planned," her voice was more melodious than ever. "Yes, only Maude did. I didn't want people to know about my 'business'. You see what I mean? Above all those doctors, nurses, nurses' aides, clerks, housekeepers, they like running their mouths all the time. Not that I was doing anything wrong, but the idea of taking a man to my house, would make their imagination run wild. Remember: I am supposed to be the *respectable* and *lovable* Fay!"

"Oh! The master plan becomes more exciting as it is being unfolded!" I thought. "We are not headed to Aunt Emma's home. Do I hit the jackpot? What do I mean by that? Will I still be treated like a patient?"

She put on the brakes just in time: the traffic lights had turned red, and she was absorbed by her explaining. The policeman standing at the street corner was ready to serve her with a summons for traffic violation; he smiled at her good reflex. Then, after the lights had turned green, she proceeded cautiously until she was out of that officer's field of vision.

"You know women," she went on, "genuine women, as you said it to Maude (she giggled)."

I thought, "What! Theses nurses did talk about me!"

"Yes, genuine women," her voice turned sententious, "they have a natural gift for intuiting a great deal of things. They are endowed with what they call the 'sixth sense'. So, Maude and I had a long talk the other day. Some point in time, you were the main subject of our conversation."

I rejoiced in myself, "I knew it!"

She went on, "Although she does not trust men in general, she believes in you. That's true, she believes in you! I've no idea of what you were talking about during my absence; however, whatever it was, you did a good impression on her and put her on *your side*. Would you believe it? She is a woman hard to please. During our conversation, she maintained I am lucky to meet such a considerate man.

"She also suggested strongly that I should be *friendlier* with you if I wanted to. Why should I get closer to you? She believed that a wonderful man is like trying to find a needle in a haystack. Of course, she wouldn't force me to go against my will; but she thought that we shouldn't be like those people who only obey social conventions and get clung to one another out of desperation. You and I are two beautiful persons who deserve each other.

"You know Maude; she can go on and on when she is in the proper mood. She told me plainly, that day, she didn't see anything wrong with your dating me. She also thought that I should go all the way. She was the one who imbued me with the idea of having you spend some time at my house to know you better through conversation. But I can tell you this now: I didn't show her that I was crazy about her suggestion which is contrary to her staidness. I have a great deal of respect for her, as if she was my natural mother. I didn't want her to stop believing in my moral standard. Inviting a man in my apartment may have all the appearance of loose living. However, I really take you for a fellow traveler in distress, who needs a moment of rest and relief—you know what I mean? From the bottom of my heart, I'd been wishing to do something likewise. Except that I was too shy to carry it out if I didn't find some encouragement from her. And I trust her; she wouldn't give me a bad piece of advice. She is a clever judge of human character. Furthermore, if something rotten happens to me, she will be the first person who will suffer the most. In other words, I always follow her 'natural instinct'.

"But I take this chance because you happen to be a very respectful man. Am I not right? You wouldn't try to go beyond the boundaries of friendship and fellowship, would you? I don't think I will be disappointed."

We reached a large intersection and made a right. Then we turned into a highway. Vehicles of all makes and shapes zoomed away; Fay's little pretty car hurtled along the road with the greatest ease. I looked at the "driver" out of the corner of my eyes; she was the very picture of serenity.

"I know what you went through when you didn't see me," she continued. "You would be in your right to think that I had betrayed you, that I didn't mean anything I had said to you for the last five months or so; but, Peter, as far as I am concerned, I will never betray you. As we are proceeding, I will tell why. Anyway, I imagine it was unbearable. You thought that I forgot you. Your mind and your vivid imagination pictured me like a little devil with a pair of horns (she giggled). Don't deny. I put myself in your shoes, and I wouldn't react any other way."

I thought that her power of deduction was amazing.

"I confess that I was also in pain," she went on. "Still I couldn't conceive of any other way to do it without drawing people's attention on our 'plan'. Remember the way my co-workers have reacted over a simple phone call! Their dirty minds see evil deeds everywhere.

"*Greatness* never comes easy.

"I repeat: as far as I am concerned, things haven't been smooth at all. Let me tell you what I've been going through since yesterday. The simple thought of your coming to my house has made me nervous. In my mind's eye, you are a warrior who is returning to his castle, safe and sound. Then the princess doesn't know how she should adorn the castle, what kind of food could please him and make him forget the hard time he had on the battlefield. In a way, you came from the worst battlefield in the world, because your enemies were dealing in crime. They had no vision, no ideals. They killed with no remorse. They are nothing but wild beasts. Yet, someone had to stand up to them and save the lives of their victims. Therefore, you are a warrior, a genuine warrior, a noble warrior who receives no instructions from anyone, but from his conscience and his love of others. You expect no reward, no recognition, and you have no fear. You predicate that evil is bad, you can't have any part of it. So I take myself for one member of mankind, who has acknowledged your greatness and bestowed a little reward on you.

"Indeed, since yesterday, I have been really feeling like a princess waiting for the conquering prince. Would you believe it?

"Then, this morning, I had to call Maude every hour on the hour, in order to find out exactly when you were going to leave the hospital so our meeting could be synchronized. Finally, I couldn't stand it. I drove to the vicinity of the hospital and was waiting for you. At various times, I narrowly missed being seen by my co-workers who knew that I had called sick; which I'd never done before. Fortunately, I brought along a large book and hid my face from view with it.

"After all, it was great fun. I felt as if I were a little girl. My heart palpitated all the time. Suddenly, you stepped on the pavement, and I saw you and I sighed with relief. I thought, 'Here is my noble warrior. He is in one piece. He is strong. He is going to make it. I will never stop believing in him'. You were standing, being engaged maybe in heavy thinking about your next course of action and about New York, the big apple. I was patiently waiting for you, since a few more minutes wouldn't kill me. Above all, I didn't want to rush things. I let you have the opportunity to say hello to the outside world, to breathe your first *polluted* air and bump against the first pedestrian. You have to be reacquainted with urban reality. I bet the streets, the pedestrians, the vehicles looked strange to you during your first two minutes or so. But, Peter, you have no choice but to reestablish yourself in the world. You have the right to be here, otherwise destiny wouldn't give you a second chance; I wouldn't exist to be your guardian angel (she giggled)."

She kept silent for a while. The traffic turned heavy in that section of Queens and required a much more cautious driving of her. Meanwhile, I enjoyed being rocked by the car rolling on the uneven macadam (although that feeling was an inferior substitute for the driver's suave and enveloping voice). I had time to turn round and admire her pretty head which seemed *too delicate* to remember all those curves and windings she was using in order to shorten the trip and avoid the flood of vehicles at the peak hour.

I was thinking that she was a *creature* of nature and a *reminder* of it when it's at its best, because of her captivating beauty radiating in the confined space of the car and her speech flowing like a limpid river. She was giving words their true functions which should go beyond the conciseness of military injunction and the sober exactness of scientific analysis, to reach a certain communion, an intimacy with reality, whatever its nature. I was captivated by her elocution which I was having time to listen to, without any interruption, and wondered about its secrets. Suddenly, I had the answer. She had realized the synchronization of reason and heart in herself. By so doing, she was capable of attempting to border on the inexhaustibleness of things, and in her effort to partially capture them, she was discovering new elements belonging to her perception. Such discovery, in its turn, was fuel for her verbal flowing. Why? She did it out of respect for her listeners who, as far as she was concerned, were entitled to some cla-rification along with her continuing apperception of reality. At this point, she was fully conscious of her doing, to expel all doubt about her intentions, to try to be fair about every aspect of the objects of her explaining. The outcome was lovely: a smooth, uninterrupted, harmo-nious melody, the very picture of her serene inner universe.

I wished the world could be populated by people like her. I only had a wish. Actually, the majority of people live in ignorance of eve-rything, even of what affects them daily, apart from the utilitarian or pragmatic aspects of it. They may enjoy a fruit. It's delicious, but how many are interested in its color, the particular texture of its peal, the seeds and their potentialities as being bearers of new trees and more delicious fruits for generations to come. It's the same when they deal with human beings. They see them, they recognize them, but do they really know them? Do they even have the desire to communicate with them? Do they feel going over the categorization, the compartmenta-lization which devises them into races, different religions, social backgrounds, to reach a mutual understanding and their common aspi-rations? Do they know that the fellow creature, who passes them on the street, is the unknown to discover, center of happiness or dread, concretion of goodness or badness, bearers of dreams, visions, ideals? Have they ever planned to join others in a huge global brotherhood? Of course not. They are rather more inclined to harm these unknown fellow creatures, to obliterate them, to try driving them away, in a vain attempt to have their peace of mind.

Speaking of human beings, as we were progressing slowly, I indulged in day-dreaming. I noticed, in that section of Queens, the alternation of life and death, their respective organization, their similarity and their difference: portions of a cemetery and house blocks almost interspersed with one another. The houses displayed their shimmering colors; the cemetery, its uniform iron gray shade. The houses bubbled over with action: men, women, children, were coming out of and going in them in one continuous stream. The cemetery awed with its lugubrious monotony and silence; except that three women and one man were walking alongside a row of tombs, in a sluggish and sad manner. Soon they arrived at their destination, which was practically a mausoleum. The mournful visitors remained still for a short while and then they bent to lay down sheaves of flowers. I imagined they wouldn't stay in that place too long, being anxious to go back to the stream of life. Yet, they allowed me to witness a continuum in the matrix of history: the living and the dead, the passing of traditions from the latter to the former, so much so August Comte asserts, "Les morts governent les vivants. [The dead rule the living.]".

I couldn't prevent myself from whispering, "The living and the dead are cohabiting in an astonishingly indifferent manner, as if they didn't have anything in common."

Fay suspiciously looked at me in a split second. But, having seen a serene expression on my face instead of an awe-inspiring one, she smiled. "Peter," she inquired, "what did you say?"

"Nothing of importance," I simply answered.

I felt the light touch of her hand on my shoulder and I was deeply moved by her attempt to appease my worries.

"Peter, everything is going to be fine," she reassured. "You will have a wonderful time in my home. I am incapable of willingly harming anyone and you. So, do your best to feel at home."

Then, after a long pause, she expanded on what she meant, "Don't worry, Peter. You are not in my way. Believe me. I am glad and honored to be your hostess.

"Let me explain something to you. Before knowing you, first by intuition, then by acquaintance, I had no transcendent purpose. By nature, I am generous. I was also content with my life or the daily routine of it. I would do a job and get paid for it. I respect people. Yet, I didn't think there was anything special about me. I was one of million gainful employed persons.

"Like any modern woman, I liked to buy clothes, shoes, jewelry and furniture. Whenever I was off, I would go shopping for anything at all, whether I needed it or not.

"Then you came. You showed me that I was empty, totally empty, and my frantic acquisition habit was nothing but an attempt to fill my inner gap. But this kind of gap can't be filled by material things, because it's not necessarily material. It's my inner world which is in a state of continuity fueled by my imagination, memory, attention, dream and other states of this nature.

"For the first time, you've made me realized something very important, which certainly fills that gap.

"My encounters with you have made me realize that we are determined as physical entities involved in the web of history. We can't survive without a minimum of food, water, air...

"We are also determined by the social setting we are living in and by some of its imperatives. It's an important factor to be aware of, because it's good for our own information—to say the least.

"However—and most importantly—, my encounters with you have taught me that I am also a conscious being. At this level, I am engaging in thinking, which has never occurred before. I am not talking about repeating clichés, ready-made expressions and opinions. Not at all. I am talking about genuine thinking allowing me to play a major part in decision-making. And, in the process of inner maturing, I surprisingly realized that acquiring gadgets, clothing and things of these kinds is no longer as important as it used to be to me. I was a toy in the hands of society. Now as a conscious being (and I am aware of it), I start participating in the history unfolding, I become a history maker (in my own little way). Isn't it wonderful? I feel wonderful! Peter! That's so great!"

"Peter, you are my teacher, you have shown me that I have a creative, an inventive power, that I can be an object of the whole social web, as I can also be an actor, a subject. I don't have to depend on others' opinions which may be often fallacious. I don't have to use clichés which I don't understand.

"In the process, I become curious about reality. My intercourse with it becomes dynamic. My awareness to which attention is added allows me to see elements of the same reality I didn't perceive before.

"Let me give you a simple example of what I am talking about. Do you know that, the other day, I was looking at the floor of my kitchen for the first time? Peter, imagine that: I used to feel the floor under my feet, to clean it in a mechanical fashion, to walk on it, but I was seeing it in some kind of unconscious, hazy way. But, the other day, I perceived it and paid attention to it. Then I saw the natural designs of the wood and realized how skillful the *Great Designer* has been. I was also grateful to the team of talented workers who did such a wonderful job to please the eyes of a perfect stranger. I was also amazed at the artistic purpose implanted in nature. I was going on and on, exploring all kinds of fascinating ideas. But I have been living there for the last five years or so. My floor was just a blurred, meaningless presence. Do you understand what I mean?

"You are my teacher, by your actions. From the first day they brought you unconscious in the hospital, I felt that you have changed the course of history. Now I know what you did. I want to be like you. Thus, what I have been doing for you is an application of the lesson I've learned from you.

"I know that you are giving me your full attention. Tell me if I am a bad student."

I breathed deeply before answering, "You are my first student, and, by a stroke of good luck, you are an outstanding one."

"But, Peter, above all, I want you to know that you are not in my way. I feel honored to be with you. I've heard about great personalities. Usually, they are historical figures. I've never met one until now."

"Since you said it, I believe it. I know that you are unable to lie (deliberately). And if you are right, I will feel so relieved."

"Why would you be?"

"Well, I would certainly understand that greatness is not an impossible dream; for, what you see in me is what you get. It's my normal way to behave."

"It's so true, Peter. It's very true indeed."

And, after another pause, she frowned.

"What is it?" I inquired.

"Nothing," she answered. "I thought I needed something from the supermarket. But I remember having bought it recently.

"You see, Peter, my new way of thinking may even make me save money. I wouldn't hesitate before to buy something I had plenty of at home."

Then, she patted me on the shoulder and laughed.

"Why are you laughing?" I inquired. "Did I do something unusual?"

"Of course not," she replied. "You've just returned from the battlefield, my prince."

"That's true."

""Didn't I tell you that you would have a big surprise?"

"Yes, you did," I acknowledged.

"Now, Peter, don't tell me I don't keep my word."

"I am still speechless."

The traffic became lighter. In fact, we could see the road stretching as far as the eyes could reach.

The *lovely driver* resumed, "Where were we? Oh, yes, Peter, honey, as I said a while ago, I am a good judge of human character. I know what you've been through and been thinking: everybody is the same. I mean everybody is selfish, greedy and heartless. In other words, no one wants to make you feel good, to wish you the best in life. That's not true. Certainly, that's not true, as far as I am concerned. I want you to spend some time with me, between now and the time you have to leave for school. I want you to make yourself at home. We will certainly share everything, except that I will take the bed, and you will sleep on the couch."

I didn't see any inconvenience with this kind of arrangement. Yet, would it be a pleasant one with time? I didn't have the opportunity to answer my own question because Fay drove into an underground garage and parked the car in her assigned space.

I opened the passenger's door and stepped out. I went around the vehicle and helped her out. It was the least I could do, being a *gentleman.*

"Thank you, Peter," she whispered. "You haven't lost your civility. You are so lucky."

Then we headed for the back door which she pointed out. We stopped, every now and then, to keep clear of cars coming in and going out. It was warm and humid. Quite a few women were also converging on the back door, after having parked their cars at their respective spots. They were wearing light and short-cut dresses which revealed usually hidden portions of their breasts and their legs.

Fay looked at me and smiled. She put her arm under mine and made me walk faster.

"Close your eyes," she *recommended*, while giggling. "Let me be your guide. I don't bring you in my apartment to be all excited. You want your peace of mind."

"Fay, I am not excited," I argued, "but astonished at the things meeting my field of vision."

She laughed heartily.

Finally, we reached the back door and entered the apartment house. A spotless lobby welcomed us. We crossed it to take one of the three elevators seen at the end. Five minutes later, we entered her apartment located on the top floor.

What a roomy and charming apartment!

Discreetly, I scanned it and noticed that it contained everything one could imagine a modern habitation should have. An imposing dining room displayed its wooden table surrounded by six chairs, a china base and deck with shining silver trays and pretty chinaware. A little further, showed up the kitchen. It was a marvel of cleanliness and tasteful arrangement. Nothing was left lying about.

On the right, appeared the living room furnished with a love chair, an armchair and a sofa bed. They were all tan and, because of that, toned down the multicolored carpet and the orange velvet drapes in the background.

Beyond, to the right, there was a closed door. I imagined it hid the *forbidden land*: the bedroom. Further down, to the left, was a half-open door. It had to be the bathroom.

I fully understood the meaning of Fay's previous confession about being a "modern woman", which pleased me a lot. It's true that I would welcome her moving towards inner self-improvement, yet I believed she deserved to live comfortably.

"This is a lovely apartment!" I exclaimed in spite of myself.

She looked at me in a surprisingly childlike way. She was so happy that she was shaking.

I was thinking about the big chance she took, letting me in her house. She didn't know me that well. She could have made a regrettable mistake. Let's take it that I was really on the wrong side of the road. I could have been a devious mind, knowing how to hide my evil intentions and my twisted mind from others. Once back on my feet, I could just resume my dangerous and senseless existence and take advantage of her good nature and abuse her and turn the pristine beauty of her apartment into a nightmare. The thought of my imaginary evil action saddened me; for, it was describing what could be happening to a nice person like my hostess.

The worse could have occurred if she loved me so much that she would go along with my foolishness and give up her career and follow me on the road to failure. Would anyone do such horrible deed? I didn't think so. I was just the victim of my gloomy imagination.

I was hoping that the chance she was taking with me would be the last one. She was in a way my mother, by participating in my rebirth. I wouldn't like to see anyone hurting this wonderful person. But, by the same token, I was rejoicing at the idea of her being lucky (which she richly deserved). I was standing in her beautiful apartment with the best intentions I had ever been actuated by. I said to myself, "This pretty lady who welcomes me in her house, who has saved my life, has given me my pride and self-confidence anew, this pretty lady, I am happy and willing to protect her against any harm coming from others and myself. She is my princess. Nothing wrong can happen to her as long as I am alive. I will make her the happiest woman in the world."

There was another reason why she was safe from that *little pig* in me (a little sleeping pig in every one of us): I was capable of containing myself. I didn't feel any uncontrollable desire for "misbehaving"; I rather became pervaded by a joyful serenity, a peaceful ecstasy, faced with this manifestation of fellowship. I had fully regained my self-esteem, my craving for intangible values, which couldn't be spoilt by lusts of the flesh or even less by misdeeds I had never had a bent for. I was strongly hoping for feeling that way as long as I was sojourning at my "beautiful Fay's" house.

Moreover, I had to save my *image*, the *image* of a *teacher* of *values*. She believed in me and bestowed upon me the highest regard in the world. She had turned me to a symbol of transcendence. I had no choice but to behave accordingly.

She went to the kitchen. Few minutes after, she called me. I went and joined her there.

"You must be hungry," she asked.

"Yes, Fay, I am," I acknowledged.

"Bravo!" She exclaimed. "I thought you lost your voice."

"I did, in the presence of such kindness on your part. Are you sure you are not an angel? Let me repeat it: I could be dead and be living in paradise; and that you've been assigned to welcome me and to reinforce the idea in me that heaven is a felicitous dwelling."

"No, Peter, you are not dead, and I am not a welcoming angel. I am instead very grateful to you. My kindness to you is a great joy for me."

"Fay, I am sincere. For a split second, you make me believe that I am dreaming. Tell me the truth. Do you really exist?"

"Yes, I do."

"You are not that angel you've been emulating, are you?"

"No, I am not."

"If you lie to me, you will lose your celestial power."

"I've never had any. But if I had, I would have done my best to keep it."

"The feeling I have is that your kindness has to be heavenly."

"Then, don't change your feeling. I will always be kind to you."

"I am so lucky."

She was busy stirring the lima beans immersed in heavy sauce.

A big piece of roasted meat was simmering in spicy juice. The beans and the rice were ready to be eaten.

"While I was waiting for you, my slow-cooker was doing the cooking," she explained. "I don't know what I would do without it."

And, after a pause, she added, "You see, Peter, you are not dead and in heaven; and I am not an angel. Why would I need a slow cooker in the divine kingdom? I would have the power to zap from desires to desires. Wouldn't it be lovely? Yet a celestial being would have to use commonsense and wisdom; otherwise, it would spend all its holy life going from wishes to wishes. Such lifestyle would be eternally boring."

Oh, I was experiencing such a wonderful time with this joyful woman!

She turned on her heels, opened the cabinet door, reached for a pepper pot and kept being busy with the lima beans. "In less than ten minutes you are going to eat," she promised. "Let me set the table."

With a motion of the hands I tried to stop her. "Let me help you, Fay," I offered. "I am going to set the table. I am strong enough to do certain things."

"No, no, no," she protested. "You will do no such things today. You are my guest, my first male guest (to be precise). You must be free from any burden whatsoever."

The diner was served. The meat was divine. Fay made it so tender that it was just melting in my mouth, like chocolate. I would have to ask her for the recipe. And the beans! I was always fond of beans, but those lima beans prepared by her were simply succulent—to say the least. The other dishes, added to these gastronomic wonders, brought me the acme of delight.

I ate so much that I became finally consumed with embarrassment. I wondered about her possible unexpressed reaction. She might believe that I was some kind of glutton, with no sense of good measure and decorum. But, instead, she was looking at me with amused eyes; her face was radiant with joy.

I went into ecstasy before this beautiful and well-meaning human being, so much so that, in my heart, I clumsily poetized my feeling in the following words:

I love you so much,
Stranger with fascinating eyes;
And you know that, don't you?
In spite of the intricacies of my person.
No, don't deny it.
You've fathomed my secret:
Through my heart you've gone,
And witnessed its muddled rhythm
Caused by your presence.

You love me so much,
Stranger with fascinating eyes;
And I know that, don't I?
In spite of the intricacies of your person.
No, I don't deny it.
I've fathomed your secret:
Through your heart I've gone,
And witnessed its muddled rhythm
Caused by my presence.

Let's love each other,
Stranger with fascinating eyes;
And tell me how to go about it,
To unburden ourselves of the dear secret.
No, don't harden yourself.
Let's be always together,
Until we carry our mutual love,
Away to the ethereal sites,
From the contingencies of life.

She snapped her fingers repeatedly. I retired from my "ethereal sites". I didn't know how long I went into raptures over my "princess", but I promised to "cool off" if I didn't want to pass off for a mentally deranged person.

"Fay, I believe I have overeaten," I confessed apologetically.

"Don't concern yourself with that," she stated. "I am glad that you like my cooking."

"Yes, I do. I've never eaten a testier and tenderer meat than what you've just served me.."

"All the good things for first male guest. Besides, after being forced to eat the food they serve at the hospital, I know you are glad to get something at least different."

We kept silent, but my mind was running full speed. I felt that I was *somebody* to receive such a warm welcome. Suddenly, I remembered that Fay had to be one of the hidden heroines and heroes they had been talking about. I also remembered that I was a student of *greatness*, *genuine greatness*, which had been unfolding under my nose. Therefore, my yearning for transcendence had been materialized.

It was then my turn to remind Fay of her *teaching status,* which she wasn't fully aware of. "Fay, there is something I would like to tell you. I am beginning to believe, at least partly, in Rousseau's conviction according to which many of us are good-natured."

She said, "I guess so, Peter. Although goodness can't be ubiquitous, but I believe it exists. Tell me, why do you share Rousseau's conviction?"

"Well, if I take you as an example, you have surpassed the normal boundaries of generosity. You could have done half of the goodness you are showering on me and you would appear great, in terms of human generosity."

"Why do you believe that I have surpassed the normal boundaries of generosity?"

"Well, Fay, I don't even know how to answer your question. There is so much I can say about your magnanimity. For example, you have given me not only the gift of life but also the first push to keep me going: you welcome me to your home; you are sending me back to college. You are a boundless source of kindness and joy. You happen to focus so many values on yourself. You remind me of the Aristotelian God who gives beings of all kinds the blessing, the privilege, the power of the first motion, the first push, the initial fillip, and they have been going on ever since."

"Peter, let me repeat it, definitely you are man of learning, which makes you a wonderful person to deal with. Are you fully aware of what you've been doing before the tragedy which struck you? That's amazing. You are capable of elevating the simplest idea to the level of a full-fledged doctrine. It has to be the result of great culture."

"Fay, there is some truth about what I've said. Now I remember. You are the second person to teach me the nature and the value of goodness."

"I teach you! Is it possible? You are not making fun of me?"

"No, I am not making fun of you. You've taught me something about kindness. You've taught me that greatness has nothing to do with making a formal speech promising an impossible heaven; it has nothing to do about noise surrounding associations claiming everywhere they are involved in charity. Greatness has to be the expression of self-denial, the recognition and the strengthening of the right of someone other than us, a perfect stranger to be happy, to get access to the basic ingredients of life. Thus a true lover of justice, fairness, compassion, would raise a storm against any attempt to deprive them from anyone, regardless of his color, religion, social background.

"While I am speaking to you, I've seen in my mind the man whose generosity can be compared to yours. It's my first teacher.

"He was a perfect stranger. I used to see him with a heavy bag of sandwiches and juices in his hand. A board smile opened up his face. He stood in the middle of the car train. He breathed deeply and, in a tone of voice that was melodious and convincing at the same time, he started his *little speech*. Yes, at first, I thought like all the train passengers that he was making a *little clever speech* to trick people out of their money, which he would use for his own needs. However, once he finished talking, he offered 'a sandwich and a can of juice to anyone who hasn't eaten all day'. He informed us that he was at the service of the homeless. Then, he also reminded the passengers how thin the veil was between a wage-earner and an unemployed homeless. He added, 'Very often there is one paycheck between the two situations'. Finally, he asked for any kind of contribution to keeping him 'alleviating the lot of those homeless'.

"One day, after having discreetly dropped a few quarters in his collecting box, I asked him where he found his strength, his love, his goodness, his generosity to continue to be a solace to others. For, he sounded like an educated person who could have landed on a lucrative position. He replied, 'Sir, one of the most joyous moments in my life is when I can feed one man, one woman, one child. I am so happy to feel really needed. I was once living in poverty and I was helped. Now, it's my turn now to help out.'

"I didn't know what else to say, except I repeated after a French author, 'Il faut faire le bien parce que c'est le bien. [You must practice the good for its own sake]'.

"By a stroke of good luck, he understood French, agreed with me and said, 'Right on, my brother!' Then he passed on to the next car train to bring his message of love and a 'sandwich and a can of juice to anyone who hasn't eaten all day'."

"That's very deep, Peter," whispered Fay.

And, after a pause, she added, "But one must recognize that you are interested in mankind to notice all this."

"Yes, Fay, I am."

We left the table. She insisted, of course, on washing the dishes herself. Afterward she joined me on the sofa, and we were sitting side by side. We listened to some of her records. The kind of music she liked responded (I should have known better) to her mitigated cheerfulness. Mozart was too "lyrical" for her, and the popular music, too cacophonous. She rather enjoyed soft, harmonious and joyful melodies.

At about eight, she suggested that we should watch television. There was a "double feature" on one of the regular channels. It was a combination of *James Bond*, *super cop* and *romance*. We made comments throughout the programs. At times we agreed, at times we disagreed with each other. But our dialogue occurred in a very relaxing way.

Then, the last televised program ended, she kissed me good night, on my cheek, in the same manner a sister would do to her brother. She went to her bedroom, not before she had given me a pillow and a blanket.

I did sleep like a baby. The couch was soft, and I was tired out. When I woke up in the morning, the sun was already up. "Good Lord!" I exclaimed.

I jumped out of the couch and tiptoed towards the bedroom to wake her up. I remembered she had told me the day before that she would have to go back to work. On my way over, I saw a note on the tea table. I picked it up and read it. It was from her.

Hi, Peter!
I didn't want to wake you up. Don't worry, I am fine.
I went to work. Breakfast is on the table. I'll call you later on. Meanwhile, enjoy yourself as much as you can.
   Fay.

I went to the bathroom and washed up. I was getting ready to plan on "enjoying myself as much as" I could.

20

What a strange and unexcited "honeymoon"! I respected the conditions of the agreement Fay had "concluded" with me: I could make myself at home, do whatever I wanted to, read, play the stereo, watch television, eat until I was satiated, take showers and kiss the hostess good day and good night on the cheek. In fact, all the prescriptions seemed to be on the positive side except one: I couldn't sleep in the bedroom with the hostess. I had to be content with the couch. I started again to wonder if the hostess was made of flesh and blood, if I wasn't dreaming, if I was till in my semi-comatose status. It could be the mental images, I had experienced, were appearing more vivid to the point of reaching a full picture of reality. At least, I was, against my will and better judgment, driving at such odd conclusion. Because, under normal circumstances, a *young couple* living under the same roof would have by then enjoyed their *honeymoon* thoroughly.

I was so confused about Fay's reality that, one day, while sitting in the living room, I called her name in spite of myself, just to hear the sound of her voice and convince myself that such a sound had to come from a physical being.

Of course, she jumped, thinking that I was *flipping out.* "Peter," she echoed me.

"Oh, I wanted just to call your name."

"Why? You know this is my name."

"I know, but it's so short and lovely at the same time. And it fits you well."

That day, I understood better the concept of social censorship which makes us often use euphemisms, words, expressions that don't quite represent the ideas and images we have in mind. So in the name of censorship, I shouldn't spoil our apparently *lovely togetherness.*

"But, Peter, of course my name fits me well," she pointed out. "I've been carrying it since the first day I was born. I've been called by it and I've grown on loving it."

"Indeed."

"But, Peter, don't tell me you want to philosophize on my name! Let me see. Well, it sounds as if it's shorthand for faith. If that's the case, would you say that a name shapes the character of its bearer?"

"No, Fay. I didn't mean to make a treatise on your name and the concept of naming in general. I wanted just to say it loud for no reason whatsoever. It could be a habit I've contracted long time ago, as I am discovering my reality bit by bit."

She patted me on the forearm. "Peter, no harm done," she added. "You can call my name any time you want to."

Other circumstances also kept reminding me of the funny aspect of that "honeymoon".

I had spoken several times with Aunt Emma on the phone. That *poor woman* got things confused and thought there was something "cooking" between Fay and me.

On our last telephonic conversation, she stated naturally, "Peter, how is your woman?"

Her voice had never sounded more West Indian, an accent she always betrayed under certain circumstances.

"You mean Fay, don't you?" I replied, after a short hesitation.

"Yes, I do. There are no other women in your life. And, I do believe you've made a wise choice. She sounds like someone who loves you a lot. Additionally, she is a decorous person. She is my choice."

I had to stop my aunt from going any further in her belief. So I rushed saying, "She is fine, but Aunt Emma..."

"And, Pete, she promised, once that she is pregnant, to come to leave with me. Of course, if the man of the house wants to."

"Aunt Emma..."

"Pete, don't get me wrong. I am happy for you. Fay is a fine lady. She is a plus in your life. Together you will conquer the world."

"Aunt Emma, I have to go," I said quickly, to stop her confusion.

"That's quite all right, Pete. I know you are very shy when it comes to speak about romance."

"Really, Aunt Emma, I have to go. I will call you later."

"You promise, don't you?"

"Yes, I do."

This pattern of conversation had been carried on between us. One day, Fay and I went to visit her. She repeated again and again that we were making a *fine couple*. She went on saying that anyone could see how much in love we were: the *amorous glances* we were covering each other with, the *discreet smiles*, the *gentle touches* of the hands, the *feeling of contentment* on our faces. My aunt was certainly *too much* and had been putting me, all that time, at a false scent, by making me believe that she was an *ignorant* of *romance*. That day, she repeated that she knew I would find the girl of my dream. She was happy for us. She wished we could come to live with her. In a matter of years, we would fill her home with the joy of our children, her "grandchildren". We had our laugh. From the bottom of my heart, I wished she could be right. But I was still being kissed on the cheek by Fay and still sleeping alone on the couch at night. Therefore, Aunt Emma would have to wait for a long time before she could welcome "our children and her grandchildren".

But that day had more surprises in its bag for me.

On our way back home, in the hallway, by Fay's apartment, we ran across one of her neighbors, another person who got things confused about my benefactor and me. She was a corpulent and beautiful lady of about twenty-five years of age. She let go the elevator she was waiting for in order to "congratulate" Fay on her being married. "No wander I couldn't see you," she mischievously added. "But you have all my blessings."

Fay looked at me, then at her neighbor. "Thank you, Rita," she finally said as a last resort. "I was planning on introducing him to my neighbors, but you know how busy I am."

"I know," the so-called Rita acknowledged, while rolling her eyes, conspiratorially.

"Well, I promise to be more sociable one of these days," Fay assured.

"That's all right, Baby. Nothing can replace happiness at home. Furthermore, everybody has experienced the fury of a nascent passion. It excludes the rest of the world, as far as the lovers are concerned.

"By the way, rumor has it that you are *expecting...*"

This time, the confusion went too far!

My hostess was about to say something, maybe a word of protestation, but, fortunately, the elevator door reopened. Before Rita got into the cage, she slapped me gently on the face and teased me, "You, little devil, it has to be you to carry her in the land of love. You must be someone special to deserve this wonderful woman. We thought she would become a nun."

She might have said something else, but the elevator carried her away.

"Rita!" Fay only said, on opening her apartment door.

We sighed both with relief. She was *off the hook*, not having to offer any explanation to her neighbor, and I was relieved from mental torture of playing the role of a loving husband.

Undoubtedly, I felt I meant something to Fay. Didn't she state that I was her *teacher*, that I had a great personality? However, I couldn't be absolutely certain of that. I hoped she didn't mean to mummify me, like a live Pharaoh, in her mind. Anyway, what she meant was one thing, and her irrevocable interdiction from mixing hospitality with romance was another thing. There was no indication in her attitude, which had signaled the imminent repeal of the interdiction. She had been the same kind of woman I had met at the hospital center, the same smiling face with sparkling teeth and the same generous person who wanted me to be "at ease" in her home, who took me for the conquering prince returning from the battlefield. She continued to attend her princess' duties, cooking my favorite meals. Then, nothing else happened.

It then became more and more unbearable to live under the same roof with a woman I loved strongly and desired too. The *little pig* in me had started to fidget about; my animal instinct was being uncontrollable. I felt guilty. I tried all kinds of distractions to cast that little pig away. I read a lot, while Fay was working. I eschewed watching television to avoid any romantic scene that would make matters worse by intensifying my drives. As far as the books I was reading were concerned, I made sure they were not love stories. I was rather indulged in reading essays on philosophy, science, technology, what, usually, we call "heavy stuff", which may temper "our appetites". But it was the first time they failed to carry me away in their quest of a deeper meaning of life, a broader spectrum of truth, a larger knowledge horizon. On each of my attempts to plunge in the ocean of their transcendence, I was pulled back by the intensity of my drives and the materiality of my body. At night, I stayed awakened for hours, hoping and expecting that Fay would come and say, "Ok, Peter, honey, enough punishment!" Every now and then a breeze blew in at the windows, and the curtains waved. I came near to jumping, thinking it was her silky gown which had preceded her.

I had nightmares too.

How many times I had dreamt of having sex with her or other women superseded her symbolically. Those dreams were so real that I woke up excited.

It was my first taste of obsession consisting in the fact that the mind keeps focusing on one object, no matter what. I imagined that if such a central point has never been reached, a feeling of discontentment would remain with the obsessed mind for life. This eventuality describes an unbearable situation.

What disconcerted me the most was the fact that I knew Fay was fully aware of my *agony*, that, in a way, she didn't give me my *full right* as a *prince*, who had been on the *road* for a long time without any kind of *tenderness*. But, it was a matter of principle for her, a demonstration of willpower, a setting an example about the possibility for two persons of mixed gender to live "in harmony", like two *sensible* and *reasonable beings*. There was nothing I could do about it. I couldn't do violence to her and rape her. I couldn't even send her a "message" by gearing our conversations to my "concern". There was no way to foresee her reaction. I knew whom I was dealing with: someone who had never, to my knowledge, entertained people with filthy jokes.

If things continued unaltered, I would rather be in the college dormitory by myself instead of being subject to such mental sufferings. This was certainly enough to make me unjustly hate a woman I loved, ascribing her "indifference" towards me to her merciless nature.

And the bedroom! Yes, the bedroom! At first, I loved it. It was the expression of its owner in terms of sense of order, cleanliness and purpose. However, as the time went by, I had taken a certain dislike to it. It was the hurdle to clear, the citadel which shielded Fay. Maybe if I could sleep in it, she and I would share the bed; if our bodies could touch each other, there would be a chemical mixture and, chances are, she would kick that "silly" interdiction of hers. But that bedroom was there with its insensible nature, its secret, its unconcerned beauty and order. It was the sanctuary of the goddess I wanted and it was *sacred*. I wouldn't be surprised if, trying to be bold, I determined to step into it and *desecrate* it and I broke one of my toes against its step, twisted my ankle or suffered from a stomachache. From that point on, I would have started being superstitious, giving soul to what was nothing but a furnished room. Yes, I knew she was a simple room, yet I couldn't prevent myself from making it responsible for my *dilemma*. At this point, I was fully conscious of the fact that my mind was terribly affected. It was the first time I completely lost my sense of objectivity and that I suffered from a mental perversion, giving soul to inanimate objects. As a matter of fact, my following course of action would testify to that.

One morning, while Fay was working at the hospital, I felt up to *desecrating* the *goddess' sanctuary* by my presence. I was doing it with the same excitement of a man who is going to make love to a virgin.

I opened the door slowly but decisively. I was expecting to hear a protecting spirit screaming, "Get out of here. You have no business being here. One more step, and I will reduce you to a statue." I smiled at my twisted imagination.

I scanned the room inch by inch.

The bed was made of solid pine. A blue fluffy bedspread with attached lace ruffles displayed its relaxing splendor. Textured drapes with blue foam backing blocked up the windows. To the right, there was a large dressing table supporting a huge mirror with the edges embellished by delicate moldings. To the left, a huge drawer chest overhung the bed.

I forgot the reason of my presence in the room. Instead, I was admiring the cleanness and the order reigning all over. It was the result of trials and errors, which finally ended up in the right arrangement of objects which could be otherwise giving to someone a feeling of mere juxtaposition. It was then the physical confirmation of Fay's inner world, a serene, peaceful, orderly world. There was nothing too flashy, but just discreet splendor. All this reinforced my love for the goddess. I wished she could be my wife at once, to enjoy such a warm and heavenly atmosphere.

I was about to continue my *inspection* of what could be my future *bridal chamber*, but, like a bolt of lightning, appeared the *secret* I wasn't supposed to fathom, the one which kept me away from the goddess' sanctuary, the picture of a handsome young man!

He seemed to be a little older than I. He was looking at me with stern and disapproving eyes.

First, I felt disheartened. My legs gave away, and I had to lean on the dressing table. Then I cried. I had been living all that time in the land of fancy! Fay had been in love with someone else. Therefore, she did, in fact, "give herself up" to somebody else's mercy. But why did she lie to me? Why did she make me believe that I was her *prince*, that she was the princess waiting for me, and that our lives had been destined to intertwine, to intermingle into each other as if such a decision had been inscribed in the matrix of reality? I bet she was engaged to that man in the picture, or they were married. What happened between them? They could have had a fight and have decided to separate from each other. That man could be a *Casanova* and give her a hard time, and she thought the best thing to do was to stay away from him, in order to keep her sanity.

However, it was obvious that she still loved him and cherished his memories religiously, in her bedroom.

Probably, she had spiritually contracted marriage with him, like those spiritualists who were supposed to wed immaterially to the seven Egyptian goddesses passing for the most beautiful women in the world.

The man in the picture, I wished him evil; I wished he could keep acting worse and worse, so, one day, Fay would come back to her senses and be free to look for and enjoy happiness.

I was also feeling guilty. I didn't know him and had no proof of his badness. I shouldn't wish him evil. I had to lose my grip on my *mental synthesis*. I had to be victim of jealousy.

Likewise, I didn't see how that man's persistent badness could be helpful to me. It was too late. Even if Fay took pity on me and let me be her lover, I couldn't be sure that she would ever love me with the same fervency and adoration she bestowed on that man in the picture. Perhaps she was incapable of loving anyone anymore. Her mind was locked up in her memories, and her cheerfulness was nothing but a façade, a screen smoke to sidetrack people. I pictured them being consumed with passion, right here, to such a par that I thought that my presence was an invasion of privacy, a total lack of discretion and respect.

The phone rang. I was in a state of panic as if, by picking up the receiver in the bedroom, Fay could locate where I was. I ran away into the living room and grabbed the other extension.

As usual, she spoke in a soft tone. Why shouldn't she? She was at peace with herself (at least in appearance). I was the one who was perturbed because I had invaded her privacy. The proof being that I was taking the consequence: I was consumed with jealousy and guilt.

I knew that bedroom would use any means available in this world to defend its goddess. That day, it filled my heart with rancorous thoughts and made hurtful any desire I would have in the future to go back in it.

"Peter, honey," she whispered, "how do you feel?"

"Ok, I guess," I replied.

I was too angry to be cheerful. Because of that, I might have answered her in a funny impolite kind of way, for, she asked, raising her voice a little, "Peter, what's wrong? Don't go pessimistic on me now!"

I knew I was wrong to upset her. After all, I shouldn't expect her to be as pure as a new born. She had to have a past. And that past couldn't be erased, nor could it lower her in the public eye. She still kept her physical beauty, her angelic smile and her sparkling teeth. She still spoke in a soft, honeyed tone of voice. She was still a self-possessed woman. Only my silly jealousy had poisoned my mind and made me see her from a bias perspective.

But, whatever I did, that jealousy got the better of me and hindered my good sense. "Fay, I have nothing that bothers me," I said in a relatively harsh manner.

Sensing that I wasn't too sociable at that moment, she conceded, "I won't challenge your answer, Peter. However, I hope to meet a cheerful Peter on my returning home tonight."

"I will do my best, Fay," I promised.

"That's more like it."

"Peter, I wish I knew what has turned you sour," she stated after a short pause. "But we are going to have a long talk, so we will clear up any misunderstanding between us. And you promise to do your best to be cheerful on my returning home."

"Yes, I do."

"I have been dealing with a Peter full of optimism, wisdom and willpower. I want him back. Do you hear me?"

"Yes, Fay, I do."

She hung up.

I sat quietly in the living room, trying to make sense out of all this. I had no reason to be jealous, since she had never promised me to become my girlfriend or wife. She took a chance to let me live with her, for a while. The love story between her and me was my own fancy. "Peter, pull yourself together," I said to myself. "Soon you are going back to school. You will get involved in heavy thinking and you will forget her."

That reasoning was still unable to soothe away my sufferings. Then, for the first time, I realized that the only medication for love is the possession of the object of it.

I had just remembered having made Fay a promise to be cheerful. How? Suddenly, I had an idea. I looked all over the kitchen and in the refrigerator for the ingredients of a *banquet* which I would prepare as the last meal in the honor of the *princess* I was about to lose forever and as a manifestation of my gratitude for being accepted as a guest by her. Luckily, for some unexplained reason, I was remembering fancy recipes Aunt Emma used to teach me and was preparing them with the dexterity of an accomplished chef.

When she rang the bell that evening, I had a strange feeling, the one which would experience a child who had misbehaved and who didn't want to face his parents. Still I had to open the door and let her come in. It was her house and she had the key for the front door. It was silly of me. "I must handle the matter like a man," I whispered. Then I opened the door.

She put her arms round my neck and kissed me. There was no doubt about the meaning of that kiss. It expressed tenderness and passion. She was in a romantic mood. She could have certainly found an equal disposition in me the day before, but, that night, I was miserable. The world appeared to me like a huge, incommensurable, somber reality that was painted in ashy color, like that cemetery in Queens. I returned her kiss with sluggish lips like the sponge I had used that morning to take a shower.

"Oh! Peter, my love! I smell something good," she asserted. "Would you by any chance cook something? I am starving."

I nodded to her.

"Yes, Peter, I am starving," she repeated. "Let's see..."

She went into the kitchen and uncovered the pots religiously. "I just can't believe it!" she exclaimed. "Pigeon peas and cornice! What's that?"

I was no longer angry, the proof being that I answered didactically, "Creole-style shrimp with rice."

"And that dish?"

"It's steak a la Diane."

"And that one?"

"It's cheese pineapple dessert."

"Let me set the table."

"I already did."

"Naturally."

It was her turn to make a huge meal. She was emitting tuneful sound expressing her satisfaction. In her excitement, she didn't notice that I was barely touching the food.

"Listen, my love," she marveled, "where did you learn to cook like that? Why didn't you tell me you were a fine cordon bleu, so I wouldn't make a fool of myself?

"Oh, Peter! You have to be..."

"What?"

"Nothing, but your modesty reaches the level of a virtue: you know many things, and yet, you don't want to flaunt your knowledge. You have to be the bearer of so many great qualities."

"Thank you, Fay."

"Then, Peter, you must be the..."

"What is it?"

"Peter, let me enjoy these gastronomic wonders."

She kept nodding her head to express her appreciation. Then she reiterated her question, "Where did you learn to cook like that?"

I looked at her. Her face was radiant, and her eyes, sparkling. She was the living expression of innocence and beauty. My anger had completely vanished. I was rather glad that my culinary skill could make her so bubbling. Could I succeed in making her love me with intensity and passion? Could I extirpate the memories of the man in the picture from her lovely head? Could she start loving someone else all over again? If yes, would I have ever forgiven her for not waiting for me to be her first lover?

She insisted, "Peter, did you hear me?"

"Well, Fay, the cordon bleu title has to go to Aunt Emma," I finally answered, "who happens to have a degree in gastronomy. As a matter of fact, she is retired from a chef's position. She started to teach me how to cook, a month after I had moved to her house. She wanted my mind to be busy all the time, so I wouldn't brood over the loss of my parents."

"So, you happen to know the fancy names of these delightful recipes?"

"Of course, I do."

"I bet you know how to prepare a lot of more dishes, don't you?"

"You wouldn't believe it! Then all at once, I remembered all these recipes, like an act of religious revelation."

"You are a dangerous man."

"Am I a dangerous man?" I panicked.

"Yes, you are, but in a very sweet fashion. What I mean is that I will have to watch you. You might be spoiling me, and I won't be able to get rid of you. Moreover, I can't afford to replenish my wardrobe, my dear Peter. If I have to eat like that, daily, I will become more than a robust woman. And you won't love me anymore. I would stop being the lovable nurse you have met about five months ago. I won't let you cook around here. I am supposed to be the woman in the house, who, by nature, is responsible for providing sweetness in profusion. You must initiate me in the culinary art."

She stopped talking. She looked at me and only then she noticed that I wasn't eating too much, which was a little surprising to her. Usually, I had a hearty appetite.

She looked at me, trying to seek out my concern through my eyes. I started again to hope for something positive to happen, to believe that it wasn't too late to capture her love. Yet, I was afraid. I didn't want to be hurt, above all by her. No matter what happened I wouldn't like to have some bitter memories of her. She was good to me! At least, on behalf of generosity, I had to respect that woman.

To break off my renewed fascination, I insinuated in spite of myself, in a sad tone, "Maybe, I won't even have the opportunity to spoil you. Very soon I have to reach my school."

She laid the fork and the knife crosswise on her plate. "Peter, don't do that!" she screamed.

"What did I do?" I inquired alarmingly.

"Don't spoil our happiness! Why do you have to remind me of your imminent departure? Daily, I've been doing my best to put it in the back of my mind. It's a painful reality I didn't want to face, and I've been doing fine, burying my head in the sand of our sweet togetherness, like a pelican. Now you come and lay it bare. That's not nice. I don't know what I am going to do without you. I become addicted to your presence."

We left the table and removed the dishes. Fay put the leftovers away into the refrigerator. On her way back, she stopped, kissed me and pulled me by the hand into the living room. We sat on the sofa, her arm around my neck.

She asked in a tone expressing concern, "Now, Peter, what in the world is really bothering you? Tell me. Am I not a good hostess? Have I mistreated you? Have I lacked respect for you? I could have unknowingly had a poor choice of words and offended you. If that was the case, I beg you to forgive me. I didn't want you to leave this house with any bad feelings. I want you to remember your stay here forever and ever. Then, Peter, darling, set my mind at ease. I am ready to apologize for any wrong I might have done you."

Suddenly, I decided to tell her my *concern*. Whatever the outcome, I had to unburden my heart. "Fay, I know you are going to be mad at me; I did something wrong," I confessed.

She opened her eyes widely to show me how "surprised" she was.

"Oh, tell me about it!" she urged. "It can't be that bad. I don't think you are capable of doing something awful (knowingly). Furthermore, you haven't left this apartment for any reason at all, except that, once, we went to see Aunt Emma (that sweet lady). Looking around me, I haven't noticed any damage to the apartment. You have instead brightened up the place by your optimism and dynamic thoughts."

"Well, Fay, I wanted so bad to see your bedroom. This morning I was in it."

She looked puzzled. "As far as I can remember, I didn't forbid you my bedroom," she admitted. "No, I didn't. You are free to go wherever you want in my home. I trust you. As you can see, I haven't locked anything at all. I have no skeletons in my closet (she giggled); while you are here, it's your house too. Honest. Peter, God is my witness; I've been spending the happiest moment in my life since we've been here. You know, it's a wonderful feeling I would like to keep forever and ever."

"...And I saw the picture of that man," I almost whispered.

She couldn't stop laughing. It was a crystalline laugh which lasted long enough to give me cause for concern. I wondered if she didn't have some kind of hysteria. Finally, it hurt me to see her making fun of me because I was jealous, that I cared about her and that I was in pain. Was there another side of her, unknown to others? Could she really be able to attract someone, make him love her passionately, then abuse him? No, I didn't want to believe that she could be so un-fathomable. Sooner or later, her true personality would have appeared.

She finally calmed down, but she was still giggling, "Peter, I am sorry to laugh so much, while I should have cried instead," she observed. "But, in a way, the whole matter sounds so funny."

Then she turned gloomy. "Peter, I know what you've been thinking about me," she went on: "I am too good to be true, or my purpose is unclear. Why did I take the burden of caring for you, while you were on the verge of death? Why did I insist on helping you get back on your feet? What I was up to? I know, Peter, that all these questions keep rolling in your head. You certainly concede that you are not in a state of immediate danger, for you would have been hurt by now. But the unknown frightens you, as it does anyone.

"If you didn't mean something to me, I could let you go without elucidating the "mystery" about me. But I want to open my heart to you as you did to me one day, at the hospital.

"Peter, I want you to believe what I am going to tell you. Promise me."

"Fay, I do," I *caved in.*

But I would rather not to, being unable to anticipate the nature of her "mystery". Very often, ignorance is a blessing. Reality, forced to reveal itself, offers its unpleasant aspects, the ones that should remain untold, in the first place. But I had no choice but to promise to believe what she was about to say. I was the one who had triggered this avalanche of emotions, I had to face it.

"I am exactly the person I appear to be," she proceeded. "I am generous. I love people to such a par that I was able to see through you, even when you were unconscious. I devoted myself to you, not out of pity, but out of something deeper which had pushed me towards you. I mean every word I have spoken to you. Whatever happens, whether, as soon as you've taken leave of me, you decide to never see me again, I want you to remember me the way you have seen me. Any deviation from that would be an inaccurate account of me."

She breathed deeply before going on, "I am a romantic little creature. I am so romantic that nowadays love, which is often fickle, will reduce me to a human wreck and will lead me eventually to suicide. I can't love someone just for a week, for a month, for a year or for ten years. It has to be forever and ever. Therefore, knowing me, I must protect myself against myself, from my almost pathologic sensitiveness, by trying to be virtuous.

"In other words, I am virtuous by necessity, as a way to function in life. You see what happened to me the other day, when I had to pick you up from the hospital! It was the first time I had ever called sick from my job. Imagine if I have to be in love with someone who wants to abuse me. I will never be able to attend any business. This is the only reason why I appear to give you a 'hard time'. But it's, I think, a first step towards something deeper, letting you share my apartment for a while. This is an informal, tacit expression of commitment? Isn't it running the risk of upsetting my undisturbed life I've been leading since I've been on my own? Why should I behave this way? Why should I expose myself to the risk of being hurt, while by nature and instinct, I should have been looking for my own pleasure? The only way I can explain my *carelessness* is that I am strongly in love with you. Yes, I must face it; otherwise, I won't be able to handle it. Love may be often equated with compulsive gambling, going from an innocent urge, an acceptable course of action to total chaos or madness.

"I've been in love with you from the first day I saw you arriving unconscious. Why? I've never had any logical explanation. But, once my heart has—so to speak—picked you out of millions of men, it has never stopped being attached *religiously* to you. Of course, I resisted, at first. I didn't want to believe what was happening to me. My reason and my fear of public opinion tried to *talk me out* of it, but in vain. I've found out ever since that reason is not always the predominant faculty of human nature. Very often, it shows up after the fact, to confirm it, to pass judgment on it and, in case of failure, to present other choices which have been available, but either unseen or dismissed by passion.

"So a funny and strange thing happened: I wasn't conscious of any change in my behavior and thought and of the fact that others could be taking noticed of my inner dilemma. I was totally wrong. They were able to discover my feelings, including Dr. Colborne who has been making passes at me as long as I've been working at the health center. Yes, Peter, I want you to know it all. I am too deep in my love to back up. Let's suppose that you were a merciless man, you could have abused me. Worse, everybody would have recognized that I would have been the author of my own dooms, since I had cared about you and brought you to my home. You could have inflicted a big wound to my heart, a wound which would never be healed until I died."

She paused for a short while. Her body stiffened slightly. It seemed it would cost her pride or something very intimate to disclose her feelings. "I am going to tell you something," she resumed. "While you were hospitalized, funny things were going on in me. All went well insofar as I was in the hospital, knowing I could see you. It wasn't even necessary to be assigned to your ward, as long as I was conscious of your proximity, of the possibility of having a peek at you from the entrance door, of knowing that you were alive, you were breathing on your own. I always had a pinch in my heart when the time came to go home. I felt so depressed, alone in the world, without your company. I almost fainted when, one day, they called 777 on you. I asked God to sacrifice me to save you, if that was the price to pay. I barely slept, asking myself if the worse had come, since you were in a life frightening stage, only a thin veil was keeping you between life and death. And I sometimes feared that my colleagues would do something wrong, just to get you out of my way. Many of them care about me. They didn't even have to mistreat you out of malice, through negligence or carelessness, but to free me from my love for you.

"In the morning, when I woke up, I looked through the window and saw the sun and greeted it with a smile. I understood then the state of mind of the earlier human beings when they deified the sun. Under the cover of darkness, anything awful, deadly might have occurred. With the sun came back hope, a sense of security, a certain rebirth, a positive attitude. So, far from you, in the comfort of my apartment, I feared that the *kingdom of darkness* could have reigned over the hospital and that I would find, in the morning, an empty bed. But the sun brought me a feeling of hope, and I kept saying, 'One more day is a step towards life'. I was confident that I would see you very soon.

"On my days off, I had no other choice but to stay home. That moment was the worst part of it. I was thinking all the time about you. Sometimes I felt something coming down from my throat to my feet. It was painful. I didn't know what to do and what would result from all that. I was scared. Like a superstitious person I was giving a premonitory explanation to my feeling, thinking that it was over, you had died. I would pick up the phone and call Maude who would reassure me, before I opened my mouth, by saying, 'Fay, my darling, *your patient* is fine.' Only then I would have a certain appeasement, knowing that she was incapable of lying to me.

"But, Peter, I am not in your mind; I can't read it either. What would happen to me if you didn't love me? So far, I have the impression of trying to force my way into your life, to impose my love on you. I have no right to do that. Your life belongs to you. As a matter of fact, my love for you can backfire and hurt me badly.

"You understand why I want you to be mine and, at the same time, I want you to stay away from me. This is the ambiguity of the situation I've been in, ever since I've met you.

"Peter, do you understand me? Do you think I am mentally deranged?

"I have told you everything."

She paused once more for breath. When she started to speak again, she did it in a tearful tone, "Peter, like you, I am alone in the world. I only have my uncle, but he is busy with his career and his family. My parents died when I was an infant. That young man in the picture you saw in the bedroom was my brother. He was in the Navy. One day, I learned that he died in the line of duty. I have nothing but memories to entertain."

I dried her tears with my palms and kissed her on the lips. Then we fondled each other. It was something which occurred instinctively, naturally. We were like two fruits reaching ripeness. A few minutes later, we were consumed with passion.

I carried her to the bedroom. To tell you the truth, I wasn't fully conscious when I stepped for the second time into the "sacred temple".

"Peter, honey," she pronounced sweetly but clearly, "we are going to reach a point of no return. I strongly want you. I am ready for giving myself up to you. But, please, don't make love to me if you are not ready to be my first and only man in my life."

I was frozen for a long time. Should I say yes or no to a condition so simply stated. But why should I say no? Since my semi-comatose state to my regaining consciousness, I had been yearning for reaching the *oval being*, the *smiling face*, the *smooth lips* whispering, "Welcome back, my angel", which lips formed with sparkling teeth a harmonious whole. My following course of action would be the answer.

Finally, we made love. It was heavenly. I didn't hurry things, not wanting to hurt the *fallen angel*. I also wanted her to believe in the possible sweetness of womanhood. At last, I wanted that moment to be remembered by both of us as long as we were living.

Anyway, she had my answer: I eloquently stated that I would be her first and only man in her life.

21

I am doing well in school. I will be graduated in a few days and
will have my BS. I have obtained a fellowship to pursue graduate studies in the field of psychology. Furthermore, as Doctor
Shaw had predicted it, I have won the national award for presenting
the best paper of the year. Ten thousand dollars will give me a good
start.

The funny thing about this award is that I have chosen a topic
which is one of the central points in Henry Bergson's and William
James' works (the author Dr. Miles accused me of emulating). To
their theses on *Stream of Consciousness* I have added what I call the
pragmatic aspect of it, an inspiration from *my discovery* of the *reason
for* Fay's *smooth* and *flowing elocution.* I have proposed that when
the *stream of consciousness* is intense, true to itself, it results in some
kind of coherent behavior, in the normal unfolding of our purposes
and our perceptions of reality. When it's troubled, our communion
with each other, as well as with the outside world, suffers. After all,

we are the filters of reality. Sometimes, we are passive filters being limited to receiving impressions, sometimes we are active, conscious filters involved in self-discovery and self-determination. Reality is there, it exists without us, yet it's a fact that it's also interpreted by each and every one of us.

Anyway, with my scholarship and my award, I feel confident; I am on my way to a more positive existence.

Everything, in fact, is going well. My discreet inquiry enables me to learn that Yolanda has married a lawyer who has been handling her parents' estates and other businesses. She told her husband the other day that her son's father was a fine young man she loved and will always love. He was *brave* and *died in the line of duty*. She had no regret for having carried his son who would keep his *memories* alive in her heart. She wasn't interested in carrying any other men's children. You know Yolanda with her hot temper, her vivid imagination and her ability to make up stories. I bet, by the time our son reaches the age to listen to and understand his "father's greatness", the story will have the size of ten volumes.

This is the way it has been and should be: honor your *departed parents* in order to enjoy longevity and blessings. This is the lesson Yolanda means to teach her son (the little man) and, later on, her grandchildren.

Of course, once in a while, you come across some punks who disagree with her. Recently, their number has tremendously increased. They have to be stopped before it is too late. What would happen if their nightmarish concept of life becomes the norm, the prevalent code of ethics, the fabric of society and government? Fortunately (at least for now), those punks end up in the camp of Tony, Paul, the *giant*, the *messenger* and their likes. They go straight to jail where they belong. Usually, they don't enjoy longevity, to speak in conformity with Yolanda's version of evolution.

I consider myself being lucky to have one big worry out of the way: this woman, being married, will soon forget about her son's father who *died in the line of duty*. I remember her *promise*, on our last meeting, before my *close call*, that she would kill me if she ever learned that I would *give myself up* to another woman. Knowing her well, her *threat* could have been not an idle one, without this change in the course of events.

Everything is going well so long as one admits that life is serrated; it has its ups and downs. Come to think of it, a woman's love for me almost caused my death, while another one's love for me pulled me from the claws of death. All things being considered, my fate seems to lie in a woman's hands. Still—as anyone else does—I prefer good luck to bad luck. So, one should always grab the former by its horns whenever one sees it. Usually, it's the only chance you have to get your grip on it. This is the reason why, before I get involved in my graduate studies or in any other kinds of activities, there is one thing I am going to do first. That thing will be enough to give me all the strength, all the happiness, all the heart I need to succeed in life: I am going to ask Fay to marry me. She won't refuse the proposal made by her first and only man in her existence.

In the meantime, my soul has resumed its sereine existence in a restored temple which has never been contaminated by deleterious drugs the streets have been saturated with (above at night, in dark alleys). My soul continues and will continue for years to come to contemplate ideals it may never possess completely.

END OF FIRST BOOK